I've lived a thousand lives
and traveled to unknown lands
on waves of italic print and ships
made from printed paper.
~ Aurora Rose Reynolds

Willow Mayson isn't ready to just dive head first into love, or at least not with any of the men she's dated.

Then she shares a single unexpected kiss with a complete stranger.

Clay Raven doesn't want the strings of a woman tied to him in any way. His priorities are his family, his job, and finding the people responsible for helping to kill his sister.

One kiss shouldn't have the ability to change that.

Even with the chemistry between them, Willow attempts to put distance between her and Clay but the guy is tenacious, until he's not.

For a guy who's never put much effort into any woman, Clay learns quickly that he's going to have to fight, chase, and manipulate his way into Willows life if he wants to be a part of it.

Then just when Willow begins to let her guard down her friend is murdered setting off a string of events that could change the course of their lives forever.

Are you ready for another BOOM?

AURORA ROSE
REYNOLDS

PRAISE FOR AURORA ROSE REYNOLDS

"No other author can bring alpha perfection to each page as phenomenally as Aurora Rose Reynolds can. She's the queen of alphas!"

~Author CC Monroe

"Aurora Rose Reynolds makes you wish book boyfriends weren't just between the pages."

~Jenika Snow *USA Today* Bestselling Author

"Aurora Rose Reynolds writes stories that you lose yourself in. Every single one is literary gold."

~Jordan Marie *USA Today* Bestselling Author

"No one does the BOOM like Aurora Rose Reynolds"

~Author Brynne Asher *USA Today* Bestselling Author

"With her yummy alphas and amazing heroines, Aurora Rose Reynolds never fails to bring the BOOM."

~Author Layla Frost *USA Today* Bestselling Author

"When Aurora Rose Reynolds lowers the BOOM, there isn't a reader alive that can resist diving headfirst into the explosion she creates."

~Author Sarah O'Rourke

"Aurora Rose Reynolds was my introduction into Alpha men and I haven't looked back!"

~Author KL Donn

"Reynolds is a master at writing stories that suck you in and make you block out the world until you're done."

~Susan Stoker *NYT* Bestselling Author

When Aurora Rose Reynolds has a new story out, it's time for me to drop whatever I'm working on and dive into her world of outrageously alpha heroes and happily ever afters.

~Author Rochelle Paige

Aurora Rose leaves you yearning for more. Her characters stick with you long after you've finished the book.

~Author Elle Jefferson

Reynolds books are the perfect way to spend a weekend. Lost in her alpha males and endearing heorines.

~Author CP Smith Bestselling Author

OTHER BOOKS BY AURORA ROSE REYNOLDS

The Until Series
Until November
Until Trevor
Until Lilly
Until Nico
Second Chance Holiday

Until Her Series
Until July
Until June
Until Ashlyn
Until Harmony
Until December
Until April
Until May
Until Willow

Until Him Series
Until Jax
Until Sage
Until Cobi
Until Talon

Shooting Stars Series
Fighting to Breathe
Wide-Open Spaces
One Last Wish

Underground Kings Series
Assumption
Obligation
Distraction
Infatuation

Ruby Falls Series
Falling Fast
One More Time

Fluke My Life Series
Running into Love
Stumbling into Love
Tossed into Love
Drawn into Love

How to Catch an Alpha Series
Catching Him
Baiting Him
Hooking Him

Stand-Alone Novels
Love at the Bluebird
The Wrong/Right Man
Alpha Law (written as C. A. Rose)
Justified (written as C. A. Rose)
Liability (written as C. A. Rose)
Finders Keepers (written as C. A. Rose)

To Have to Hold to Keep Series
Trapping Her

Adventures in Love Series
Rushed
Risky
Reckless

NEW YORK TIMES AND USA TODAY BESTSELLING AUTHOR

AURORA ROSE
REYNOLDS

Until Willow
Until Him/ Until Her series
By Aurora Rose Reynolds

Published by Aurora Rose Reynolds

Cover design by RBA Designs
Cover photography by Wander Aguiar
Formatting by Christina Parker Smith

AURORA ROSE
REYNOLDS

To my best friend and biggest fan I love you to the moon and back Mr. Reynolds, and I'm forever grateful that I get to spend this lifetime with you.

Until WILLOW

M A Y
James Trevor

Asher & November

Trevor & Liz

Hanna
Cobi

July
June
May
December
April

James
Dean
Tia
Conner

BELIEVE IN

S O N

Susan   Elizabeth

Cash & Lilly

Nico & Sophie

Jax
Ashlyn

Hope
Jasper
Edward
Toby
Destiny

Willow
Harmony
Bax
Talon
Sage
Nalia

Ava
Lillian
Alistair
Nash

THE BOOM!

Willow

One

$\mathcal{S}$ITTING ACROSS FROM Alec, I tap my fingers against my martini glass as he stares at his cell phone and types frantically. Pressing my lips together as I study him, I wonder how long it would take him to realize I was gone if I just got up and left.

My guess? Twenty minutes, if not longer.

He and I have been dating for a few weeks; he's a nice enough guy who checks all the appropriate boxes. He hasn't stood me up, hasn't once looked at another woman when we've been out, he opens car doors and as a bonus he's good looking. The thing is he's as boring and as obsessed with work as every other man I've dated. And, I mean, I get it–work is important but so is enjoying life.

And if I'm honest I'd like a man to be a little obsessed with me–I mean, not stalkerish–but I wouldn't mind finding a guy who puts me first, who makes it clear that he can't get enough of me–a man who gives me his undivided attention when we are in the same space, especially when we're out on a date at a fancy restaurant and I've put in the effort of actually dressing up for the occasion.

With a sigh, I look across the dimly lit restaurant and spot the sign for the restroom with an arrow pointing down the stairs. Maybe a couple of minutes away from the table will give him time to finish with what he's doing and give me time to get out of my head.

"Hey." I reach across the space between us and touch his hand and his head flies up. "I'm going to use the restroom before our food comes. I'll be back."

"Sure." He gives me an apologetic smile. "And I'm sorry. There's just a lot going on at work."

"No worries." I muster up a smile and scoot out of the booth. "I'll be right back."

"Sure." He checks me out as I stand and his eyes darken, letting me know he is not completely oblivious to me.

I walk across the restaurant then navigate down the stairs in my heels. When I reach the bathroom, I go inside, and since one of the stalls is already occupied I use the other. It takes a second to get the heavy wooden door to close but once I get it locked I take care of business, then try to open the door. It doesn't budge, so I push it harder, and it still doesn't move.

"No way." I shove my arm into it like I'm a linebacker causing pain to race across my shoulder to the back of my neck, then kick the door as hard as I can. Nothing. "Oh my god." I bang the door and yell for help getting no response, then look around the entire frame of the stall finding that there is only about a ten-inch gap at the top and nothing at the bottom. Taking a breath, I try to calm down and think, I don't have my phone so I can't call anyone, but someone will have to come in here eventually. Right? Right. Crossing my arms over my chest I wait, then wait some more. Without a watch or clock, I don't know how much time has gone by, but it had to have been at least fifteen minutes, if not longer.

Starting to get anxious I look at the top of the stall then at the toilet. Maybe, just maybe, if I stand on the seat I can reach the top. Carefully, in my heels that are slick on the bottom, I place one foot on the edge of the toilet, then jump up as high as I can, barely catching the frame with the tips of my fingers. Using all my strength I pull myself up then swing my leg catching the toe of my black platform sandal on the frame. Without a doubt, I look like an idiot, but when I get my leg over, I use that to pull me up, only to find myself squished between the roof and frame of the stall. Wiggling, I squeeze through the tight space, then drop my legs and then look down as I hang there.

It's not far, but I'm still about a half a foot off the ground. I let myself fall and thankfully I land on my feet, though my right ankle wobbles causing enough pain to make me gasp. I limp over to the sink then blink at my reflection in the mirror. My hair and my black body-hugging wrap-around top is covered in dust. I glance down, finding my black jeans are just as dirty as the rest of me.

Great!

I wash my hands then attempt to dust myself off, getting the worst of it before washing my hands again and leaving the bathroom. When I get back to the booth Alec looks up at me from his plate that is already half eaten. I slide into my seat.

"I got locked in the bathroom."

"I was wondering where you were. I was about to send a search party." He laughs.

My throat prickles with annoyance because he obviously didn't care enough about me being gone to send someone to make sure I was okay, or even come looking for me himself.

"This isn't going to work." I mutter to my self and turn to grab my cell phone along with my bag then jerk my head around when his hand grabs my upper arm.

"I didn't mean anything by that. I was just joking."

"I know." I pull my arm back then dig into my bag for some cash, finding two twenty-dollar bills. I place them on the table with him watching, then start to scoot out of the booth.

"You're leaving?"

"Does it even matter if I'm here?"

"Of course it does."

"Alec, we hardly see each other, and when we do, you're normally distracted by work or talking about it."

"My job..."

"Is important–believe me, I know." I tell him gently because I don't want to end things on a bad note. I mean he is a nice guy, he's just not the guy for me. "I'm sure I'll see you around." I get up and then, without sparing him another glance, I walk through the restaurant to the front door and out.

Thankfully I drove myself, since he was coming to dinner straight from work, so I head for my car that I parked in the lot just down the street. When I get behind the wheel, I ignore the excessive pings from texts Alec is sending, turn on my engine, then back out of my parking spot. After I turn out of the lot, I hear the rumble of a motorcycle engine and on instinct I check my mirrors. With my heart in my throat, I watch as a black Harley, with it's driver matching the bike in a black jacket and helmet, cut off the SUV that was behind me. With their shield down I can't see their face, but I can tell the man driving is not a small guy. Still, no matter how big he is, riding a bike can be dangerous, and I'm half-tempted to yell out my window that he should be more careful.

I keep an eye on him in my rearview as I drive toward my condo, but when I'm halfway there, I spot the sign for a liquor store and decide at the last minute to stop and get a bottle of wine, so I'll have it for the bath I plan on taking as soon as I get home. I turn into the lot, noticing the motorcycle pass, then search for a place to park.

I wander the isles in the store, trying to figure out what I'm in the mood for. Merlot is normally my go to but there is something about a hot bath and Rosé that goes together perfectly. After a good ten minutes of debating, I end up getting both, then check out and leave the store with my bag in hand. As soon as I step outside, I notice two guys dressed similarly in jeans and hoodies with baseball caps; they're standing near the rear of my car next to a large black SUV with tinted windows. A prickle slides down my spine as they turn to look at me, and I'm half tempted to spin around and go right back into the store.

"Hey baby." A deep voice calls out and I look to my side finding a man approaching me, a man that is dressed exactly like the guy on the Harley minus the helmet. He's big, probably over six feet with broad shoulders, dark hair that's cut low on the sides, longer on top, with a thick well trimmed beard covering the lower half of his face and tattoos that I can see peeking over the collar of his shirt. "You didn't tell me you were stopping here."

"Umm." My brows dart together, and I turn to check and see if there is someone behind me because I have no idea who he's talking to. When I turn back around, he's in my space–like all the way in my space and next thing I know his large palm is wrapped around the back of my neck and he uses it to pull me forward. Stunned stupid I do nothing as his soft, warm lips cover mine and he kisses me. I should not feel a zap of electricity snap to life between us or find this kiss hot considering I have no idea who he is. Still, the muscles in my lower belly twitch in response, then my core clenches when I feel his tongue drag across my bottom lip. Gasping I put my hand up against his chest to push him back, but he doesn't let go or at least not completely.

"Don't fight me, not with those guys watching," he whispers against my lips and my body stills.

"Good girl." He mumbles lifting his head and tucking my face against his chest under his chin while wrapping his free hand around my back. My heart pounds franticly against my ribcage and I'm sure I'm going to pass out as I listen to car doors slam and an engine start. "They're leaving the lot now." He rumbles holding me for a second longer, before letting me go and taking a step back.

"You kissed me." I know those should not be the first words out of my mouth, but I've never felt what I just felt when kissing anyone, and I don't know what to do with the fact that I swear my world spun when he was kissing me.

"And you kissed me back." He shrugs before he turns and walks off.

"I did not kiss you," I hiss at his back, then panic when he walks to my car and squats down so he can reach under the bumper. "What are you doing?'

"Hold on." He moves his hand around then holds it out to me a couple of seconds later, and I see that he has a small, round, metal device in his palm that's about the size of a quarter.

"What is that?"

"Tracker." He drops it on the ground between us then crushes it with his scuffed up black boot.

"A tracker?" I shake my head. "Why is there a tracker on my car?"

"Pretty girl, young, nice body." His eyes wander over me slowly. "They could get a few grand for you a night or sell you off at auction to the highest bidder."

"What?" I breathe, sure that I heard him wrong.

"There's fucked up people in this world, babe, and a lot of them would do just about anything to make a buck. Good news is I've been watching them and caught them watching you."

"Auction me to the highest bidder?"

"Like I said, there's some fucked up people in the world." He moves his gaze to my car. "I'll follow you back to your place and make sure you're locked in for the night."

Absolutely not. "I don't think so." I take a step back from him then swing my purse around and drop my eyes to it and dig out my cell from the bottom along with my car keys.

"When they realize they don't have a signal to the tracker they're gonna come back, and could just follow you."

"Or this could be some weird set up and you're in on it." I narrow my eyes on his. "You playing the savior, trying to make me comfortable, only to turn around and do what you said they were going to."

His expression darkens and he takes a step toward me. "Do not put me in the same box as those motherfuckers."

"I don't know you." I hold my ground, refusing to cower, even though it's difficult when faced with all his scariness up close. After a long stare-down, I drop my eyes to my cell, find my dad's number and press call. It rings once and my body relaxes when he picks up.

"Hey kid what's up?"

"Are you in Nashville?"

"Yep, are you okay?"

"I'm not sure," I mumble, then explain to him what happened with the guys and the tracker.

"I'll be there in five. Go wait in the store until you see me pull up."

"Okay."

"Love you."

"Love you, too. See you soon." I hang up and spin on my heel and head across the lot.

"When is your man gonna be here?" Mr. Scary-guy asks, stepping in sync with me.

"My dad will be here in five minutes." I peek over at him, and he grunts something under his breath. "You don't need to wait with me."

"I know. Still going to do it." He opens the door to the liquor store, and I stand next to the glass window and watch, hoping my dad hurries up. The man at my side doesn't say a word, but then again, he doesn't need to speak for me to know he's here. His presence is almost overwhelming, and it feels like he's sucking up all the oxygen, which is making me light-headed.

It takes less than five minutes for my dad to arrive and the minute he pulls into the lot on his Harley, I push open the door, then notice an SUV roll in right behind him.

"Fuck," my new shadow mutters.

I glance up at him. "What?"

"Nothing." He walks toward the SUV while I go to where my dad is swinging off his bike.

"Hey kid." He greets me with a hug that lets me know that everything is going to be okay then asks. "Who's the guy?"

"I don't know." I look at the man in question and watch him talking with the two guys who pulled in behind my dad. I don't recognize either man but it's obvious by the familiar way that Mr. Scary is talking to them that they know each other. Both men are around his age and good looking, one with dark blonde hair, clean cut in jeans with a Henley under a vest, and the other wearing an outfit similar to my dad's and Mr. Scary's. The second man has longer dark hair and scruff on his jaw and looks a lot like the man talking to him. "You brought reinforcements?"

"There's been some issues recently with women being targeted, I was with them when you called." He lets me go. "They wanted to see if the MO is similar."

"Oh."

"Where's the tag?"

"On the ground behind my car." I follow him to the back of my ride where he bends to pick up the metal disc off the ground and the three guys come to join us.

"Where did you go tonight?" Dad asks.

I shift on my feet feeling all eyes on me. "I was at Cabriana's with Alec."

"You're still seeing that guy?" Dad questions.

I roll my eyes. He never liked Alec, not that he had a reason not to besides the fact that I'm his daughter and Alec is a man.

"Not after tonight," I mutter then add, "and before you ask, no, he didn't do anything. It just wasn't working." I hear two distinctive chuckles and force myself not to look at the man standing at my side, once again sucking up all the oxygen.

"How'd you know she'd been marked?" Dad asks, focusing about a foot above my head at my side.

"This is my brother, Clay." The guy with dark blond hair speaks up.

I know my eyes widen because they look nothing alike, like *nothing* alike.

"As family we've spoke about what's been going on in the city recently."

"I was on my bike when I saw someone tag her car. I decided I'd follow," he says, leaving out what he told me, that he was watching them, which I find interesting.

"You didn't think about calling it in?"

"Nope," he says easily.

I rub my lips together when my dad's expression turns scary.

"This isn't a game."

"I'm aware," Clay bites out.

I'm almost tempted to step between him and my father, but instead I ask, "So is it the same kind of tracker used in other cases?"

Clay's brother takes it from Dad and flips it over in his hand. "Looks like the others to me." He hands it to the man next to him.

"I'd say it's the same." He hands it back to my dad then meets my gaze. "Did you get a good look at the guys?"

"Not really." My nose scrunches. "They were both average looking white guys." I shrug wishing I had more information, but the truth is I was distracted by the man at my side about two seconds after I spotted them standing next to my car.

"What about you?" my dad asks Clay.

He crosses his arms over his chest. "The man who placed the tracker was not one of the men who were here."

"So, they might not be connected," I surmise.

"I wouldn't say that," Clay's brother says softly. "These guys tend to work in teams."

"There has also been a string of carjackings over the last few months. The tracker could have been placed in order for them to find your car later and steal it," the guy with dark hair explains.

"So, no one has any idea what was intended." I lift my hands and let them fall to my sides. "Should I be worried?"

"You should always be worried," Dad says.

I glare at him. "That's not helpful."

"I taught you to always be aware of what's going on around you and to trust your gut if something doesn't seem right."

"I know but I'm asking if this tracker situation is something I need to be worried about right now. Will whoever put it on my car put another one on it?"

"I wish we could give you that answer, but we can't." Clay's brother says, then adds, "all you can do is stay vigilant."

"Great."

"Why don't you stay with me and Mom tonight?"

"Brodie is out of town until tomorrow, I'm keeping Jeb for him until he gets home, and besides Leah is home so I won't be alone." I watch him let out a frustrated breath, probably because he doesn't like Brodie who happens to be a guy I dated a while back but stayed friends with, and he knows he can't force me to stay with him and Mom, even if he really wants to.

"All right, I'll follow you home, but if you go out this weekend, I want you to tell me when and where you're going."

"I can do that." I agree then look at Clay's brother and the man with him. "Nice meeting you two."

"Tucker." Clays brother says.

Then the other man adds, "Miles."

I give both of them a smile, then glance up at Clay. "Thanks for looking out for me."

"No problem." He jerks up his chin.

With nothing else to do I turn to my dad. "I'll wait for you before I pull out."

"Yeah, kid I'll be just a minute." He lifts his chin.

I hustle over to my car and get in behind the wheel. After putting my bags in the passenger seat, I start the engine then look at the rearview mirror at the men still behind my car, talking. I have no idea what is being said but neither Clay nor my dad look very happy, which is making me curious. After a minute, my dad walks off with the other guys, and Clay stands there watching them go, then turns his head. Our eyes meet in my mirror, and I bite my lip then drag my eyes off his. I put my car in reverse then check the mirror to make sure it's clear. When I see it is, I back up, then pass my dad, hearing the sound of his bike pull up behind me along with another. When I look in the mirror again, I see my dad and Clay riding side by side and a sense of *déjà vu* washes over me. My grandma's always said that *déjà vu* is just a way of something bigger than us letting us know that we are on the right path. I just don't know what that means for me in this instance.

Clay

Two

HEARING SOMEONE BANGING on my front door, I drop the weights in my hands to the mat at my feet and grab a towel off the weight bench. As I make my way across the concrete floors, Skye falls into step with me, with her ears up and her tail wagging.

"What's up?" I greet Tucker and Miles as I swing open the door then turn to head for the kitchen.

"What the fuck was that yesterday?" Tucker asks as I grab a bottle of water out of the fridge.

"What the fuck was what?" Dayton asks, looking a little worse for wear as he steps out of the room he's been crashing in since he got into town a couple of days ago.

"Were you out all night?" I raise a brow his direction.

"Yes, *Dad*." He squints his eyes. "Why the fuck do you need so many windows?"

"I like the light." I put the bottle to my lips and tip it back.

"Are you going to ignore my question?" Tucker bites out, planting his hands on his hips.

I wipe my mouth with the back of my hand. "Yesterday I was helping you out."

"You know you're supposed to be invisible. We can't catch these guys if we don't have a trail to follow." Tucker points out.

My jaw clenches. He's not wrong; I've been laying in wait for months, waiting for these guys to slip up, and yesterday when I was sure they did, I fucked up. I shouldn't have stepped in, I should have just got the information I needed to put the pretty brunette on radar, then let the situation play out, but there was something about her that clawed at my insides and urged me to protect her.

"Not sure it'd be wise to use Nico Mayson's daughter as bait anyways." Miles mutters.

Tucker's jaw clenches.

"And you wanna talk about blowing my cover? What the fuck was that with you telling him I'm your brother?" I ask.

"You don't know Nico. If I hadn't stepped in, you'd likely be in jail on some charge he made up until he could figure out who you actually are, and he would find out," Tucker bites out.

I raise a brow at Miles.

"He's not exaggerating." He shrugs.

"I'm obviously missing something," Dayton says, looking between us.

"You're not missing much, we're still at square fucking one when it comes to tracking down anything new about Arya." Miles walks to the couch.

The water in my empty stomach settles like a lead weight. Arya became my sister when I was twelve and ended up in the same foster home as her, Tucker, Miles, and Dayton. The family we lived with was better than some of the other foster families I had stayed with in the past. We never went without food and always had a bed to sleep in, though they made it clear from the beginning that we were not a part of their family, they had kids of their own and were only doing their duty as god-fearing people by taking in unwanted children.

And each of us had been passed along through the system so often at that point we were use to being the outcasts, so we formed our own family within that family, until one day we came home from school and found out that Arya, who had just turned thirteen was being adopted by a couple that lived out of state. By that weekend she was gone, leaving all of us who were helpless to do anything to keep her from going.

For the first year after she was adopted, we would get letters in the mail from her almost weekly, but eventually those letters started to come fewer and farther between until they stopped all together with no explanation as to why. That's when Tucker, Miles, Dayton, and I made a pact that as soon as we aged out of the system, we would track her down.

Only we had no idea at that time what we would uncover when we did finally find her.

"Clay." A hand lands on my back. I snap out of my thoughts and look at Dayton who has moved from the island to stand next to me. "Did you hear what I asked?"

"No." I finish my water then walk across the kitchen and drop the bottle in the recycle bin.

"I asked if you checked the chats to see if this woman you stepped in for had been requested by someone?"

"I checked last night, and couldn't find anything."

"I'm still not sure they were tagging her," Miles says from the couch across the room. "Over the last few months numerous car thefts have taken place, and in the cases where those cars are recovered before they could be scrapped, there's been a tag just like the one you found yesterday."

"That doesn't explain the two guys waiting for her outside the liquor store."

"Maybe they weren't waiting for her, maybe you just want a lead so bad you thought they were." He holds up his hands as my jaw clenches. "It's understandable–we're all fucking tired of waiting for a lead, man."

"So, what do you guys have, anything since I was here last?" Dayton asks, looking between Miles and Tucker.

"Two new missing person cases were opened up, one–a sixteen-year-old girl with a history of running away, the other–a dancer at a club called "Teasers". Neither woman has used their phone, credit cards or had contact with anyone since disappearing and we have no leads."

"So, a young impressionable girl with an obvious history of some type of family issue—" he holds up one finger "—and a girl with a job in an industry where women have been known to be victimized." He holds up a second finger. "Both of those are like blood in the water for the type of predator we are hunting." He looks at Miles and Tucker. "Do you know the woman from yesterday? Does anything about her history give you an inclination that she would be an easy target–a woman who wouldn't be missed?"

"We don't know her, but we know her father. He's close with all of his kids and loves his wife." Miles looks at me and smirks. "And given the way he was ready to go for Clay's throat yesterday, I'd say he'd burn down the world to find the person responsible if his daughter went missing."

"He wasn't a fan of yours?" Dayton asks me with a grin.

I press my lips together. The truth is I couldn't give a fuck how Willow's father felt about me, but I could appreciate the way he showed up when his daughter called him. A lot of people say they love their kids but saying those words and putting action behind them are two different things.

"You need to stay clear of her," Tucker says.

I turn his way. "Pardon?"

"I saw the way you were watching her, and I'm telling you that you need to steer clear. We work with her father and they're obviously close. We don't need you blowing up our shit just to get your dick wet."

"Who the fuck are you talking to right now?" I take a step toward the living room and Miles flies up off the couch stepping between us while Skye goes on alert and comes to stand next to my side laying her weight against my calf.

"You–I'm talking to you." Tucker taunts, knowing just how to get under my skin having had sixteen years to perfect it.

"I'm going to tell you this only once: do not ever try to tell me who I can fuck or spend time with."

"So, you are going to go there?"

"If I do, it's none of your business."

"Fuck! What the fuck did I tell you?" he asks, pointing at Miles who just shrugs. "You can't be okay with that?"

"He doesn't need my permission." Miles sighs.

"Okay, lets all calm down." Dayton steps in front of me.

"I'm calm." I cross my arms over my chest. "You need to talk to him."

"You know Clay would never do anything to jeopardize us reaching our goal." He turns his back to me so he can face Tucker. "Right?"

"Right." Tucker mutters, flexing his hands.

"Then chill. We all want the same thing, we're on the same team, so fighting amongst ourselves isn't going to help us right now." He looks around at us. "Are we good now?"

"We're good." I let my arms fall to my sides.

"Tuck?" Dayton sighs and Tucker lifts his chin. "Fuck, why is it that I'm still keeping you two from killing each other?" He walks to the couch and falls lazily into it. "Have you been dealing with this bullshit since I've been gone?"

"All the fucking time, and it's worse now than it's ever been." Miles sighs, taking a seat next to him.

Dayton looks at Tucker. "Are you still pissed at Clay because of the shit Naomi pulled?"

Leave it to Dayton to call Tuck out like the lawyer he is.

"She was drunk," Tucker mutters.

I shake my head. "Brother, you know I love you and I'm all for you trying to figure shit out with your wife, but you know that's a fucking lie." I scrub my hands down my face. "She might have been drinking but she was not drunk."

"She'd been going through a lot since the miscarriage."

"I know." My tone softens because fuck I know that him loosing that baby gutted him. His wife–I'm not so sure, she seemed almost relieved when talking about the miscarriage. Then again, everyone deals with loss differently, so what the fuck do I know?

"She had been drinking, she needed a shoulder to cry on and Clay gave her that." He looks at me. "She told me what she did as soon as she got home."

I know she did, and I know that shit was only because I made it clear that I was going to tell him no matter how much she cried and begged me not to. To this day I still don't know why she showed up on my doorstep. Yes, we had gone out on a couple of dates before her and

Tucker got together but it was never serious. And after she married my brother, we were cordial at best and only really spoke in a group setting. Finding her outside my door had caught me by surprise, but I love my brother, and knew that they had gone through something difficult, so I didn't tell her to leave like I should have. No, I invited her in and about ten minutes into her being here I knew I fucked up when she tried crawling up my body to get to my mouth.

"So, you get that Clay wasn't at fault?" Dayton raises a brow.

"She was vulnerable."

"And you think I took advantage of that?" I let out a hollow laugh.

"You knew we'd been struggling."

"I'm not doing this." I head across the loft toward my bedroom then stop and spin to face him. "Actually, let me say one thing."

"Clay." Miles groans but I keep my eyes locked on Tucker's.

"I don't want your wife, and I think it's probably about time that you came to terms with the fact that maybe you don't want her either."

"Fuck you, man, you live your life uncommitted to everything and everyone. You don't know shit about marriage or relationships."

"I've never been married but I know that the person you choose to be with is someone you should actually want to fucking *be* with."

"You don't know shit."

"That's where you're wrong. I know you're miserable, I know you make a lot of excuses for your wife's behavior, and I know that you're taking that bullshit out on the wrong person." I let out a deep breath. "Now I'm gonna shower." I leave my brothers in my living room without a backwards glance and walk into my room with Skye at my side. I strip out of my clothes as I head for the shower knowing one thing for sure, nothing good is going to come from that confrontation and if anything, it just caused more of a rift between Tucker and me.

FUCK!

Willow ⸺ Clay

Willow

Three

"*AND* NEXT THING I know he's kissing me," I say, watching my best friend and roommate's eyes widen as I tell her about what happened with Clay.

"Are you serious?"

"Yes."

"Did you kiss him back?"

"Absolutely not." I wave my hand out and her eyes scan my face.

"Your mouth is saying you didn't, but your face is saying something else."

"My mouth and face are both saying the same thing."

"Okay." She presses her lips together. "So, what happened after that?"

"He goes to my car and for obvious reasons I'm like, 'what are you doing?' Then he pulled out a tracker from under the back bumper."

"What?" she gasps, and I cringe. "Why would there be a tracker on your car?"

"I don't know, I called my dad, and he showed up with some guys and get this…" I wait for a little flare. "One of them was that guy Clay's brother."

"Are you living in a movie?"

"It felt like it." I hop up on the counter next to where she's cooking some kind of fancy pasta dish that will no doubt be amazing. "So anyways the guys looked at the metal thing then said they couldn't be sure that it was a tracker for me or just for my car."

"For your car?" She frowns.

"I guess that there's been some car thefts recently and they use the tracker to find the car later." I shrug. "I looked it up online and it's happening in lots of big cities."

"You do have a nice car."

"I do." I agree because my Audi is top of the line and the only thing in my life that I have ever splurged on. It took me months to finally decide to purchase it and that was only after about a dozen pro/con lists. To say I have a difficult time making long-term decisions is an understatement. But to be fair, I never want to regret anything, so I always take time to make sure that what I'm doing is the right thing.

"So, are you safe?"

"Yeah, I mean I've been keeping an eye out and haven't noticed anything strange or anyone following me."

"Good," she says quietly, then meets my gaze and asks, "so you and Alec are done?"

"Yes."

"And how long before he turns into one of your best friends that you dog sit for and try to match up with someone you think would be perfect for him?"

"Very funny." I roll my eyes.

"It's a serious question. You date all these guys then find a reason to break up with them only to befriend them in the end. You have to admit it's a little odd."

"Did you miss the part where I was trapped in a bathroom forever and instead of him coming to find out if I was okay, he had dinner by himself?"

"Okay, I can admit that sounds bad."

"Exactly, and it's not odd that I'm friends with my exes, they're nice guys, they're just not the guys for me."

"I'm just saying you're the only woman I know who is not only on speaking terms with all of her ex-boyfriends but actually friends with them."

"And again, they are all nice guys." I shrug. "Really It's easy being friends with them, I mean I hooked up with them, yes, but I didn't have sex with all of them so it's not really awkward."

"I still don't understand how you are still a virgin."

"I'm not a virgin." I laugh.

"Okay a reincarnated virgin then."

"That's not a thing." I smile. "And you know why I'm not going there again." I remind her and her face softens in sympathy.

"Not all guys are like he who shall not be named."

"I know but there are some who are, and I'd rather not find out that what I thought was something special was just some guy telling me everything I wanted to hear so he could get in my pants."

"Do you think you've actually given any of the guys you've dated over the last few years the chance to prove that?"

"Yes, I mean I don't think it's too much to ask a guy to actually show up, to be present and to make me a priority. I don't need to be the most important thing in his life, but I do need to be in the top three." Okay, that last part might be a lie. I do want to be the most important thing to the guy I fall in love with, then again, I think that desire comes from seeing my parents' relationship along with all the other couples I know. *A girl can wish right?*

"You're right you deserve that." She gives me a soft smile.

"And so do you," I remind her, then hop down off the counter when my cell starts to ring. When I see that it's Carly, a friend of mine from work, calling, I slide my finger across the screen and put my phone to my ear.

"Hey."

"Hey, what are you doing tonight?" she asks, and I look at Leah.

"Leah and I are getting ready to eat dinner, and veg out on the couch with a show."

"Oh." She sounds a little disappointed.

"Is everything okay?"

"Yeah, it's just this guy I met online asked me to meet him at a bar and I want to go but don't want to go alone because he's going to have friends there."

"Hold on a sec." I pull my phone away from my ear after she says okay then put it on mute and wave my hand out to get Leah's attention.

"Do you feel up to going to a bar tonight? Carly is supposed to meet some guy, but she doesn't want to go alone."

"Sure," she shrugs, and I shake my head because I know she doesn't really want to go but is agreeing because I'm asking.

"We don't have to, we can stay here and hang out like we planned."

"I honestly don't mind going out for a while, but I can't stay out late since I have to work early."

"Okay." I click the phone off mute and put it back to my ear. "All right me and Leah will meet you there."

"Seriously?" Carly asks, sounding relieved.

"Seriously, just text me the name of the bar." I take the plate of pasta Leah hands me. "What time are you heading there?"

"I think he said he wanted to meet at nine. There's some band in town playing that is supposed to be good."

"Awesome, we'll see you there."

"See you there." She hangs up and I drop my phone to the counter then follow Leah who has her own plate to the living room.

"So what time are we meeting her?" She flips on the television.

"Nine and we'll just Uber, that way we don't have to fight to get parking downtown."

"Sounds good." She grins. "Now should we watch some Viking hotties attempt to take over England?"

"Is that a trick question?" I curl into what has been my section of the couch since we purchased it and dig into my food. After the first bite I look at my best friend. "I still don't know how you're not married yet."

She laughs. "Because I eat like this and look like this." She pats her thigh.

"Stop it. You know you're gorgeous." And she is–between her long, blonde hair, big blue eyes, freckles that give her an unusual flare, and curves in all the right places, she's the whole package. But sadly, my beautiful friend has a mother and a father who have made her hate her body which is just as perfect as she is, and no matter how much I try to convince her differently she can't or won't accept it. Like this pasta dish we're eating tonight, I'm sure tomorrow she will be up early to get to the gym to work it off.

"I hate your mom." I grumble and she lets out a long breath, then without a comeback she turns to the TV as our show begins to play.

Knowing the conversation is done I dig into my five-star shrimp and pasta dish and devour each and every delicious bite while I watch a group Vikings attempt to take over the world and only partly wish I could go back in time because things like hot showers and women's rights did not exist back then.

DRESSED IN A pair of jeans that flare at the ankle, platform booties, and a tight lace top that shows just a hint of cleavage under my short leather jacket I get out of the Uber Leah and I rode in, then hold out my hand.

"Can you make it out?" I laugh as she scoots across the long backseat in her jeans that are as tight as mine.

"Yes." She laughs with me when she finally gets her heels on the ground. "Thanks." She turns to smile at the driver totally missing that he was just checking out her ass.

"Sure, have fun ladies." He waves before we slam the door. When we step up on the sidewalk, I scan for Carly who said she would meet us out front of the bar.

"Do you see her?" Leah asks and I shake my head.

"No, do you?"

"Wait isn't that her?"

I look to where she's pointing and have to do a double take. I haven't known Carly for long, we've only been working together at the bank for about six months, but she looks nothing like herself tonight. Not only is she wearing a full face of makeup with her hair done up big, but her outfit is something I'm honestly surprised to see her in. At work she's always in slacks and button downs and when we've hung out outside of work, she normally just dresses very casually in jeans and a sweater or a t-shirt. Tonight's outfit is none of that. No, her skirt is short, her heels are high, and her top is low cut showing a good amount of cleavage. I mean she looks beautiful, I'm just shocked because it's so different then her norm.

When she spots us, she starts to wave, then walks our way through the crowd on the sidewalk. "Oh my god, thank you guys so much for coming."

"You look awesome." I give her a hug that she returns before stepping back and running her hands down her sides.

"It's not too much?"

"Not at all."

"Thank you." She lifts her shoulders and smiles like a little kid who's excited. "I'm just so nervous, I haven't been on a date in so long and I swear this guy is perfect and I just want tonight to go good, you know?"

"I'm sure it will be great." I give her a reassuring smile. "So, are you meeting him inside?"

"I think so." She looks around then cringes. "I didn't ask."

"Well, we can go in and see if he's here. What does he look like?"

"Tall, dark, and handsome." She laughs then pulls out her phone and clicks away before showing Leah his photo on the screen.

"Oh, he is hot." Leah grins and I nod my agreement because the guy is good looking with dark hair and that whole clean cut but still edgy look.

"Right." She tucks her phone in her bag. "Well, I guess we can go in and if he can't find me, he'll call."

After showing the bouncer at the door our ID's we walk into the bar that is, not surprisingly, packed full of people. Not only are there tons of men and women but there are three separate groups of girls who are all dressed similar, who I have no doubt are here for a bachelorette party. This is only the first floor, so I'm sure there are more on the other two levels.

"Oh my god, he's here." Carly spins around to face us. "Do I look okay?"

"You look awesome."

"Are you sure?"

"Yes," I laugh, grabbing her hands. "Do you want us to go over with you?"

"Umm, I don't know." She glances over her shoulder quickly. "I think I should probably go alone at first, don't you?"

"That would probably be good." I squeeze her hands. "You got this, and we are here if you need us."

"Thank you so much." She gives us both a goofy smile, then spins around and starts walking across the bar. It doesn't take the guy long at all to notice her, then again, a lot of other men in the room stop to watch her as well.

"All right so what do you say you and I get a drink." I suggest to Leah when Carly's date gets up to greet her with a smile and a sweet kiss to her cheek.

"Yes, please." We head to the bar and after we both have the vodka sodas we ordered, we start to head for a standing table but stop when Carly waves us to come over to where she is.

"Girls, this is Matthew." She tips her head back to smile up at him. "Matthew, this is my co-worker and friend, Willow, and her roommate Leah."

"Nice to meet you both." He holds out his hand for each of us to take and I'm honestly a little disappointed by how weak his grip is. I mean I know that's stupid but working in the banking industry I've found that men who have strong, firm handshakes tend to be more sure of the things they want in life and in relationships. And men whose handshakes are weak tend to be wishy-washy about everything.

"You, too." I take a sip of my drink.

"So, you work in banking as well?" He takes a seat and pulls Carly to stand between his legs, which seems really intimate when he's just met her. Then again, she doesn't seem to mind at all, judging by the contended smile on her face.

"I do."

"She's the investment manager." Carly tells him and he tips his head to the side as he studies me.

"You're a little young to be in that job."

I pretend not to have heard him because I seriously hate when guys say things like that–I mean if I had a penis, I doubt they would feel the same.

"So, what do you do?" Leah asks him.

"I work in shipping."

"Shipping?" I know she's frowning without even looking at her.

"My company ships high value items all over the world."

"That sounds interesting."

"It's mostly me sitting at a desk making calls and doing paperwork. What about you, what do you do?"

"I work for Vanderbilt." She tells him and I barely hold back a laugh because only my best friend would be so nonchalant about the fact that she's actually a doctor at one of the most prestigious hospitals in the United States.

"Cool." He takes his attention off us when someone shouts his name and I look across the bar and watch two guys walk our way. When I look back at Matthew, who is starting to get up, and moving Carly who is still standing between his legs, so she doesn't stumble.

"Hey, guys." He greets his friends with handshakes and pats on the back, then motions to us three girls.

"Willow, Leah and–" he wraps his arm around Carly's waist, "my girl Carly. Ladies this is George and Lev."

I give both guys a small wave. Soon all the guys seem to forget we exist and start to talk amongst each other, so us three girls group together at the edge of the bar and watch the band. Like most of the bars downtown that hire artists to come in and play, they put their own spin on popular country songs making it easy for people to sing along and want to stay a while. After some time, Matthew and his friends come over to join us and I can tell by Carly's demeanor that she's happy to have his attention back.

As the music plays, I look at Leah and notice that she looks a little pale.

"Are you okay?"

"I actually have a headache." She squints at me. "I think I'm gonna call it a night."

"What's going on?" Carly asks, leaning into us to hear over the music.

"Leah has a headache."

"Please don't leave me." She latches onto my arm, and I feel her fingers dig into my skin through my jacket.

"Stay." Leah grabs my attention. "I'll be okay."

"Are you sure?"

"Of course." She glances between Carly and me. "You guys have fun."

"Okay." I give in. "But I'll wait with you outside until your car arrives."

"Fine, *Mom*." She rolls her eyes.

"I'll be right back." I tell Carly after Leah says goodbye to everyone.

"Promise you're not leaving me." Carly grabs my hand when I start to walk away with Leah.

"Promise, I'll be right back." I give her a reassuring smile then take Leah outside and wait with her on the sidewalk until her Uber arrives, then give her a hug. "Text when you're home."

"I will. Have fun." She gets into the back of the car, and I watch until it's out of sight before I head back into the bar and find Carly where I left her.

"Thank you for staying." Carly wraps her arm around my shoulder, and I slide mine around her waist.

"No problem." I give her waist a squeeze then look up at Matthew when he steps up behind her.

"Do you ladies want another drink?"

"Yes please." Carly gives him her order, then he looks at me.

"I'll have a vodka soda."

"Coming right up." He walks to the bar with his friends and we both watch them go.

"So how are you feeling now that you've met him?"

"I don't know, it's hard to get to know someone in this kind of environment."

"True."

"But he's hot and is buying us alcohol, so I'd say he's okay," she laughs, taking her attention off me to look back at the stage.

I inwardly sigh wondering what the heck is wrong with me that I can't find such simple attributes attractive when it comes to men.

Willow

Four

COMING AWAKE THE first thing I notice is my head pounding, the second thing I notice is that even with my eyes still closed the light is so bright I can see it through my closed eyelids and the third thing is a softness of the blankets and scent of some kind of oddly familiar deep musk I'm wrapped in.

My heart starts to pound as I lay with my eyes closed because I know something is wrong–very, very wrong. The bed I'm in feels nothing like my own but it's still obvious that I'm in a bed. Doing a scan on my body, I can tell my jeans are off and I'm no longer in the top I had on last night but can feel the soft material of the t-shirt I'm wearing. What I don't feel is any pain or discomfort between my legs, which is a relief.

What the hell happened?

My throat gets tight, but I fight back the urge to panic because I have no idea what the hell it is I'm about to face when I finally work up the courage to open my eyes.

After a deep breath, I squint my eyes open and look around at what seems to be a giant room with brick walls, windows that take up one entire side from floor to ceiling, with a few industrial but expensive looking bedroom pieces around the huge space and the bed I'm on in the middle. Slowly I sit up, not sure that I won't puke because my stomach is rolling like I drank way too much. But I don't remember having more than two drinks last night. Hearing a jingle that almost sounds like car keys I look toward the heavy-looking door and watch a large dog that looks similar to a wolf get up off the concrete floor with a quiet groan and starts in my direction with its head low, ears back and tail down.

"Hey, puppy," I whisper, trying not to show fear because I know that's the first thing animals can sense. Holding out my hand when the dog comes to the edge of the bed that seems like it's sitting on the floor, it sniffs my fingers then nudges them with its nose. Taking that as an invite to touch him or her, I slide my fingers up its snout and rub the top of its head then behind its ears. Really, I've never seen a more beautiful dog in my life; its eyes are a blue so clear that they look like a glacier, and its coat is a mixture of greys, blacks, whites, and taupe that would blend in perfectly if out in the wilds of Alaska with ease. "What's your name?" I slide my hand around it's collar until I find the tag then look at the silver medallion with the name Skye on one side and a number on the other. "Skye." I say quietly and its tail begins to wag. "I wish you could tell me what I'm about to come face to face with." I say quietly then look to the door and brace when I hear the handle start to turn.

Not sure if I should play like I'm still asleep or go on the defensive and get up out of bed, I sit frozen in fear as the door is opened.

My lips part and I swallow hard as a man walks into the room with his phone in hand, and a scowl on his handsome face as he types away on it. I had no idea when or if I would ever see Clay again, so I'm taken aback to see him, wearing only the tattoos that cover his torso and arms and a pair of sweatpants that have been cut off at the knee.

As he walks across the room distracted by his phone, I scramble to remember something–anything from last night that might clue me in on how I ended up here in what I'm guessing is his bed, wearing his shirt.

When he places the phone on top of the dresser, Skye makes a huffing sound and he turns around, his eyes landing on mine.

"Why am I here?" I grip the blanket between my fingers as he walks toward me.

"You were being loaded in some guy's car outside a bar last night when I came across you."

"What?" I breathe, sure that I heard him wrong.

"You were out of it, totally wasted."

"I only had two drinks last night." I rub my lips together. "I don't remember much of anything after the second one. Was there another woman with me?"

"No other woman. I asked if you knew the guy you were with, you said he was your driver, but you couldn't tell me his name. He told me he was taking you home, but you were so out of it that the address you gave didn't make sense." He crosses his arms over his chest. "He and I shared a few words, I got you out of his car and brought you back here."

"You brought me back here."

"Yep." He shrugs. "How are you feeling?"

"What's a level up from like *death*?"

"Not sure there is anything worse than that."

"Hmm." I look around. "Did I have my bag with me?"

"No bag, no cell."

"Great." I scrub my hands down my face and fall to my back, now more concerned with what happened to Carly then anything else. A warm, heavy weight lands on my stomach. My eyes fly open, and I look down.

"She likes you," he says, and I focus on him across the room as I rub the top of Skye's head.

"She's sweet."

"She's badass."

"Whatever you say." I fight back another round of nausea and squeeze my eyes closed.

"I know you don't want to, but it would probably be good to get up and put something in your stomach."

"Do you want me to puke in your bed?"

"Not particularly."

"Then let's not mention that again." I open one eye and find him closer to the bed than he was before and still very shirtless. "Am I wearing the only shirt you own?"

"Yep." I catch his smile before he bends, putting his fist in the bed next to me. "You need to get up and put something in your stomach."

"Okay." I agree quietly, even though I have no desire whatsoever to leave his bed. "Do you know where my clothes are?"

"No." He grins, and I narrow my eyes on his. "They're in the dryer in the bathroom."

"Thanks." I wait for him to move so I can get up, but he doesn't. With a huff I push to sit up and then toss my legs over the side of the bed opposite of him and place my feet on the floor. When I stand my legs shake, my head pounds and my stomach rolls, but I still find it in myself to make sure and pull down his shirt as I stand. "Where's the bathroom?" He motions to a closed door, and I walk across the room to it. When I walk inside, I use the restroom then go to the sink and turn on the water before I look in the mirror. I cringe at my appearance; my makeup isn't so bad, but my face looks pale and drawn like I went on a bender.

There's a knock on the door and before I can even call out, it's opened, and Clay is stepping inside. "Here's a fresh toothbrush, and if you want, feel free to jump in the shower."

"I don't want to intrude more than I already have."

"Towels are above the washer/dryer." I nod and his eyes scan my face. "What bar were you at?"

"Boots."

He jerks up his chin in acknowledgement, then leaves without another word.

I look at the glass-encased shower with its multitude of nozzles. I should probably not feel comfortable enough in this man's house to get naked, but I still find myself grabbing a towel and taking off my clothes, placing them on the vanity. Before letting the water warm up, I step under the spray in the shower and instantly feel a little better as the cold water washes over me. I use the stuff he has in bottles that smell like him to wash up and close my eyes as I try to remember what happened last night. I know Carly and I were having a good time and that the guys were around, but it's like after I was given that second drink everything is a black void. And I don't even want to think about what would have happened if Clay hadn't come across me.

When I get out of the shower, I dry off and brush my teeth before I go to the dryer and take out my jeans and put them on, deciding to just to wear his shirt rather then fuss with the top I wore last night.

With my hair wrapped in a towel I take my stuff with me, leave the bathroom, and find the bedroom empty, so I make my way to the door and pause to take a deep breath before I open it.

I step out into another huge open room with brick walls, more windows, sturdy looking furniture, and low leather couches. With one look around, it's clear that a man lives here, but that man has seriously good taste. Seeing Clay in the kitchen area I pad that way and he stops what he's doing to watch me.

"Any chance I'm getting my shirt back before you leave."

"Nope."

"Looks better on you anyway." He motions for me to come to him. As I take a seat on one of the barstools, he places some kind of green looking drink on the counter along with a glass of water. "That will help with the hangover."

"Thanks." I pick it up and take a sip. "It's not half as gross as I thought it might be."

"Good." He smiles and darn, but he really does have a nice smile.

"I know it's asking a lot of you, but would you mind taking me home. I would call a cab or a friend but…"

"You don't have your purse or your cell."

"Yeah." I lick my lips. "That and I know Leah, my roommate, is working today so she won't be around to even pay for my cab when I get there."

"Who were you out with last night?"

"A friend from work named Carly. She was meeting a guy she only talked to online and didn't want to go alone so me and Leah met her there." I rub the top of Skye's head when she comes over and rests her head on my lap. "Leah took off early with a headache, so it was just me and Carly."

"That's not safe, babe."

"Yeah, I'm getting that, *babe*." I say sarcastically and he presses his lips together apparently not finding me funny. "Sorry."

"Any memory of what happened to your friend and her date?"

"No."

"Do you think she would leave you?"

"Maybe, I honestly don't know, we've only hung out a few times and it's always been just dinner or if I've had her over to my house."

"Right," he mutters, seeming even more annoyed.

"You said I was getting into a car."

"A man was putting you in his car, you could barely hold your head up."

I shake my head. "All I can think is that was one of the guys who was friends with Carly's date."

"He had friends with him?"

"Two guys." I rub my forehead between my eyes wishing this headache would go away. "I can't remember their names though, we didn't really talk."

"Maybe your friend will remember."

"Maybe, I just wish I had my phone so I could call to make sure Carly's okay."

"Do you have her number at your house?"

"Yeah." I meet his gaze then drop my voice. "Do you think I should call the cops?"

"I called my brothers, they're getting the tapes from the bar you were at."

"Brothers?" My brows dart together.

"Finish up your shake, I'm gonna get dressed then I'll take you home." He walks toward his bedroom, and I turn on my stool to watch him go. I know I didn't mishear him–he said "brothers" meaning he has more than one who works as a police officer. I mean, I don't know him so I guess I shouldn't feel like that's a big deal, but I can't help but feel like it is for some reason, and I'm not supposed to know.

Getting up with my drink, I wander into the living room with Skye following at my side and go to a wooden shelf with framed photos on it. As I look at the pictures, I wonder who the couples and the families are, they look too perfect, like they've been photo shopped and Clay or his brother Tucker aren't in a single picture.

Is this even his house?

When I hear the door open behind me, I turn expecting to see Clay but instead I watch a good-looking man wearing glasses, a t-shirt, and basketball shorts with rumpled hair stumble out of a room.

"Fucking stupid light," he groans, almost bumping into a couch as he squints, his eyes closed.

A giggle bursts from between my lips as I watch him fumble his way around the living room furniture cursing, and at the sound he stops dead in his tracks and turns to face me. "Who are you?"

"Willow." I smile and he drops his eyes to my shirt–or I guess it's Clay's shirt.

"Oh fuck," he mumbles.

I tip my head to the side. "What?"

"What are you doing here?"

"I brought her home last night." Clay cuts in and the guy looks his direction.

"He didn't like *bring me home* bring me home, I was drugged." My nose scrunches. "Or I think I was drugged."

"You were drugged?"

"I don't know."

"Did you call Miles and Tucker?" he asks, looking at Clay.

I do the same.

"They're on it." Clay tells him, then his eyes meet mine. "Ready?"

"Yeah." I walk to the kitchen and set down the cup, then remove the towel from my head and look around for somewhere to put it.

"I'll take it." Clay grabs it tossing it onto the island, then motions to the door. "Your shoes are there."

"Thanks." I start to put them on while both men go into the bedroom where I can hear them talking in hushed tones. Curiosity has me wanting to eavesdrop, but just as I start to move to get closer to the door, Skye blocks my way and leans into me with her heavy weight.

"Let's go." Clay grumbles when he comes out of the bedroom, dressed in jeans, a long sleeve shirt with a vest over it and boots.

I nod and grab my stuff from the counter then turn to wave at his friend when he says goodbye. When we leave his place, he leads me to an elevator, and we take it down to the first floor. I expect us to be in a lobby of some kind, but instead, the doors open, and I find that we're in a warehouse that is still under construction; piles of drywall, buckets of paint and other items are scattered around the large, open space while plastic sheeting blows in the wind coming through the open windows.

"What is this place?"

"It used to be a factory, eventually the first three floors will be apartments." Clay wraps his hand around my upper arm, helping me step over discarded pieces of wood with nails sticking out of them.

"The building owner let you move in with it looking like this down here? I feel like this is a lawsuit waiting to happen."

"I'm not planning on suing myself," he says, and I glance up at him, which means I'm not watching where I'm going and end up stumbling slightly. Thankfully, he still has a hold of me, so I don't fall on my face like I could have.

"Thank you." I sigh then squeak when he stops and lifts me off my feet in one quick motion. Wrapping my arms around his neck on instinct, I blink as our eyes meet up close, caught off-guard by his nearness and just how pretty his eyes are. Not only are they a very unusual blue green but the lashes surrounding them are dark and long. Clearing my throat, I place one hand against his chest. "I can walk."

"I'd rather not have you sue me when you break your pretty neck," he mutters, stepping around a stack of paint cans. "Those shoes are dangerous."

"No, they aren't." I look down at my boots. "They look high but that's just an illusion."

"Whatever you say."

He reaches a set of metal double doors that curve at the top, then places me on my feet so he can open them. When we step out onto the sidewalk, I realize that we are near the river and an old train yard downtown.

"This way." He points me to the right where there a few cars parked along the sidewalk, then takes his key out of his pocket and the lights on a red jeep that has been decked out flash.

When he opens the passenger door for me, I get in and look around. The vehicle is new, even the plastic mats on the floor are still covered with the paper from the dealership. Another mystery.

When he's behind the wheel, I rattle off my address, then we sit in silence as he drives us across town. I want to ask about a million questions, but I get the feeling that he wouldn't answer them, so I keep my mouth closed. Getting to my building doesn't take long because traffic is so light, and when we arrive, he finds a place to park, and I start to tell him thank you for the ride but before I can even open my mouth, he's out the door and slamming it shut.

"I don't need you to go in with me." I tell him as I hop down from my seat after pushing open the door.

"I want to hear what your co-worker has to say about last night."

"Okay, but I need to go to a friend's place to pick up my key since I don't have my bag. Do you want to wait for me in the lobby?"

"I'll go with you." He follows me to the building and lucky for us a couple is leaving as we are walking up to the door, so the guy holds it open, allowing us entry.

I press the button for the penthouse when we get on the elevator, and hope like heck that Brodie is home and not at soccer practice or out with friends. The ride up to the top floor feels like it takes forever with Clay sucking up all the air in the small space, so when we arrive and the doors open, I drag in a relieved breath.

"Hopefully he's here." I mumble to myself as we head down the hall to the door at the end and then knock twice. I hear movement from inside, then the turn of a lock and a moment later Brodie is opening the door, wearing only a pair of black boxers.

"Hey what are you doing here?" he asks me, then looks to my side and frowns at Clay, who is so quiet that I would forget he was here if his presence didn't seem to cause my cells to vibrate with his nearness.

"I need my spare key, I got locked out of my place." I tell him then laugh as his Great Dane, Jeb, bounces out of the apartment and starts to dance around my feet, almost knocking me over when he hops up on his back legs so he can get his face in mine. "Hey handsome." I give him a hug then try to control his snout as he begins licking my face.

"How'd you get locked out?" Brodie asks, handing me a key as he takes control of Jeb.

"Long story."

"You can tell me about it over dinner," he suggests.

I shake my head. "I can't tonight, but maybe later in the week."

"I'm out of town." His expression softens. "Remember, you're keeping Jeb."

"Oh, I thought that was next week."

"It is next week." He looks to my side when Clay makes a grunting noise. "And you are?"

"This is my friend Clay. Clay, this is Brodie." I wait for them to shake hands or something but neither does anything but stare at the other.

Okay, awkward.

"Are you still keeping Jeb for me?"

"Of course." I frown, wondering what's wrong with him. "I'll send you a text tomorrow."

"All right." He looks like he wants to say more but changes his mind and steps back into his apartment. "See you tomorrow."

"See you tomorrow." I agree then with my key in hand and Clay at my back I walk to the elevator and press the button to go down to the fourth floor.

"Your ex?" Clay asks.

I look up at him. "Yep."

"And you watch his dog?"

"He's a friend."

"I bet he is."

"What's that supposed to mean?" I narrow my eyes on his.

"Nothing."

"I help him out when he's out of town for work." I defend, then get annoyed with myself because I owe this man no explanation.

"And you have dinner with him?"

"Did you miss the part where he's my friend?"

"I missed none of that, babe."

"Good, *babe*." I snap then stomp out of the elevator as soon as the doors open. I know my annoyance is irrational, I've had that same kind of conversation with Leah a million times, but coming from Clay, it feels different. Or maybe it is a culmination of his comments and Brodie's reaction to him. Honestly, I'm too exhausted to figure any of it out right now.

When we reach my apartment door, I use the key to let us in, flip on some of the lights and leave Clay standing in the living room as I go to my bedroom. After grabbing my work laptop off my bed where I left it, I take it with me to the kitchen and start it up. It takes a minute to find Carly's number in the database and when I do I turn to look at the man standing in the middle of the room looking around.

"I need a phone, I don't have a landline."

"Security in this place is shit and you don't have a landline."

"Security is actually great in this building, and no one has a landline nowadays."

"I have one."

"Okay, *Grandpa*, congratulations. Now, can I use your phone?"

He comes to where I'm sitting, and I fight the urge to show any kind of reaction once he's in my space and leaning into me.

"Say, 'Please'."

"Can I use your phone, please?" I say even though the word "no" is on the tip of my tongue.

He stands back and reaches into his pocket, pulling out his cell phone. "Was that so hard?"

Yes, it was, but I can't figure out why I have the urge to push back, or why everything feels difficult when it comes to this man. After unlocking it, he hands it over and I notice the screen saver is a photo of a little dark-haired girl with bright pink bows in her hair with her arms wrapped around Skye's neck.

"My niece," he says.

I look up at him shocked that he gave me that so easily. "She's adorable."

"She's trouble," he says with a soft look on his face.

My stomach flutters. Damn, but I like that look on him. I duck my head and pull up the phone pad so I can dial Carly's number. When the phone starts to ring, I put the call on speaker, figuring it will be easier for him to just listen rather than having to relay what she said.

"Hello." Carly answers, sounding like she just woke up and I instantly feel a sense of relief.

"Hey, it's Willow."

"Oh, hey." There's a hint of surprise in her voice. "I didn't recognize the number."

"It's a friend's phone." I bite my lip then ask. "Did you get home okay last night?"

"Yeah, is everything okay?"

"I don't remember much, it's like I blacked out."

"You had a lot to drink." She laughs.

"Did I?" I frown. "I don't remember taking more than a few sips of my second drink."

"Matthew kept buying us drinks all night." She giggles and I hear what sounds like a smack then a grunt. "He probably bought us like ten each."

"Oh." I rub my forehead. "Do you know how I left, like who was taking me home?"

"I ordered you an Uber because your cell phone died."

"You did? Did you walk me out to meet it?"

"No, you said you were okay and that I should stay with Matthew." The phone goes quiet for a second. "Are you okay?"

"Yeah, I'm just trying to piece things together." I close my eyes wishing I could remember what happened. "And one of his friends didn't walk me out?"

"No, they had already taken off by that point."

"Right." I mumble. "Sorry for interrupting your morning."

"Are you sure you're okay?"

"Yeah, I'm fine, is Matthew there with you now?"

"He is," she whispers sounding happy.

"Okay, enjoy your time with him and I'll see you tomorrow at work."

"See you then." She hangs up and I stare at the phone not sure what it is I'm feeling.

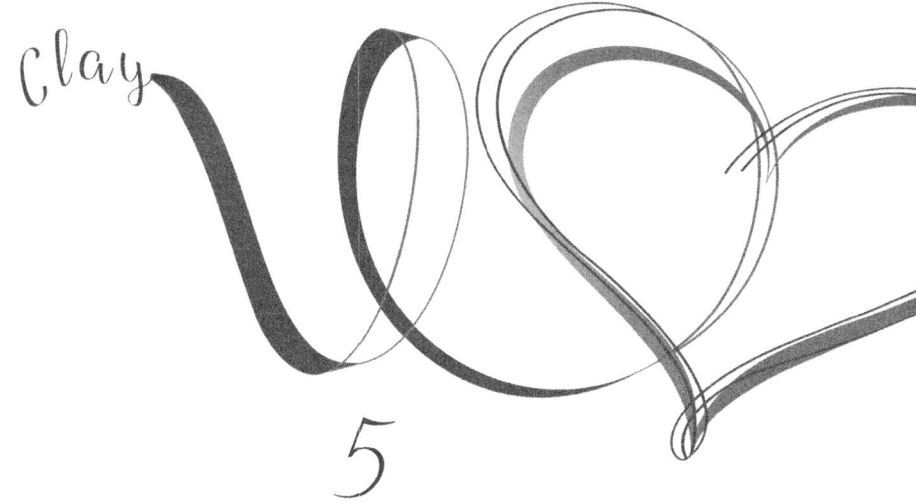

Clay

5

$\mathcal{S}$LIDING MY CELL out of Willow's hand I tuck it into my pocket then place my fingers under her chin. My gut clenches when I see the look on her face, and I bite back the urge to let her know what I think of her friend. It's obvious that the woman she was with last night couldn't give a flying fuck about what happened to her and that she only cared about herself. But right now is not the time to bring any of that up.

"I swear I don't remember drinking that much."

"You might not have; how well do you know that girl?"

"Carly?" Her brows drag together.

I clench my fists to avoid reaching out and touching her.

"Like I told you, we work together and have hung out a few times."

"So, she could be lying."

"Why would she lie? She said I called an Uber and she sounded worried." She slides off her stool and walks around into the kitchen, opening the fridge. "Do you want some?" She holds up a refillable jug of water.

"I'm good." I pull out my phone when it starts to ring then slide my finger across the screen and put it to my ear. "What's up?" I ask Miles.

"Cameras at the bar were conveniently down last night, but the closing bartender did leave a bag behind the counter after closing up and it's Willow's."

"Was there a phone with it?"

"Yep, in the bag."

"Where are you now?" I question.

"Where do we need to be?"

"I'm at Willow's."

"You always did love playing with fire," he mutters, then adds, "shoot me a text with her address."

"Will do." I hang up then type out a quick message, letting him know I'll meet him downstairs.

"What's going on?" Willow asks and I meet her gaze.

Fuck, even fresh-faced and as tired as she obviously is, she's still fucking beautiful.

"Your bag was at the bar and your phone was in it."

"Seriously?" Her shoulders sag in relief.

"Yeah, but the cameras were down so there is no way of knowing what the fuck happened while you were there."

"Maybe Carly is right, maybe I drank too much," she says.

She doesn't look convinced.

"Do you normally drink until you can't remember shit?"

"Never." She pours herself a glass of water and chugs it down before pouring another. "But I don't see Carly lying about something like that."

"You also don't know her well, babe, and it's obvious from the outside looking in that she's a shit friend."

"You don't know her."

"Neither do you."

She makes a noise in the back of her throat that is both cute as fuck and frustrating to hear, because it's obvious she doesn't want to hear me say it even if she's thinking it herself.

"Do I need to go somewhere to pick up my purse?"

"Miles and Tucker are dropping it off."

"Your brothers, you mean." She raises a brow and I lift my chin. "They didn't tell my dad that they were both your brothers."

"We're not blood, we grew up in the same foster home." I tell her and her expression fills with sympathy.

"Oh."

"I'll meet them downstairs and bring your bag up." I turn to head for the door, but her next words stop me in my tracks.

"I won't tell."

I look at her over my shoulder.

"It's obvious that you don't want people to know that you guys are related." She clears her throat. "So, I won't tell anyone."

"I'd appreciate that." I turn and leave her in the apartment, not sure what to do with whatever-the-fuck is happening inside my chest. A few minutes after I get downstairs, Tucker and Miles pull up in their work-issued SUV and they both hop out. With one look at Tucker's face, I can tell he's pissed, but he's just going to have to get the fuck over it. I was curious about Willow before finding her last night, but the moment I saw her in my bed this morning, I knew that it wouldn't be the last time I'd see her there. And now the urge to have her is stronger than it was.

"I tried to tell him to stay in the car." Miles greets quietly when he gets close enough to hand me Willow's purse.

"You just can't fucking help yourself, can you?" Tucker clips, walking up on us.

"Tuck, chill man." Miles sighs.

"He's gonna blow our shit up; do you not see that?"

"You're gonna blow our shit up because you can't get a fucking grip on your emotions," Miles tells him, then looks at me. "How's Willow feeling? Did she get a hold of the friend she was with last night?"

"She did. Her friend claims they were both wasted and that she doesn't know who Willow left with—-just that Willow told her to stay with the guy she met up with and that she was getting a ride. The friend didn't bother checking to see who that ride was."

"Good friend," Tucker says.

I'm glad that he and I can agree on at least one thing. "The cameras were down at the bar?"

"They said they've been having issues with them for a while now."

"So, we got nothing," I surmise.

"Not one fucking thing," Miles confirms.

"I don't think we need to put our energy into this situation," Tucker says.

I focus on him. "What situation is that?" I cross my arms over my chest as I stare him down.

"Willow."

"I gotta agree with him on this," Miles says, then adds, "she's not the normal victim, she has too many people who would be looking for her if she came up missing. You know these guys like to find women who are easily forgotten and don't draw a lot of attention."

I want to deny what he's saying, but he's right, Willow doesn't fit the normal profile of someone who would be trafficked, and I've been unable to find anything online that would lead me to believe she's been requested by someone. "All right, so where are we at with the sixteen-year-old and the dancer?"

"We're still chasing down leads," Tucker says, visibly more relaxed than he was moments ago. "We have a couple of people that have refused to speak to us. They might open up to you."

"Get me their information and I'll see what I can get."

He jerks up his chin.

"I'm gonna take this up to Willow." I look between my brothers and share some honesty. "She knows who you two are to me."

"Fuck, I knew it." Tucker scrubs his hands down his face. "If people find out, we're going to have a lot of questions we won't be able to answer."

"She's not going to tell anyone."

"You better hope for our sake she doesn't," he mutters before turning and walking away.

"I hope she's worth it." Miles sighs, taking off after Tucker.

I watch both of them get back into their SUV, then head back into the building not even having to use the key in her bag because, like when we arrived, someone is leaving, and they just let me inside.

How her dad let her move in here is something I do not fucking get, not with how protective he seemed. People are way too trusting, which means someone could easily get inside then make their way through each floor until they find a door unlocked. Even the top floor, which I would guess is the most expensive unit in this building, can be easily accessed with the press of a button.

When I get upstairs, I knock, then wait a minute and knock again when she doesn't answer.

"Sorry, I was changing." She swings the door open a second later, no longer wearing my shirt and her jeans but instead a sweater that has fallen off one shoulder and a pair of shorts that match in the same soft looking material.

"Check this and make sure nothing is missing." I hand her bag over and she squeezes it against her chest.

"Thank you." She turns for the living room while I close the door.

"It doesn't look like anything is missing," she says while digging through the black purse, then pulls out a wallet, opening it up. "My credit cards and the little bit of cash I had are all here, and my phone is dead." She holds it up as she tips her head back toward me. "Carly wasn't lying."

"Good news."

"Yes, and the best part is I won't have to spend the day canceling all my cards and getting a new phone." She gets up, then goes to the kitchen. "This is yours." She hands me the shirt I put on her last night when we got back to my place. "Thanks for letting me borrow it."

I jerk up my chin and she shifts on her feet, it's odd seeing her unsure when earlier she was tossing her attitude around. "You gonna call your dad and tell him about last night?"

"If I do, he might lock me up." She rubs her lips together and wraps her arms around her middle. "I don't want him worried if there is nothing to worry about especially when him and my family are getting ready to leave town."

"Might be smart to let him know, just in case, and you should avoid going out unless you can trust the people you're with."

"That I can agree with you on." Her hands fall to her sides. "And thank you again for last night, I don't even want to think about what could have happened to me if you hadn't shown up."

My gut twisting and my hands balling into fists catches me off-guard. What happens or could happen to her shouldn't matter to me, but there is no denying that the thought of her being in harm's way makes me see red. "I want you to take my number and use it if you ever find yourself in a situation where you feel unsafe."

"That's very kind but–"

"It's not something that's up for debate." I cut her off, taking a step toward her. Her pupils dilate. "And I don't have time to play cat and mouse, so I'll make it clear here and now that I want you in my bed."

"Wha – What?" she stutters, taking a step back away from me.

"I know you heard me."

"I did." She shakes her head. "I just–I just don't know who just comes out and says something like that."

"Someone who doesn't like games." I hold her gaze, then spin when I hear the door behind me start to open, and place her behind me.

"It's just Leah," she whispers, grabbing my arm as she steps around me. "Hey, you're home early."

"Some drunk puked all over me, so I had to leave early so I could come home and shower and wash my hair properly." The woman who must be Leah answers without even looking in our direction, as she closes the door and kicks off her shoes. "I checked in on you this morning, but you weren't in bed, and you didn't—" Her words taper off when she lifts her head and her eyes land on where I'm standing behind Willow.

"Umm, this is Clay." Willow says, peeking back at me, then she bites her lip before looking back at her friend. "He brought me home."

"Clay, as in liquor-store-Clay?" Leah asks, sounding surprised.

"Yeah," Willow confirms.

Leah looks at me. "Ugh, nice to meet you."

"You too." I jerk up my chin.

She focusses on her friend. "So, I take it last night went okay then?"

"Honestly, I can't remember much after you left, and I had my second drink."

"You can't remember what happened?" she repeats on a horrified whisper.

"No."

"Where did you sleep last night?"

"At Clay's, he came across me when I was getting in someone's car, and I don't remember any of that either. All I know is I woke up in his bed."

"Did you call the police?"

"Clay filled them in, and I called Carly. She said we drank a lot."

"But you don't remember drinking a lot." Leah says, then shakes her head. "And getting wasted to the point of blacking out isn't really your style."

"I know."

"Do you want to go to the hospital?"

"No." Willow holds up both her hands. "I'm fine."

"I don't like this. Are you sure you're okay, that nothing—"

"I know. I don't like it either," Willow cuts her off. "But I really am okay."

"What did the police say?" she asks.

Willow looks at me for how to answer.

"They don't have much to go on, the cameras at the bar were down."

"I knew I shouldn't have left you last night." She starts toward her friend then stops in her tracks looking devastated. "I can't even hug you—I smell like puke."

"I'll hug you after you shower."

"Okay." She lets out a breath then looks at me. "Thanks for looking out for her." Her eyes go to Willow. "I'll be out in a few, we'll order something. I'm starving."

"Sounds good," Willow says softly.

We both watch her friend head across the room. Once she's behind her door Willow walks to the front door and opens it up.

"Although I appreciate your earlier offer, I'm going to have to pass," she says, turning to face me.

I cross my arms over my chest. "My earlier offer?"

"I'm not interested in the whole 'me in your bed' thing."

Pink rushes up her cheeks making her look adorably fuckable. "You're cute when you lie."

"I'm not lying, I have no interest in being your bed buddy or your booty call."

"What are you interested in being?" I let my arms fall to my sides and start walking toward her.

"Nothing," she lies, avoiding eye contact.

"I told you I don't like playing games." I stop when we're toe-to-toe and she shifts nervously.

"I'm not playing a game," she whispers.

I grin.

"Why are you smiling like that?"

"Because I'm starting to think this game might be fun." I lift my hand and touch my fingers to the underside of her jaw, hearing her sharp intake of breath. "I'll be in touch."

"What?" she asks as I step out of the apartment.

"See you around, Mouse."

"Clay," she calls to my back then shouts, "I'm not playing a game."

"I know," I shout back over my shoulder then hear her make a frustrated sound right before the door slams.

Yeah, this might be fun.

$\mathcal{W}$TH MY FEET aching due to the heels I chose to wear today, I take a seat at my desk and start up my computer so that I can log out of the banking's online system and shut down my desktop. Like most Mondays, the day was busy from the time the bank opened until I walked out the last client and locked the doors behind them just minutes ago.

"Hey."

At the sound of Carly's voice, I lift my head and watch her smile, looking unsure as she steps into my office. "I wanted to come check on you. We haven't had a chance to talk all day and I felt horrible after we hung up yesterday. I'm sorry I didn't walk you out. I should have done that."

"I'm good, and no need to feel bad," I reassure her with a smile.

"You got home okay, right?"

"Yeah," I leave out the part about waking up in Clay's bed because each time I think about that, his statement about wanting me in his bed comes to mind, and I just can't go there.

"Okay." She frowns. "We really overdid it."

"Apparently," I mutter, and she laughs, seeming more relaxed than she was just a few seconds ago. "So how did things go with Matthew?"

"Good." She smiles, ducking her head. "We spent the day in bed yesterday, then had dinner last night."

"That's great."

"Yeah, I think he's coming over this evening and we're going to go out."

"Wow, he's not messing around."

"I guess not," she agrees, blushing. "Do you want to go out with us? I think we are going to do karaoke."

"Sorry, I can't. Brodie is heading out of town, and I need to meet up with him because I'm keeping Jeb while he's away." Even if I didn't have actual plans, I still wouldn't go, not after what happened Saturday night. I hate that I can't trust her now, but that's one thing Clay and I can agree on. Women should always stick together when they are out because you never know what could happen.

"He's lucky you are nice enough to keep his dog for him every time he goes out of town."

"I don't mind. It gives me the feeling of having a dog without having all the responsibility." I smile when she laughs.

"Well, I should go and finish closing out my till so that I can clock out."

"Sure, and have fun tonight."

"I will." She gets up and gives me a smile before she heads out the door.

Once I'm done closing down my computer, I grab my purse from my desk drawer, then do a walk through of the bank. When I know everything is as it should be, I head into the main lobby where everyone is waiting.

"Are you all ready?" I ask, as I walk to the door with the key in hand.

"We've been ready," Troy, the lead teller, says grumpily as he pushes out of his chair.

I just avoid rolling my eyes. A year ago, I was working at a bank near my parents when a job for the head investment manager for the office in Nashville came up and I applied. I honestly didn't think I would get it, but was happily surprised when I was told that I did. What I didn't know was that Troy, who's always worked at this branch, was shooting for the same position and angry that they brought someone from the outside in. And every day he makes it glaringly obvious that he thinks I'm lacking and that he could do a better job.

"Well, now you're free." I give Troy a polite smile, then open the door and say goodbye to everyone as they leave before I set the alarm and lock the door with the master key.

After I get into my car, I start heading toward downtown and curse the amount of traffic there is. The only downfall of leaving my old job was that I had to give up small town life and my ten-minute commute. Having visited New York City numerous times, I wouldn't say traffic in Nashville is the same or really even close, but it still takes forever to make it from one side of the city to the other during rush hour, which is so different from where I grew up.

I reach my building thirty minutes later and pull into the parking garage, then park in my space, making sure that my tag is on the mirror before I get out because the one time I forgot it, my car was towed. And since I had no idea that was even something that could happen, my first thought was my car had been stolen and that was not a fun experience first thing in the morning when I hadn't had enough coffee and was already running late for work.

When I get to my apartment, I let myself in, making sure to be quiet in case Leah is sleeping. Her schedule has been all over the place the last few weeks due to a shortage of doctors and nurses at the hospital, and there are days she doesn't even come home at all, and just crashes there between her shifts. So even though I don't exactly love her mom, I'm glad that she will be on a forced vacation for a couple of weeks while she helps her parents who just moved from Colorado to Florida.

Going to my room I kick off my heels and take them into my closet, then change out of the wide leg pants and button down top I wore today, and put on a pair of sweats and a long sleeve, oversized top. After tying up my hair, I slide on my flip flops, then get my keys and head right back out the door and take the elevator up to Brodie's place.

I knock when I arrive and a moment later a pretty redhead opens the door wearing one of his jerseys and what seems like nothing else. When she doesn't greet me but just gives me a narrow-eyed look, I pray for patience. Since about two weeks after I ended things with Brodie, this exact situation has played out more than once. The first time it happened

I waited for the curl of jealousy to creep up on me from knowing he was with another woman, but I felt nothing—absolutely nothing except for frustration with him, for putting me and that woman in such an awkward situation.

"Hey, is Brodie here?" I smile then press my lips together to keep from laughing when Jeb shoves the woman aside to get out the door and greet me.

"You big lug." I give Jeb a hug, then grab a hold of his snout to try and avoid him getting his tongue anywhere near my mouth.

"Who are you?" the woman asks.

I start to tell her that I'm Brodie's friend but snap my mouth shut when the man of the hour comes up behind her dressed but looking like he just got out of the shower.

"Shit, sorry, I didn't realize what time it was," he says.

"It's all good." I look at the woman. "I'm Willow. Nice to meet you."

"Is she your sister?" She ignores my greeting and looks up at him.

"You gotta go, Cali, I need to hit the road," he tells her without answering her question.

She pouts out her bottom lip. "Will you call me when you get back into town?"

"Yeah."

Honestly, I've never seen the same woman at his place more than once, so I doubt that's the truth. It makes me sad for him that he keeps looking for love in the shape of a vagina, especially when he deserves so much more.

"Okay, I'm just going to get my stuff." She leans up to kiss him but at the last second, he turns his head, so she just catches the corner of his mouth, and either she doesn't notice or maybe she just doesn't care.

After she gives me a look that says, "he's mine," she disappears into his apartment rolling her hips.

I barely avoid rolling my eyes in return.

"Sorry about that." He takes a hold of Jeb's collar and holds open the door for me.

"It's not the first time one of your girls has been here when I've shown up." I grab Jeb's leash off the hanger next to the door and hang it around the back of my neck.

"We need to talk," he says, then mumbles something under his breath when Cali comes out of his bedroom holding a piece of black material in her hand while still wearing his jersey, but also wearing a pair of jeans and heels.

"I hope you don't mind that I keep this," she giggles, holding the golden top away from her body.

"Actually..."

"He has like a million, of course he doesn't mind," I cut him off before he can respond.

She actually smiles at me like we're friends. "Cool." She skips to where he is and grabs his hand. "Walk me out."

"Sure." He mumbles then looks at me. "Be right back."

"I'll be here."

"Bye." Cali says to me, and I wiggle my fingers at her, then go to the kitchen and grab Jeb's dog food and start to pour some of it into a large zip lock bag to take with me.

"You know that was my favorite jersey," he says when he steps back into the apartment a few minutes later.

I shrug one shoulder. "Since you will probably hurt her feelings in just a few days when you don't call or text her, consider it a pre-fuck-up apology gift."

"She's a puck bunny, Willow, she knows the score."

"She's a woman with feelings, Brodie, and you don't know what she knows." I shake my head.

"I know she was using me the same way I was using her."

"Ew." My nose scrunches. "Don't say that; it makes you sound like a douche." I grab a new bag of Jeb's treats from his cupboard then look over at Brodie when he doesn't say anything, but I feel the energy in the kitchen seem to shift, become heavier. "What?" I ask when I find him looking at me funny.

"You don't care."

"What?"

"You don't fucking care," he shouts while tossing his arms in the air, a move that causes Jeb to bark.

"Care about what?"

"Me, that I'm fucking other women," he yells, and I blink, completely stunned by his outburst. "It doesn't fucking matter to you at all."

"Wait." I hold up my hands while shaking my head. "Are you—have you been doing this whole having-women-over-every-time-I-show-up as a way to try and make me jealous or something?"

He doesn't answer. Instead, he just stares, and I know I'm right.

"Oh my god." I whisper.

"It didn't work."

"Of course it didn't." I shout then laugh without humor.

"This isn't fucking funny, Willow."

"It's actually hilarious, Brodie." I rub my hands down my face. "Your way of trying to win me back, or whatever it is you think you're doing, is to shove women in my face." I look around wishing there was something close by to throw at his stupid, fat head. "We broke up because I couldn't handle the constant distance, lack of communication, and the amount of women always hanging around. I told you that." And I did, I told him early on that his constant traveling and then not even calling or texting while he was away was an issue, and he did nothing to change it, so I protected myself by ending things because I didn't want to end up hurt if I did let him completely in.

"No, you broke up with me because you can't commit to fucking anything in life."

"Screw you." I hiss

"You didn't do that either," he roars, and I take a step back, not out of fear but out of the realization that I messed up. Leah was right. I shouldn't have started spending time with him again after things between us ended, but I cared about him and didn't want to not have him in my life anymore. I was so stupid.

"I think." I start softly. "That you need to find someone else to keep Jeb after you get back from this trip."

"Willow…"

"It was selfish of me to think that we could be friends." I cut him off as guilt rolls through me. I never once considered how he felt and maybe I should have. I mean he was the one who told me that he was in

60

love with me, and I just didn't believe him, his actions didn't back up that claim but maybe he was in his way.

"I love you, don't you see that?" he says gruffly.

But I don't—I don't see it. I mean he was fucking someone else right after we broke up and has screwed a dozen women since then. If he really cared about me, it wouldn't have been so easy for him to move on, right?

"You never even gave me a shot—a real shot before you gave up on us."

"I'm sorry." I rub my lips together. "But I have nothing to offer you but friendship."

"I don't want your fucking friendship," he shouts, and Jeb barks again, jumps up on his hind legs, obviously worried about his human.

"Okay." I say quietly then ask. "Do you still want me to keep Jeb or—"

"I'll find someone to keep him," he bites out.

I nod, then slide the leash from around my neck and place it on the counter before I turn and walk to the door.

"It's always so fucking easy for you to walk away."

I don't acknowledge his final comment, as I step out of his apartment and close the door behind me. I don't have it in me to fight with him and I know it wouldn't do any good anyway.

When I get back into my apartment, I open the door and find Leah sitting on the couch in the living room.

"Hey, I was just going to text to see if you'd be home for dinner," she says, watching me walk across the room, then she frowns. "Where is Jeb?"

"I don't think we're going to see Jeb anymore." I plop down next to her, and she lets out a breath.

"What happened?"

"Brodie flipped out, got mad that I haven't been jealous of the women he's sleeping with, then told me that he loves me and that I can't commit."

"Wait, you need to repeat that," she hisses, pissed on my behalf.

Darn, but I love my best friend.

"I guess he thought that me showing up and finding women in his place over and over again would cause me to realize that I'm in love with him or something." I close my eyes and let my head fall back against the couch. "And I don't want to hear I told you so, but I should definitely stop being friends with the guys I've dated."

"Willow." She leans her head on my shoulder.

"Maybe I'm broken," I whisper and feel her jolt.

"What?"

"I felt nothing, even the first time I saw him with someone after we broke up. I wasn't jealous or sad. And the other guys I've dated? It's been the same. I mean I care about them, yes, but that's it. I just care about them—nothing more. None of them have ever had the power to hurt me."

"Maybe they didn't earn that."

I turn my head as she lifts hers off my shoulder.

"What do you mean?"

"I mean they didn't earn the amount of trust it would've taken to be able to cause you emotional pain. That doesn't mean that there is something wrong with you. You're just protective of your heart."

I rest my head on her shoulder hoping she's right, because the more I think about it, the more I wonder if I'm even capable of letting myself fall in love with someone.

Willow

Seven

GRABBING AN EMPTY cart outside the grocery store, I drop my bag in the basket then head through the automatic doors. After smiling at the girl behind the lotto desk when she greets me with a cheerful hello, I head to the produce section. Normally I do my grocery shopping on Sunday, but since I was feeling like I had been hit by a truck, I ended up just lazing about that day, then yesterday after my run in with Brodie, Leah and I ended up ordering in dinner and just hanging out. Today I don't have a choice, I need to pick up food for the week so that I don't starve or end up eating fast food every night. And lucky for me, I got off work early today so I'm able to get it done then go home, make dinner, and then call it an early night. Something I desperately need.

While dumping a bunch of bananas in the cart I hear a cute little giggle come from close by and do a scan of the area around me, then freeze when my eyes land on Clay standing a few feet away. My pulse skips a beat and butterflies take flight in the pit of my stomach. There is absolutely no denying that I'm attracted to him, but who wouldn't be? Remembering his parting words from the last time I saw him, I duck my head and start to push my cart away, hoping to go unnoticed. I'm brought to a halt when the bottom of my sweater snags on something. I look down to see what I've gotten hooked on, then blink when a cute, very-familiar-looking, little girl smiles up at me from under the edge of the table with a banana in her hand that she's obviously been attempting to open.

"Winter?"

Hearing Clay's deep voice causes a tingle to travel down my spine and I watch the little girl, who must be Winter, giggle then place her finger in front of her lips, telling me to be quiet.

"Hey, do you need some help with that?" I whisper.

She nods, causing her dark hair to fall slightly into her eyes. Having been around other kids her age, which I'm guessing is about five maybe six, and having seen when one of them has decided to do this exact thing in the store, I turn to where I last saw Clay and find him with a panicked expression on his face as he looks around. Then his eyes land on mine.

Without saying that Winter is in front of me out loud I point to the table and watch his shoulders relax before he heads my way. Crouching down in front of Winter, I take the banana from her. "These things are always hard to open."

"I know," she whispers, and I hand her the banana back once I got the skin peeled back, then feel my skin prickle with awareness when Clay crouches down next to me.

"Were you hungry?" he asks, grabbing Winter's tiny wrist and using it to gently pull her out of her hiding space to stand between his legs.

"Yes, I told you I wanted a banana."

"I know but I was going to pay for them first." He chuckles smoothing her hair back from her forehead.

My ovaries trip all over themselves watching him be so gentle with her. Oh goodness, I need to get out of here.

Clearing my throat, I start to stand, but Clay's large hand wraps around my thigh causing my breath to hitch in the back of my throat.

"Where you running off to, Mouse?" he asks.

I narrow my eyes on his at the nickname.

"She doesn't look like a mouse," Winter informs him.

"What does she look like?" he asks her.

"Kind of like a princess." She reaches over to touch my hair.

"I think you might be right." He smiles at her. "Winter this is Willow. Willow, my niece, Winter.

"Nice to meet you Winter, I love your name."

"Thank you." She smiles as Clay stands and grabs my upper arm to help me up or maybe to keep me from running off because he doesn't let me go even after we are both standing. "Do you know how to make lasagna?"

"What?" I smile at her not sure where that question came from.

"Uncle Clay can't cook." Winter informs me with a mischievous smile.

"Take that back." Clay starts to tickle her, making her giggle.

"No." She giggles louder.

I laugh.

"I need to feed this munchkin and she refuses to eat pizza, corn dogs or anything a normal kid would eat."

"That's because it's all over processed," she tells him in her little voice.

"You're not wrong." I agree with her, and she smiles smugly at Clay as if to say, "I told you so".

"Well, if you agree with her, you can help me make her a non-over-processed meal."

"Wh—what?" I sputter and he grins.

"Unless you're seeing your boyfriend tonight."

"You have a boyfriend?" Winter asks me.

"No, I don't."

"Uncle Clay doesn't have a girlfriend either. Daddy says he's a player." She looks adorably confused, then shrugs her shoulders. "I don't know what sport he plays though."

"Your dad talks too much," Clay mutters.

I bite my bottom lip to keep from laughing.

"I know." She looks between Clay and me. "You can be Uncle Clay's girlfriend."

Oh lord

"That's no—"

"That's a great idea," Clay tells her, cutting me off.

I swear it feels like my eyes are going to pop right out of my head.

"You can start your role as my new girlfriend by helping me make dinner tonight."

What the hell is happening?

"And we can play with my new doll house." Winter claps excitedly.

"Before you play, you need to study for your spelling test and do your reading."

"It's not fair that I have to work all day at school then have to work more when I get home." She lets her head fall back on her shoulders with a groan.

"Sorry, kid, but I don't make the rules." Clay rubs the top of her head then looks at me. "So, what do you say, Mouse, are you up to helping me out tonight?"

Good lord no, and I totally plan on saying that even as Winter puts her hands together in prayer and says "please" over and over again, but when I open my mouth the word "yes" comes out. "I mean—"

"Come on." He bends down and grabs the handle of a small red basket that has a few things in it off the ground and tosses it into my cart before taking command of it. As he begins pushing it through the produce section I stare at his back while listening as Winter tells him that she wants to have asparagus with the lasagna that I'm now apparently helping him make.

Seriously what the hell is going on?

"Willow?" Hearing my name, I turn and curse my luck when I spot Jayson standing near the salads display. Jayson, a guy I dated a few years ago, was someone I broke up with because he was flighty, then befriended because he might have sucked as a boyfriend but was super nice and always fun to hang out with.

"Ugh, hey Jay how's it going?" I ask as Clay and Winter circle back to where I am.

"It's funny seeing you here." He smiles, walking toward me, shaking his shaggy blonde hair out of his face. "I was going to call you tonight to see if you were up for seeing a hockey game next weekend."

"Oh, umm, I'm actually umm busy next weekend." I tell him feeling highly uncomfortable as I feel Clay's eyes bore into the side of my head. "Maybe another time?"

"Yeah, for sure." He smiles, then looks over to where Clay is standing and lifts his chin. "What's up dude?"

"Nothing much." Clay says.

A small hand wraps around mine and I look down to my side at Winter.

"Can we finish shopping? I'm starving."

"Ugh yeah." I give her hand a squeeze then look at Jay. "I'll see you around."

"Totally, babe." He grins.

I bite my bottom lip and allow Winter to drag me away.

"Another boyfriend?" Clay asks quietly when Winter basically drops me off at his side.

Of course, I pretend I don't hear him and instead I walk past him and then, with Winter bouncing at my side, chatting up a storm, I hustle through the rest of the store tossing things into the cart that I need, along with stuff for lasagna, hoping like heck that I don't run into anyone else I know.

Less than fifteen minutes later Clay pushes the cart full of his groceries out of the store, and I say his groceries because as I was trying to sort through what was mine and what was his at checkout, Winter, being helpful just started tossing everything on the conveyer belt together. Then when it came time to pay Clay maneuvered me out of the way and paid for it all. And since there's no way I'm taking anything home he paid for, I'm once again stuck without groceries.

"I think—" I stop at the back of Clay's jeep where he's putting all the bags in his trunk, while Winter climbs into the back seat, "I should just—"

"Follow me to my place." He cuts me off as he looks over and meets my gaze. "I was thinking the same thing, we can sort out the groceries there."

"That's not what I was going to say." I step back so he can shut the window then tail of his jeep. "I just think this is probably not a great..."

"You're not running are you, Mouse?" He cuts me off stepping into my space, towering over me.

"Stop calling me that!" I snap.

"Get in your car and follow me or I'm putting your ass in my jeep and leaving your ride here."

"Yo—You're unbelievable," I sputter. "Who do you think you are?"

"Ten."

"What are you doing?"

"Make your choice—your ride or mine. Nine."

"You can't be serious, I'm—"

"Eight."

"Stop counting down like—"

"Seven."

"Oh my god you're—"

"Six."

"Stop it."

"Five." He crosses his arms over his chest.

"Can you please just be reasonable this is ridiculo—"

"Four."

"You're so annoying." I throw my arms in the air.

"Three." He raises a brow and I start to panic because I can tell that he's not going to stop and if I don't give in, I'm going to be stuck at his place without my car.

"Fine I'll follo—" My words end on a gasp of surprise when he suddenly wraps his hand around the back of neck, jerks me forward and covers my mouth with his. The kiss completely knocks me off kilter, and just like the last time he kissed me, I'm caught off guard by the zap of electricity that zaps to life between us.

"See you at my place," he says as soon as he rips his mouth from mine.

I touch my fingers to my lips that feel somehow branded by that kiss.

He squeezes the back of my neck that he still has a hold of, and I blink up at him.

"I'll wait until you're in your car."

I nod and quickly turn on my heels then wobble off to my car like a newborn baby deer, my legs feeling like Jell-o and my hands shaking like I drank to much coffee.

Once I'm behind my steering wheel, I start my car, put it in reverse, and back out of my spot. I pull up behind Clay and wave at Winter when she waves at me through the back window, then like an idiot I turn out of the parking lot right behind him and follow him to his place.

After reaching his building a few minutes later, I park behind him on the street that is crowded with construction vehicles and notice a couple of guys enter through the front doors wearing hardhats. I grab my bag then meet Clay and Winter at the back of the Jeep as they start to unload the grocery bags and Winter puts a glittery backpack on her back.

"Willow." Hearing my name shouted from up above me I tip my head back and look up.

"Seriously?" I mumble when I see Tony leaning over the side of the building with his sunglass covered eyes pointed down at me. Tony and I went out on a few dates a couple of years ago. It never went anywhere, but he did become a friend I've met up with on occasion. He's also a guy I tried to hook Leah up with, but she refused to go out with him because she thought it was weird.

"You've got to be fucking kidding me," Clay grumbles.

"You have to put a dollar in the swear jar," Winter sings from his side.

"Ugh, hey Tony." I wave and he grins, slipping off his green and blue tinted sunglasses.

"I thought that was you."

"Yep, it's me." I let out a breath, wishing that a brick would just fall off the building and put me out of my misery. Leah was one hundred percent right about me befriending all my exes, because today has been so flipping awkward.

"What are you doing here?"

"I'm—"

"She's here with me. Aren't you're supposed to be working?" Clay shouts, stepping up next to me.

I watch the color drain from Tony's face. "Oh shit, right, sorry. See you around, Willow."

"See you, Tony." I rub my lips together then look at Winter when she tugs on my arm.

"You know a lot of people."

"Yeah, I have a lot of friends."

"I have a lot of boyfriends, too." She smiles happily then takes my hand as Clay grunts something. "Come on I'll show you how to get to Uncle Clay's house." We step inside the open building where men and a few women are milling about working and she lets me go to bounce over to a box near the door that is filled with hardhats.

"I'm starting to see a theme, Mouse," Clay whispers against my ear.

I shiver and turn to glare at him. "Stop calling me that."

"Never." He smiles at me up close.

His expression does something weird to my stomach. Refusing to think about what that feeling is, I turn my attention to Winter when she comes back to us carrying two bright orange plastic hats.

"We have to wear these." She hands me one of the hats and then puts one on her head. "Uncle Clay says he doesn't have to because he has a hard head."

"I believe that." I tell her and she shrugs, then takes my hand once more leading me through the maze of boxes, piles of wood, paint cans and building supplies to the back of the building where the elevator is. When we reach it, Clay touches his cell phone to the panel on the front which causes the door to open up and once we're all inside, Winter presses the button for the fifth floor. When the doors open again, we enter a familiar hallway and take a right to the only doors on the floor and Clay uses his phone again to let us inside his place.

The moment we step through the door, Skye is there to greet us, first going to Winter to get a hug that makes my heart melt, then coming over to me.

"Hey girl." I squat down to rub my fingers through her thick fur, and she makes a chuffing sound as she nuzzles my neck. Once I've given her a proper greeting, I stand and look around. Without the hangover I had the last time I was here I'm able to truly appreciate just how beautiful the vast space is. And I imagine that his entire home must be the size of the area downstairs that is currently being worked on which makes me curious about what is behind some of the doors that are closed.

"Kick off your shoes and get comfortable, babe," Clay orders me as he walks to the kitchen with the shopping bags.

Winter drops her backpack, takes off her hat and leaves it next to the door along with her coat.

Since I still have on the heels I wore to work that might not be killing my feet but aren't exactly comfortable, I slip them off, then pad across the warm concrete floors in my stockings. I then take off my coat and lay it over the back of the couch along with the fitted suit jacket I wore over the silky button-down top I tucked into my pencil skirt.

"Willow, do you want to see my doll house?" Winter asks from across the room grabbing my attention.

I start to tell her "yes", but before I can get my mouth open, Clay cuts me off.

"Reading first. You know your dad will have my ass if you don't get your homework done."

"Aww come on, I just want to show her it."

"Sorry kid." He shakes his head.

She lets out a groan, but still goes to her backpack and digs through it, taking out a book before going to the couch.

As she plants herself on one of the overstuffed cushions, I walk to the kitchen where Clay is unpacking the shopping bags. When his eyes come to me, a very inconvenient tingle slips down my spine.

"Come here, babe," he says quietly.

I keep my feet firmly planted where I'm standing. "Do you want to show me where everything is? I should get the lasagna started since it will take some time."

"No, what I want is for you to come here."

I let out a breath of frustration, not with him but with myself, because lord, I want to listen to him and that is so not like me. "Clay."

"All right I'll come to you." He stops what he's doing and walks toward me.

I tense, not sure that I'll be able to handle it if he kisses me again. Putting my hand up to stop him when he's close, he drops his eyes to my hand and smiles then lifts his hands toward my face, and I hold my breath not sure what he's up to. Then a weight is lifted off my head and I feel all kinds of idiotic as he places the hardhat I was still wearing on the counter next to me.

"So nervous, Mouse," he says softly, then leans in, his lips brushing against my ear where he whispers. "I won't attack you with Winter here, you're safe for a bit."

He leans back and I wonder if it's obvious that my heart is pounding so hard it feels like it might jump out of my chest.

"Come on." His hand grasps mine and he leads me to the bags on the counter. "Just tell me what you need and what you want me to do."

Clearing my throat, I look at the stuff on the counter, then with a deep breath, I get started on making dinner, not even bothering to ask how I got myself into this situation. It's obvious that I've fallen into some strange alternate reality like that movie where the guy had all his ex-girlfriends show up to show him where he went wrong in life.

"Have you spoken to your friend from work, the one you went out with?" Clay asks while going over to the oven and turning it on to preheat.

"Yeah, but not much because work's been busy, but she's still seeing the guy she met at the bar that night, and she apologized for not walking me out of the bar when we went out." I look over at him. "And I check my car before I get in it for any kind of tracker and haven't found one, so I don't think someone was after me but instead after my car."

He gives me a look that is filled with what can only be described as pride. "Smart girl."

"I was raised by a man who takes personal safety to a whole other level; he'd be disappointed if I wasn't proactive." I grab the boxes of no boil pasta and open them up.

"I can appreciate that." He comes up next to me and watches as I finish mixing up the ricotta cheese mixture that will go between each layer of pasta.

"So do you really not know how to cook, or do you use that as a way of making women feel sorry for you, so they end up in your kitchen."

"I worked at a steak house growing up. I can cook a steak, bake a potato, and make a few sides. Lasagna isn't something I ever learned how to make, and since it's not something I'd normally eat, I have no desire to learn."

"Your niece eats it, you should learn for her." I meet his gaze.

"If I did that, I wouldn't have been able to make you feel sorry for me." He winks.

I swoon like an idiot.

"Now tell me about all these men who know you. Have you dated all of them?"

My stomach drops and I drag my eyes off his. I want to lie because that is what society has told us women to do, to lie about how many men we've dated or slept with, especially when a man asks us that question. But I fight back the urge to do that. Why is it wrong for me to explore my options and search for the right person for me? I mean, even if I had sex with all these guys, what would really be wrong with that? Men sleep with tons of women and get nothing but a pat on the back while women are shunned and looked down on like they are somehow tarnished.

Screw that.

"I have. I've dated a lot, and kept most of the guys I've been out with as friends because they are good guys."

"Do you end it or do they?"

"What does that matter?" I look over at him and he shrugs.

"Just wondering if it's your MO to run."

"I do not run."

"Mmm." He makes a sound in the back of his throat then takes his eyes off me when Winter climbs up onto one of the stools at the counter across from us.

"I'm done with my reading."

"Good job are you ready to practice for your spelling test?" he asks her and her shoulders slump.

"If I have to."

"You do. Go get the stuff, we'll make it quick."

"Okay." She gives in and hops off her stool.

I finish with the lasagna. Since it's late and making lasagna from scratch would take hours, I did a quick bake one. A couple jars of good quality pasta sauce, fresh mozzarella, ricotta, and no bake pasta. It's something my mom would throw together when I was a kid and something I honestly forgot about until we were at the store. While Clay begins to go over Winter's words with her, I dust the top of the dish with cheese then carry it to the oven and place it inside where it should bake for forty-five or so minutes. As I start back to the counter, I glance over at Clay and find a smile on his face as he watches Winter jot down the word "because" on her paper, and a burst of *déjà vu* washes over me almost causing me to stumble.

"You okay, babe?" He looks over at me.

I nod then busy myself with cleaning up, refusing to mentally get into why I keep having *déjà vu* whenever I'm around this guy.

"Can I play now?" Winter asks as Clay spins her mock test around to look over it.

When he's done reading her the last word, he says, "Go for it, kid." And lifts his chin.

"Are you coming, Willow?" She looks at me.

I smile at the adorable expression on her face. "Yes, in just a second."

"Yay." She jumps off her stool and bounces across the living room to a set of double doors that she shoves open.

From where I'm standing, I can't see much, but I can see the large doll house she told me about earlier.

"Her dad is?"

"Miles."

I nod remembering how much I thought that he and Clay looked alike, and if I didn't know and just saw them together, I would have thought that Winter was Clay's daughter, so that makes sense.

"On days he works, I pick Winter up from school and she comes and hangs with me until he gets off."

"That's sweet."

"What can I say, I'm a sweet guy."

"I somehow find that hard to believe." I mumble and he chuckles. "Where's her mom?"

"She lives in Denver."

"Oh." I rub my lips together not sure how to respond to that.

"She flies in as often as she can, and Winter spends the summer and some holidays with her. It sucks, but it works for all of them." He pushes away from the counter then takes the towel from my hand, tossing it onto the counter. "Come on, I'll clean up in a bit."

"Okay." I follow him across the space to the double doors where we find Winter sitting on the floor in front of her dollhouse. She's wearing headphones but focused on Skye, who is lying next to her on her back getting a belly rub. I take my eyes off the two of them and blink. I thought the rest of the house was big, but I was wrong, this room is huge, and a dream hang out spot for kids and adults alike. Not only is there a giant TV with comfortable looking couches and a bar set up with rows of liquor bottles, but there is also an entire kids' playground and I'm not talking about one of those rubber ones some people have inside their houses when their kids are little. No, this one has a full-sized slide that drops into a pit of foam, swings, and monkey bars.

"Holy cow." I breathe when I spot a mock treehouse tucked into the corner of the room that is so tall it almost reaches the ceiling.

"I had this all built when Miles and Winter were staying here before their place downstairs was finished. I haven't had the heart to take it all out," Clay says.

I focus on him. "It's very cool." I shake my head. "So, they live in the building?"

"Yeah, he and Winter live on the fourth floor, which is divided into two apartments. Dayton will eventually share the fourth floor with them when his place is finished, and he moves here."

"Dayton?"

"You met him the morning you slept here. He still lives in Denver, so he's not always around, and when he is, he crashes in my guest room."

"So, he's your brother?" I guess, and he lifts his chin. "And you live in this building, are renovating it, and have all your family moving in here, so either you're a builder or the leader of some kind of cult."

"No cult." He laughs. "I have a few properties around the US and other investment properties but I'm not a builder," he says, but doesn't add more making me even more curious about him and who he is. I mean I deal with people starting businesses, buying property, and moving huge chunks of money around every single day and know how much things cost. And this place alone was probably close to twenty million dollars if not more and that's not including all the remodeling he's done and is doing. That's a whole lot of money to have at your disposal...

"Willow," Winter calls, dragging me from my thoughts.

I turn to look at her and find her with her hand held out with a doll in it. I walk over and take a seat on the ground next to her and take the toy she gives me. "You can be the mom."

"Sure." I place the doll in the house then start asking her in a funny voice if she's made her bed and done her chores, which makes her start to giggle and run her smaller doll around the doll house. When she eventually gets bored with the dollhouse, she takes off across the room to climb on the playground equipment and I can't help but to join her. It's been forever since I've slid down a slide or gone across monkey bars, and I honestly forgot how fun it was and why I always looked forward to recess and the park on weekends when I was a kid. As I chase her all over, I feel Clay watching the two of us and glance over to where he's standing with his arms crossed over his chest at the edge of the foam pit. Like he feels me looking at him, his eyes meet mine and the smile he gives me causes an odd feeling to fill my chest. And if I didn't already know I was in over my head, that would be one hundred percent clear now.

Clay

Eight

$\mathcal{W}$ITH THE FIREPLACE on and the lights dim, I look between Willow and Winter then down at the cards in my hand.

"Do you have a hammerhead shark?" I ask Winter, and she groans before handing me her card. I smile as I place my full set on the table next to my others.

"Do you have a starfish?" Winter asks me and I glance down at my hand then shake my head no.

"Are you cheating?" Willow asks me under her breath, and I look up from my cards and find her eyes narrowed.

"We're playing Go Fish, Mouse, why would I cheat?"

"I don't know but three times now Winter and I have asked if you had a card and you've said no, then three times you've asked us for those same cards when it's your turn and gotten a full set. It's a little suspicious."

"Very suspicious." Winter agrees from where she is sitting on the opposite side of the coffee table on the floor.

"Show us your hand." Willow reaches out quickly trying to take my cards, but I pull them back just before she can grab them.

"Do you really think I would cheat at a kids' game?"

"If you're not cheating just prove it." She gets up and comes to stand in front of me holding out her hand and Winter starts to giggle.

"I think you're the one who's trying to cheat." I use the length of my arms to keep my cards just out of her reach when she grabs for them again.

"Seriously, Clay, let me see your cards." She leans into me which places her breasts in my face and, if it wasn't for my niece a few feet away giggling, I would not stop myself from nipping her through that thin fucking shirt she's wearing, wrapping my arms around her waist, and putting her under me on the couch.

"What's going on here?" Miles asks, stepping into the house.

"Daddy." Winter shoots up from where she was sitting and runs across the room to him.

"Hey cupcake!" He lifts her off the ground and kisses her cheek. "What are you guys doing?"

"Playing 'Go Fish' and Uncle Clay is cheating." She informs him as I get up.

"He's always been a cheater," Miles tells her, placing her back on her feet then he looks my way and lifts his chin before focusing on Willow. "Hey, Willow."

"Hey." She places her hands in front of her and wiggles her fingers together.

"Willow made lasagna for dinner." Winter tells him taking his hand. "It's not as good as Mommy's but it was still really good, and Uncle Clay saved you a plate in the microwave."

"Baby, we don't say things like that." Miles tells her as she pulls him toward the kitchen and Willow laughs but quickly covers her mouth.

"I said it's really good."

"I know but you could still hurt someone's feelings," he tells her, and she looks over at Willow scrunching her nose.

"Sorry, Willow."

"It's okay, my mom's is better too." Willow tells her and Winter smiles up at her dad like *I told you so.*

"All right kid, did you study for your spelling test and do your reading?"

"Yes." She sighs and he looks at me.

"She got everything right on her practice test."

"All right, pack up your stuff, we need to get home so you can take a shower before bed."

"I want to take a bath."

"If you take a bath, you won't have time to watch one of your shows after you're done."

"Fine, I'll take a shower." She gives in and starts to gather her books and things off the counter. I go to the microwave and take out the plate I saved for him that's covered in plastic wrap and hand it over.

"Willow's here?" he says quietly.

"She is."

"Is this going to be a regular occurrence?"

"If I get my way, yes."

"Let me guess, she's not making that easy." He smirks as his gaze goes past my shoulder.

I turn to find Willow in the middle of putting on her jacket.

"Where are you going, Mouse?" I ask her and she freezes then slowly turns to face me.

"Umm." Her eyes ping to Miles then back to me. "I need to head home." She rubs her lips together. "I have work early in the morning." She finishes buttoning up her coat then starts toward the door where her shoes are.

"Damn, didn't think I'd ever meet a woman in such a hurry to get away from you," Miles mutters under his breath.

I glare at him.

"Will you be here tomorrow?" Winter asks her.

"Sorry, honey, normally I don't get off work until after five or six so probably not."

"Aw, but I liked having you here; it was so fun."

"It was so much fun." Willow leans down to give Winter a hug.

"Good luck with that." Miles says before walking toward the door. "All right kid, give Uncle Clay a hug. We gotta go."

On cue, Winter runs across the room to me and throws her arms around my waist squeezing tight.

"I'll see you after school." I tell her, rubbing the top of her head, and she nods, then zips to where her dad is. I head behind her, grabbing a hold of Willow's wrist before she can try to follow them out the door, which I know she's planning on doing.

"See ya around, Willow." Miles says, dropping his gaze to where I'm holding onto her before smiling at me. "See ya, brother."

Shaking my head I close the door behind them, then turn toward Willow, and she takes a step back holding her hands up between us. "I really do need to go."

"I bet you do." I take another step toward her. "You keep running, babe."

"I'm not running, I just—" She cuts herself off and glances around, looking frantic.

"You just what?" I raise a brow and take another step toward her.

"I'm not interested."

"You're not interested?"

"No, I mean, don't get me wrong, you're great and hot, plus you have that whole mysterious thing going on, but I'm just not into that right now."

"You're not into that right now." I bite back a grin.

"Stop repeating what I'm saying."

"Babe, you're into me, just admit it."

"No, I'm not." She shakes her head, while doing everything she can to avoid making eye contact.

If I didn't know that was a lie, my ego would be bruised, and if I wasn't so curious, I sure as fuck wouldn't be wasting my time. But fuck, this woman has taken up all my headspace since the moment I met her, and I know in my gut there's a reason for that.

"You are."

"You're so full of yourself," she huffs.

"You're here."

"Yeah, because you forced me to be here." She tosses her hands into the air.

"You could have drove home when we left the parking lot at the store." I point out and she balls her hands into fists. "But you didn't do that, you followed me home."

"Okay, I will admit I did do that." She nods. "But that doesn't mean

I'm into you."

"Come here, and let me get my mouth on you and I'll prove you're into me."

Her eyes widen and she takes a step back. "No! No more kissing."

"Scared?"

"You're so cocky." Pink spreads up her cheeks.

"You know I'm right."

"You're not and also, it's rude to just kiss a woman."

"Not if that woman is into it." I stop in my tracks and cross my arms over my chest. "I'll make you a deal."

"What?" she asks, sounding weary.

"I'll back off, you can go back to dating all these guys who obviously don't have what it takes to hold your attention, if you can kiss me without showing any kind of reaction."

"That's ridiculous."

"You're the one who said you're not into me, so prove it."

Swallowing as she stares at me, I can see the wheels in her head turning as she tries to figure out if she can do it, then I watch determination fill her gaze, so much of it that I almost laugh.

"Okay, fine." She rubs her lips together. "But only one kiss."

"Come here." I wait and it takes a few seconds for her to start slowly walking toward me. I can tell she's nervous by the pulse beating rapidly in her neck and the way her pupils have dilated. When she's close, I let my hands fall to my side then wait to see what she will do when we're toe-to-toe. My fingers twitch at my side as her hand moves to my jaw and she leans up on her tiptoes bringing her mouth closer to mine. Ducking my head, I listen to her sharp intake of breath at the first brush of our lips, I tell myself that I should go slow, but the need to prove my point takes over. Curling one hand around her waist, I pull her hips into mine, then slide my other hand up her back and into her soft hair. The noise she makes in the back of her throat has my cock hardening behind my zipper and she loses whatever control she was clinging to. As my tongue slips into her mouth, she presses her tits into my chest and digs her nails into my biceps. Whatever apprehension she had when she agreed to the deal crumbles to dust at our feet and she gives in, letting instinct and desire take over. I fight back a groan when her fingers find their way under my shirt. I start working on the buttons of her coat wanting to touch her.

"Clay," she gasps, letting her head fall back to her shoulders as I trail my lips down her neck to her collarbone.

"Right here." I get her out of her coat and let it fall to the floor, then bite back a curse when her fingers slide under the edge of my jeans skimming the head of my cock that is begging to be released. The noise she makes when I cup her breast is one of the sexiest sounds I've ever heard in my life, and I can't wait to hear it again.

"Oh god." She pants and I duck my head and pull her breast into my mouth through the thin material of her top. "I—oh lord." She gasps then within the blink of an eye she's feet away from me looking dazed with her lips swollen and her eyes glassy. As her chest heaves, she looks around then she quickly rushes to grab her coat then across the room.

"Willow."

"I have to go." She grabs her bag off the floor by the door and I stalk after her as she swings the door open. Grabbing her bicep when she hits the button for the elevator, I swing her around to face me and the look of panic and tears in her eyes catch me by surprise and cause my gut to clench.

"Hey, what's all this about?" I gentle my tone and watch her eyes slide closed.

"I can't do this." She tries to duck her head, but I capture her jaw.

"Will—"

"I don't want this." She cuts me off and I watch a single tear slide down her cheek before she pulls away from me and the elevator doors open. As she gets in, I stand there for a moment then get in with her. "Clay."

"I'm just walking you to your car." I press the button for the main floor, and we ride down in silence. When the doors open up, I make sure she makes it through the maze of shit all over the place then lead her down the sidewalk once we get outside.

"I'm sorry," she whispers as we reach her car, and she swings the door open.

I don't know what the hell is going on inside her head, but it's obvious that me pushing her right now won't work in my favor, so I keep my mouth shut and then force myself to let her go as she gets in her car and drives off.

$\mathcal{Y}$OU KNOW THOSE people who always say, *"It could be worse"?* Well, those people are all idiots. Not only am I questioning if I made a huge, gigantic, colossal mistake running away from Clay when he ruined me forever for any other man on this planet with one stupidly amazing kiss. I'm also pretty sure that kiss and me backing out of our deal set off a series of unfortunate events in my life to remind me on a daily basis just how idiotic I am and that it, in fact, can be worse.

It's been four days since that kiss and every single day something bad has happened. The day after the kiss, I finally got the license plate for my car in the mail that I've been waiting anxiously for since my temporary one was expired. Of course, I put it on my car not even thinking about the tag number until Leah pointed out that morning I took her to the airport that 8DX-247 looks like it says, "Ate dicks twenty-four seven". Now, I can only imagine what anyone behind me in traffic is thinking.

Then yesterday I went to the mall after work so that I could return a pair of jeans I bought and, while I was getting off the escalator, my shoelace, which I didn't know was untied, was sucked up by the teeth at the bottom of the escalator and after getting my foot out at the last minute, half my shoe was gone causing the whole machine to break down. After that near death experience, I ended up going home with only one shoe, a migraine, and the pair of jeans I didn't get to return.

But no that run of bad luck just couldn't be enough. I shake my head as I stare at my empty parking space, the one where my car normally is, and exactly where I know I parked last night when I got home. Apparently yesterday when I got home after the mall fiasco, I forgot like an idiot to hang my car tag on my rearview mirror, so they towed my car. Or, at least, I hope that is what happened, because honestly, I can't remember if I hung the tag, but I do know I didn't check to see if there was another tracker under my car.

With a curse I head back into the building, hoping like heck that the front office is already open so that I can ask them about my car, because if they are not, I'll have to spend the next however long calling each and every tow company in the city to see if one of them has it.

When I get inside, I make my way through the maze that is the inner building and thank my lucky stars when I find the office open, and Libby, one the girls who runs the front desk, sitting in her chair behind the counter.

"Hey." I greet her out of breath as I step inside, and she lifts her head and smiles at me.

"Hey, Willow."

"I was wondering if you could tell me if my car was towed." I walk up to the counter, and she frowns.

"I don't think so." She stops whatever she's doing and starts to type something into the computer, then a second later she looks up at me and cringes. "It was towed last night. There's a note that no tag was displayed."

My shoulders slump and she offers me a sympathetic smile. "In other news the system is supposed to change soon, and you'll have a sticker to add to your window so it's always there."

"That's good." Not helpful now but still good. "Can I get the number for the company who towed it?"

"Sure." She jots it down on a sticky note and hands it over to me.

"Thanks."

"Yep, anytime." She gives me another smile before I turn on my heels and head out the door. When I reach the street, I dial the number for the tow company and let the person know that I will be on my way in just a few minutes. Then I call my job to let Katy know that I'm going to be a little late. Thankfully, my boss is understanding about the whole thing and just tells me to take my time.

An hour and one hundred and fifty dollars later, I park in the lot of the bank and grab my bag from the passenger seat, then head inside. I don't even bother going to drop off my lunch in the fridge before I head straight to my office. Like Mondays, Fridays at the bank are always busy with everyone trying to get all their banking done before we close for the weekend and me being late even just thirty minutes after the bank opened is too much time.

"Did you get your car sorted?" Katy, who is the bank manager, asks, walking into my office as soon as I take a seat behind my desk.

"I did, thanks for covering for me." I flip on my computer.

"No problem, also I got an email from Carly this morning and she won't be in today or next week. Her father passed away and so she is going to Florida to be with her family," she says, and my hands freeze on my bag. I might not have been best friends with Carly, but I know she mentioned that her dad died when she was in high school and that her mom passed away a few years ago, and she never mentioned her being remarried.

Clearing my throat, I shake my head. "I'll call her when I get a break."

"And I know you normally take care of your own calendar, but we've had a potential new client contact us and he asked if he could set up a meeting with you today since he's going to be going out of town next week."

"Okay, do you know what time he's supposed to be in?" I ask trying not to get annoyed that someone who probably has a whole lot of money was able to get an appointment today when I know for a fact that my schedule for the day was already full.

She glances at her watch then looks at me. "It should be anytime now."

"Great." I plaster a smile on my face.

"I'll bring your client in when he arrives."

Okay, so whoever it is has a lot—like a ton—of money because normally Katy doesn't bother herself with meeting any new potential clients.

"Thanks." I give her another smile then watch her walk out of my office before I dig through my bag for my cell phone. Once I have it in hand, I type out a quick text to Carly, asking if she is okay and if she needs anything. For all I know she has a stepdad or father figure she didn't mention and is grieving that loss and I just can't imagine what she might be going through if that is the case.

As I place my phone and purse in the bottom drawer of my desk, there is a tap on my open office door, and I look up. It takes about five whole seconds for me to register who is standing next to Katy, and when I do, I urge myself not to pass out.

I tried to convince myself that I would be okay if I ever saw Clay again after that kiss but it's obvious that I'm not, not even a little. My heart pounds, my palms start to sweat and my nipples pebble in response to his nearness and the memory of how good it felt having his mouth on me.

"Willow, this is Mr. Raven." Katy introduces, placing her hand on Clay's bicep while looking up at him like he's a world-famous movie star.

"Thank you, Katy." Clay tucks one hand into the front pocket of his suit pants and smiles at her. "Miss Mayson and I know each other."

"Oh." Katy looks at me.

"It's a small world." I stand up without pushing my chair back, which means I hit both my thighs on the underside of my desk then fall back into my chair.

"Are you okay?" Clay asks.

I wave off his concern. "Yep, fine just fine."

"Are you sure?" Katy asks as I rub the tops of my thighs.

"Yes, just having a little bad luck the last few days."

"Well, let me know if you need anything, I'll be in my office," she tells me then looks up at Clay. "It was very nice meeting you Mr. Raven and if you need anything at all be sure to let me know."

"Clay." He holds out his hand and she takes it.

"Clay," she repeats, sounding breathless as she looks into his eyes.

"Thank you, Katy." I say a little louder than I need to, and she jumps slightly and blushes as he lets her hand go.

"Right, yes. I'll be in my office." She leaves, shutting the door, and I stare at Clay trying to ignore the fact that I just got jealous of him touching another woman's hand.

"Mouse," he says, unbuttoning the button on his suit jacket.

"What are you doing here?"

"Chasing you, like always." He walks toward me, and a nervous flutter fills the pit of my stomach.

"You came to my job?"

"You can't run from me if I'm here as a client." He takes a seat in the chair across from me and leans back, placing his ankle on the top of his knee, getting comfortable. "And since we need to have a conversation, I figured this would be the best place to do that."

"Katy is going to be very disappointed that you won't be banking with us."

"I don't give a fuck about Katy."

I press my lips together.

"You wanna know the most important thing I learned growing up?"

I lift my chin and his eyes bore into mine.

"That if you want something, you have to fight for it and if it comes easy it was probably too fucking good to be true to begin with." He lets his foot fall to the floor as he sits forward.

"Clay."

"I also learned to stop fighting when there is nothing to fight for, which is why I'm done," he says softly, gently even.

But even as soft and as gentle as his voice is, I know in that instant that he's saying he's done *with me,* and a pain so harsh it feels physical crashes into my chest, causing my breath to get stuck in the back of my throat.

Lost for what to say or do, I watch him get up and button the button of his suit jacket. I see his mouth move as he comes around the side of the desk to stand over me, but don't hear a word he says. But I do feel the touch of the tips of his fingers to my face as he runs them along the edge of my jaw before he turns and walks out of my office, shutting the door before he goes.

I don't know how long I sit there, it could be minutes but it's most likely seconds before Katy steps into my office.

"Oh no," she whispers as soon as she sees my face. "I was going to ask how the meeting went, but I can tell by the look on your face that it was not good." She shuts the door. "Are you okay?"

Shaking my head no, I then start to nod yes because I can feel my throat starting to itch and if I admit how upset I am, I know I'll break down and cry. I can't cry, not at work, and not over a guy I hardly know.

"I'm fine." I croak and she comes over, placing both her hands on the top of my desk.

"Good, that's good, honey." Her voice is quiet as her gaze locks on mine. "Learn and learn quickly that men are assholes, and they don't deserve your tears."

I want to tell her that Clay isn't an asshole. Is he bossy? Yes. Pushy? Absolutely. Overbearing? Definitely. But an asshole? Not even a little. Since the first moment we met I've felt safe when I was with him, desired from a single look, and protected in a way that only my father has ever made me feel. I know without knowing that if I was out with him and got locked in a bathroom, he would be searching for me before his meal arrived and he would never use jealousy as a way to get my attention or a reaction from me. He's the opposite of every single man I have ever dated and I'm starting to realize that I might have screwed up horribly not telling him the truth which is he scares the crap out of me. Because the truth is I know exactly who he is, and I maybe even knew it the second we met. I might not have wanted to admit it, but it was like something inside of me recognized him, as cheesy as that sounds. That said I don't know that I'm ready for what will come if I open myself up to the possibility of us. For so long, I've dated men that didn't have what it would take to keep hold of my attention—maybe it was even on purpose, though unconscious. I've enjoyed my life just as it is, and I know that if I give in, everything in my life will change in an instant. And I don't know that I'm ready for that.

"Are you going to be okay to make it through the rest of the day or do you need me to tell everyone that you caught a bug and are taking off the rest of the day?"

"I'll be okay," I say quietly, because even as sweet as her offer is there is no way that I want to go home to my empty apartment to sit there alone with my regrets for the rest of the day. It's bad enough that I'll have to do that this weekend, with Leah gone to her parents and my mom and dad out of town for a cruise around Alaska with my siblings, their spouses, and their kids. I'm on my own.

"All right." She nods. "I still think you should take a few minutes before your next appointment and go splash some cold water on your face."

"Thanks, Katy." I stand and walk around my desk as she goes to open my office door. I don't spend much time in the bathroom and by the time I get back to my office my next client is there waiting. Thankfully with how busy the day is, I don't have a lot of time to dwell on what happened with Clay, but I know when I leave work that will all change.

STANDING IN FRONT of the wine selection in the grocery store I debate which bottle I should pick up for dinner at my cousin April's this evening. Like she somehow knew that I needed a distraction tonight, she sent me a text this afternoon asking if I wanted to come over, and, of course, I immediately said "yes." Since she got married and had her daughter, she spends a lot of time in Vegas, where her husband owns a popular club and where his family lives. I've missed her. Plus, I'm hoping to talk to her about Clay, since I know that when she got with her husband, she wasn't exactly ready for him or how much her life would change after they got together. And it would be good to hear her opinion on things, especially knowing she won't sugar coat it just to make me feel better.

"Willow."

Hearing my name in a cute familiar voice, my heart sinks, and my breath freezes. Slowly, I turn, and when I do, I watch Winter hop, skip to where I'm standing. Before I even have a chance to prepare myself for impact, she runs into me and throws her arms around my waist causing me to fall back a step.

"Hey you." I touch the top of her head and she tips her head back to smile up at me.

"I thought it was you." She giggles then looks back over her shoulder. "I told you it was Willow." She yells.

Relief floods my veins when not Clay, but Miles grins at his daughter.

"You were right." He walks over then lifts his chin, reminding me so much of his brother. "Hey, Willow."

"Hey, Miles," I say softly then I look down at Winter. "How was school this week?"

"Great, and I totally aced my spelling test." She smiles proudly.

"You did?"

"Yep." She nods.

"That's awesome. Congratulations."

"Thank you. Uncle Clay was going to take me out to ice cream, but he left."

"He left?" I repeat, hoping like heck I heard her wrong.

"He'll be back next week," Miles says softly.

I lift my eyes off his daughter to meet his gaze.

"He just had to go take care of some business back in Boulder."

"Oh." I should not feel relieved. Should I?

"Do you want to have ice cream with us? We're going to get all the stuff to make sundaes. Daddy said I could get whatever toppings I want, even gummy worms," Winter says.

I can't help but to smile at her excitement. "I would love to, but I'm having dinner with my cousin tonight." I smooth my hand over her soft hair. "Maybe another time."

"When Uncle Clay gets home?" She holds her hands together and looks up at me with big pleading eyes, making it impossible for me to tell her no.

"We'll see, okay?"

"Okay." She lets me off the hook then grabs her dad's hand. "Bye, Willow."

"Bye, honey." I smile at her and say goodbye to Miles then watch them walk down the isle and disappear around the corner. When they are gone, I pick up a bottle of red wine, figuring it's a safe bet, then head to check out. As I'm standing in line, my cell phone beeps, telling me that I have a message. When I pull it out of my bag, I'm relieved to see that it's from Carly, although I'm a little surprised she didn't call, because she is one of the few people I know who rarely texts.

Carly: I'm in Florida with my family. Thanks for checking in. I'm okay.

"Ma'am are you ready?" Pulling my eyes off my phone I look at the cashier and she holds out her hand.

"Sorry, I spaced out." I place a smile on my face as I pass her the bottle, while a strange feeling settles in the pit of my stomach.

"That's okay." She rings it up, asks for my ID then tells me the price. After I pay, I take the bottle in hand and walk out of the store, and pull up the message again as soon as I get into my car. The text is simple enough, and like I said, Carly and I are not the best of friends. I don't know everything about her, but I can't remember her ever mentioning any of her family besides her parents, who had passed away.

With my fingers hovering over the keypad, I try to figure out what to write back, then decide it will just be better if I call her. After pressing the green dot next to her name, the phone starts to ring and ring and ring again, until the call is cut off, and I'm sent to voice mail. With a deep breath I wait until it's time to leave a message then I just ask her to call me, and tell her that I'm worried about her, and that I just want to hear her voice to know she is okay. Sure, that I'm overreacting, I hang up and hope like heck that she actually calls me back and puts my mind at ease.

With no other choice but to wait, I tuck my phone away, start my car, then head out of my parking space and the lot of the grocery store.

When I get to my cousin's house thirty minutes later, Carly still hasn't called me back, so I send her a text basically repeating my voicemail because if she is like some other people I know—namely myself—she won't actually check her voicemails, but instead deletes them without even hearing what they say.

With nothing left to do, I get out of my car with my bottle of wine and head up to the front door of Aprils house and ring the bell. Not even two seconds go by before the door is open and I'm greeted by her and Malia, who has grown so much since the last time I saw her.

"You're here." April engulfs me in a tight one-arm hug while Malia latches onto my hair that has gotten too close to her chubby little hands.

"Oh my god, you need to put her in some Tupperware to keep her tiny, she is already so big."

"I know." She pouts, kissing Malia's chubby little cheek before passing her over to me and taking the bottle of wine. "Maxim is out back on the grill."

She leads me through the front of the house, which is absolutely spectacular, the entire place looks like it was cut right from the ad of some high-end magazine.

"I'm so glad that you were able to come over tonight," April says as we walk into the kitchen.

"Me, too." I bounce Malia on my hip while she babbles away. "I figured that you guys would be in Vegas for the winter."

"If I did that, my parents might actually murder my husband. They hate their grandchild being so far away."

"And you," I point out.

She shakes her head. "No, I mean I know they miss me, but ever since that little one came into this world it's been all about her. They don't even ask how I'm doing anymore, and Maxim's parents are not any better." She grins. "So, tell me everything. What have you been up to? I don't even remember the last time we really even had a chance to catch up."

"Everything is the same. My life is definitely not as exciting as yours." I laugh when Malia tugs on my hair to get my attention.

"So, you're not dating anyone?"

"No." I rub my lips together and her eyes narrow.

"You're lying. What's going on?"

"Well, there is someone, but I messed up, and I'm pretty sure he's done with me."

"If he's done with you then he's not the one for you." She rolls her eyes.

"I guess you're right."

"Now tell me, how did you mess up?" She opens a bottle of wine and pours us each a glass.

As I tell her about Clay, how we met and everything that happened since then, her eyes widen, her lips part, then a smile curves her lips. The smile broadens when I finish with what happened today in my office.

"So now I'm not sure what to do because if I do talk to him, he could tell me that he wants nothing to do with me, which would suck even more than not knowing that."

"Or it could turn out that he is playing the long game and hoping that you'll admit to yourself that you like him and go talk to him, which is what I think you need to do."

"I have admitted to myself that I like him, I just—" I shake my head. "I don't—"

"You're scared." She lifts her glass out towards me. "Welcome to my world. Honestly, I will be the first to admit that the idea of falling in love with someone and starting a life with them scared the shi—" she glances at Malia, "bejesus out of me and let's not even talk about having a baby. I was so sure I was definitely not ready for that. But now that I have Malia and Maxim, I can't imagine my life without either of them.

"I love that for you," I tell her softly, then turn when I hear the sliding glass door in the kitchen open.

"I stayed out as long as I could because I could tell there was some serious girl-talk happening." Maxim walks in, holding a tray of food.

April laughs then accepts a kiss from him as he comes to stand next to her and places the tray on the counter.

"Hey, Willow."

I smile. "Hey."

"We were just talking about men and how crazy you make us," April informs him.

"Yeah, I figured that's what it was." He lifts her glass of wine from her hand and takes a sip. "So, who is this guy? Is it the hockey player you were dating?"

"No, not Brodie." I shake my head and leave out what happened with him because I don't need anyone else telling me that I shouldn't have befriended him after I broke things off. "His name is Clay."

"Clay." Maxim tips his head to the side as he stares at me. "What's his last name?"

"Raven." I tell him something that I just learned this morning. Really,

I'm sure that April would think that I was ridiculous right now if I told her that information. Or if I told her that I don't even really know what he wants from me besides "me in his bed" as he so rudely put it. Lord, maybe I need to stop overthinking this, because for all I know all he wanted was to get in my pants and when he saw that wasn't going to happen, he cut his losses.

"That's a unique name," Maxim states sounding odd.

"It is." April agrees then asks. "Do you know him?"

"I don't believe so." He turns away and she frowns at his back.

"Why do I think you're lying?" she asks him.

"Why would I lie?" he returns, going to the oven and opening it up to pull out what I'm guessing are potatoes wrapped in foil.

"I don't know." Her eyes widen as she asks. "He's not a bad—"

"No." He shakes his head.

"Drugs?"

"No." He repeats.

I frown at the two of them, trying to figure out what the heck it is they are talking about, because I'm so lost.

"Then what?" she asks.

He glances at me. "How well do you know him?"

"Not well. I know he has brothers, has money and is in construction or property, honestly, I don't know much."

"Fuck," he mutters.

My brows dart together. "Do you know him?"

"Not personally, but my family is aware of him."

"And that means?" I ask as April freezes in place.

"I don't think I should be the one telling you his secrets," he says, and something about his tone causes the hairs on the back of my neck to stand on end.

"She's not in danger because of him, is she?" April asks, sounding freaked.

Her reaction totally freaks me out.

"No," he says instantly, sounding beyond sure. "Let's just say that if he is who I think he is, she's never been safer and will never be safer than when she's with him."

"Okay, that's good." April nods, wrapping her arms around her middle, then she looks at me. "That's good right?"

"Who is he?" I ask as my heart starts to beat funny and my palms start to sweat. Knowing what I know of Maxim and his family, there can only be a few reasons why he said that his family is aware of Clay. Not friends with him—but aware of him. And although I don't know what that means exactly or how I should feel about it, something tells me that Clay is someone who lives in that grey space between good and bad—a man who looks like he was born to be on the back of a motorcycle, or dressed in a suit at the front of a boardroom.

"He'll have to be the one to give you that information," he tells me.

Just by the look in Maxim's eyes, I know that he is not going to budge. So, whoever Clay is and whatever his story, it isn't something I'm not going to learn tonight, or maybe *ever* for that matter.

Willow

Ten

PARKED OUTSIDE OF the apartment building where Carly lives, I stare at her car then look at her door, as I try to figure out my next move. For the last three days I've sent her texts, called her number, and got nothing in response, and as of yesterday her phone was off and going right to voicemail. That worried me, but now I'm totally freaking out, because this evening before I was leaving work, Katy stopped by my office to let me know that Carly sent in a letter of resignation that was effective immediately without an explanation as to why she was quitting.

And I know that people quit their jobs and cut off contact with ex-coworkers every day, but normally there's a lead up to that happening—some catalyst that sets things into motion. But with Carly, nothing is adding up, as far as I know she was loving living in Nashville, and from what she told me, she had made a couple of friends at the gym she goes to plus she had just started dating Matthew and seemed really excited about him.

So why would she just leave then quit her job?

Grabbing my cell phone out of my bag and taking my key with me I get out of my car and head up the walkway to Carly's front door. After knocking, I wait, then place my ear against the door after I knock again. Hearing nothing inside I look down at the door handle and my heart starts to beat a little harder. Placing my hand on it I turn my wrist and nothing. It's locked which both relieves and disappoints me.

With a defeated breath I start to head back to my car, but stop when I glance down at the flowerbed that runs along the path to her front door. A while back, I remember her telling me that she got locked out of her place and her rental company charged her fifty dollars to show up on a Sunday to let her in, so she was going to buy one of those rocks you hide a key in.

Maybe just maybe—

I don't know how many rocks I pick up before I find the one that is made out of heavy plastic, but when I do I hold my breath as I flip it over and slide open the hidden compartment. Seeing a key inside, I shake it out onto the palm of my hand then tuck the rock inside my pocket so I can put it back when I'm done.

As I go to the door and put the key in the lock, my hands start to shake, and adrenalin makes my heart race when the lock clicks open. Slowly I turn the knob and push the door in. I stare into the darkness of her apartment then reach inside and flip on the light. Not seeing anything out of the ordinary, I carefully step inside, leaving the door open, just in case I need to make a quick exit. From where I am I can see that nothing seems to be out of place, which puts me slightly at ease. I take a few more steps and look around. There's a sweater laying on the back of the couch and a book open upside down on the armrest like she was using it to keep her place. What there isn't is moving boxes or anything else to say she was getting ready to pack up. I turn on the light in the kitchen, and besides two wine glasses that are filled with water in the sink, nothing is there. Stepping out of the kitchen I look at the bedroom door then back at the front door to make sure that it's still open. I know it's stupid, since I've been in here for a couple of minutes already and no one has jumped out, but my gut is telling me to get out. When I reach the bedroom, I turn on the light and before I even step into the room my heart sinks. At the end of the bed is Carly's purse, the purse she had saved to buy and was so proud of. Slowly I walk over to it like it's a snake that might strike out at me and my hands shake worse than they already were as I open it up. When I find her wallet, and her keys inside, my throat starts to burn.

Backing away from it I take my phone out of my pocket and dial nine one one.

STANDING ON THE curb outside of Carly's apartment with my arms wrapped around my middle, I listen to the two officers who showed up as they talk quietly a few feet away.

From the moment they showed up they have made it seem like I'm overreacting, that it's totally normal for a woman to just disappear and leave her life behind. Neither of them have acknowledged that something is amiss, and honestly, they have seemed more concerned with how I got into Carly's house without her permission than her being gone. If my dad weren't in Alaska, I would call him and ask for his advice, but he doesn't even have cell service where he is right now, so I'm on my own, and now I'm not even sure that I won't be arrested.

When headlights land on me, I turn and watch a large, black SUV pull up and relief hits me hard when I see Miles in the passenger seat with Tucker behind the wheel. As they park, I let my arms fall to my sides and wait for them to get out.

"Willow," Miles calls when he opens his door.

I swallow as he walks to where I'm standing.

"What happened?"

"Carly's missing. She emailed and said that her dad passed away, but her dad died like forever ago. Then today, she quit, and I've tried calling her like a million times, but she never answered." I ramble not sure that I'm even making sense. "Something isn't right. I knew something wasn't right, so I came over here to—" I shake my head. "I don't know. Then I remembered she had a key in one of those rock things." I pull the plastic rock out of my pocket to show him. "So, I let myself into her place and her purse is in there along with her wallet and her keys." My throat gets tight.

"Take a breath for me," he says gently as he takes my arm and pulls me away from where the officers are standing, and Tucker comes over to join us after hanging up on a call. "Okay, now who is Carly?"

"We work together at the bank." I dig my nails into my palms. "She moved here a few months ago from Florida."

"All right and you said her dad passed away?"

I shake my head no, but then nod yes. "Yes, she said she was taking a few days off because her dad died, and she was going to be with her family."

"But you don't think that's the truth?" Tucker asks and I meet his gaze.

"No, she told me once that her dad passed away when she was a teenager and her mom never got remarried." I shake my head. "We're not the closest of friends, so I don't know if she considered someone else her dad or something but—"

"It's okay. Breathe." Tucker rubs my arm.

I nod and try to breathe, but honestly, I feel totally overwhelmed right now, and I know that if they don't take this seriously, then Carly might not ever have anyone looking for her.

"You said she quit her job?"

"Yes, tonight we got an email from her, and she resigned."

"So, you came over here to check on her?"

"I didn't know what else to do. She hasn't been answering my calls or texting me back and I just wanted to make sure she was okay." I lift my shoulders as I feel wetness slide down my cheeks.

"So, you used her key to get inside?"

"I just needed to know if she was really gone or if something happened to her." A chill slides down my spine and my stomach churns. "If she's in Florida, why wouldn't she take her purse?"

"Okay, I'm gonna have you sit in our SUV where it's warm." Miles says as lights roll across us. On instinct, I turn to see who is here and my chest gets tight when I see Clay park his jeep right behind the SUV Miles and Tucker showed up in.

As he gets out, his eyes land on mine and even with the distance between us I can see concern in his gaze. I don't know what comes over me, but I take off running toward him and don't stop until my body crashes into his.

He lets out an "Ooff" on impact, then not even a second later his arms wrap around me tight.

Circling my arms around his middle I burrow my face into his chest and a fresh set of tears fall from between my lashes.

"Baby," he whispers, palming the back of my head and holding me tighter. "I got here as fast as I could when Tucker called me."

I nod, unable to speak, not that I'm sure what I would say even if I could talk. After dinner with April and the weekend with my thoughts and regrets, I talked myself into going to him, and just telling him the truth. I planned on doing that tonight but once Katy told me about the email from Carly, I found myself driving to her place as soon as I left work.

"Come on, let's get you warm."

He lets me go and places his hand in the middle of my back and walks me to the passenger side of his jeep then opens the door.

Once I'm in the seat he cups my cheek and his eyes scan over my face. "You gonna be okay while I go talk to my brothers?"

"Yes." I sniffle as I dry my tears with the sleeve of my sweater and his face softens before he leans over me shoving the keys in the ignition and starting the engine.

"Be right back." He touches his lips to my forehead with a kiss that is so soft, it feels like a whisper, then he lets me go, steps back, and shuts the door.

I watch him walk up to the house where his brothers and the other two officers are talking, then I drag my eyes off them and fiddle with the heat to turn it up. It's not that cold tonight, fall is just starting to really creep in, but I feel chilled to the bone and beyond exhausted, like I've run a marathon.

The minutes tick by as the guys talk, then the two uniformed officers take off in their squad car, leaving Miles, Tucker, and Clay on the porch. When the three of them disappear inside, a sense of unease washes over me and I look around. Unlike the building I live in, Carly's apartment complex is open, and her neighbors have already started decorating for Halloween which will be here in just a few weeks. Normally, I'd love the orange and purple glow of lights and spooky decorations, but tonight they do nothing to put my mind at ease.

I swear I see the shadow of a tall figure move behind a tree. I reach over to the keys in the ignition, shut it off, then shove open the door and hop out. I run to the front door of the apartment that is open, the light like a beacon in the dark. Then, just like I did when I was a kid and I thought there was something under my bed, I jump over the threshold into the light of the apartment where nothing bad can get me.

"What happened?" Clay asks as all eyes come to me.

I right myself. "I—I thought I saw someone behind a tree." My chest heaves and my heart pounds as he walks to me, ducking his head and placing his face close to mine.

"Someone was out there?"

"It was probably my imagination." I glance between all three men, who don't look at all convinced—and I know they aren't when Miles pulls his weapon and heads out the front door with Tucker right behind him. "I really think I just freaked myself out," I say quietly, meeting Clay's gaze.

"We'll let them figure that out." He wraps his arms around me tucking my face against his chest.

I don't know how long we stand like that, but soon a throat is cleared, and I turn my head to find Tucker standing in the doorway.

"We didn't see anyone out there. Miles is grabbing some evidence bags and stuff from the car."

"You guys believe me?"

"Why wouldn't we?" Tucker asks.

I shrug. "Those other officers made it seem like Carly leaving her bag and stuff wasn't a big deal."

"A woman with no apparent reason to run away from her life is a big deal," he says.

I relax into Clay's hold, beyond relieved that they believe me. "Am I going to be arrested?" I ask.

Clay growls. "Why the fuck would you be arrested?" His hold on me becomes almost suffocating.

"Because I broke in here."

"You had a key." Tucker tells me, then adds, "Your friend told you about it and said you could use it anytime you needed to get in."

"She—"

"She told you that you could use it anytime you needed to get in." He gives me a stern nod.

I nod along, because it's obvious that's what he wants me to do, and honestly, knowing Carly, she would be okay with me using her key to get into her apartment. Or at least I think she would have.

"Do you need more from Willow tonight or are you and Miles good here?" Clay asks.

I tip my head back toward him.

"You're good to get her home." Miles says, stepping inside the apartment, then his eyes come to me. "We'll wanna talk to you tomorrow and get a full statement."

"I'll bring her to the station when she gets off work," Clay tells him.

Miles lifts his chin in agreement before Clay ushers me out of the house.

When we get outside, he looks at my car then his. "Where are your keys?"

I pull them out of my pocket, and he takes them from me.

"I'm gonna pass these off to Miles. He can drive your car then drop your keys off when his shift's over."

I start to open my mouth to tell him no, that I'm not going to his place with him, but instead I give in. There is no way I'm going to be able to sleep tonight, and I really won't be able to do that with Leah gone. Plus, he and I need to talk, so being with him will give us a chance to do that.

Ten minutes later, with him driving and me in the passenger seat with my bag and my coat on my lap, I look out the window as he heads toward the city. When he takes the exit that leads to my building, instead of getting off at the one that would take us to his place, I look over at him. "Where are we going?"

"Taking you home." He glances over at me quickly then continues talking as he focuses back on the road. "I'll get your number for Miles, so he can call you when he's downstairs with your keys, and you can let him in."

Closing my eyes, I turn my head toward the window, as that weight on my chest that's been there for days gets heavier. I don't know why I assumed that him showing up tonight was something more than what it was. I should have realized that he's just that guy, the kind of guy who would show up when his brothers call. The kind of guy to offer comfort and give forehead kisses to a woman who's freaked about the fact that her friend is missing. He's not the kind of guy to make a statement like he did days ago in my office and not follow through on the promise he made of leaving me alone.

"Right. Of course," I whisper, all the courage I built up to talk to him, to tell him how I feel is gone just like that, in the blink of an eye.

"Mouse," he calls.

I open my eyes. "Yeah?" I don't even bother looking at him as I watch building after building pass by out the window.

"If you open that door even a little, baby, I'm not backing off again. I'm shoving that shit wide open."

I turn my head his way, as he slows to a stop at a red light, and my heart starts to pound against my ribcage.

"You gotta be sure you're ready for that though."

He turns his head my way and the moment our eyes lock, that weight on my chest eases just a bit. "You scare me."

"I know I do." He reaches over, grabbing my hand, holding it between us. "Now tell me—do you want me to take you home or do you want to come home with me?"

As I stare into his eyes, I know there is no turning back if I agree to go home with him. And as scared as I am to let him in, and to see what happens, I know that I would despise myself for not taking the risk.

"I want to go home with you," I say quietly.

He brings my hand to his mouth and brushes his lips across my knuckles, then places my hand on his thigh. After he flips on his blinker and turns in the direction of his place, he covers my hand with his and keeps it trapped there the entire drive.

It doesn't take long to get to his building, and, after he parks out front, he gets out then walks around to my door, meeting me there as I slide out of my seat.

"Have you eaten dinner?" he asks, taking my hand in his as we walk down the sidewalk.

"No, I went right to Carly's when I got off work."

"I'll order us something when we get upstairs." He places a hard hat on my head after we step inside, and I almost tell him that he should be wearing one too, but keep my mouth shut and let him lead the way across the expansive space of the first floor that now has more than a few wooden-framed walls up.

"Where's Winter?" I ask when I see a small pink scooter leaning inside the elevator when it opens up.

"Her mom is in town, so she's with her." He looks down at me then lifts the hard hat off my head after we step onto the elevator, and he presses the button for his floor. "She told me that the three of us have an ice cream date."

"I ran into her and Miles at the store on Friday when I got off work."

"I heard. I also heard from Miles that she tried to convince him to ask you out because you don't have a boyfriend."

"She's sweet."

"She is, but that's never happening," he grumbles.

I fight back a smile.

When the doors open, we step off and go through it, and as soon as he lets us in, Skye greets us with a happy dance around our feet. Dropping my bag and my coat to the ground, I squat down to give her some love, and she presses her nose into my neck and chuffs in happiness as I rub my fingers through her thick fur.

"I missed you, too." I give her neck one last hug then stand and kick off my heels near the door as she follows her dad into the kitchen area.

"What are you in the mood to eat?" he asks, pulling out a stack of menus from one of the drawers.

I walk over to meet him at the counter. "I'm good with whatever you want."

"Pizza would probably be the quickest."

"Sure, but can we get buffalo wings too?"

"We can." He reaches for his cell phone on the counter. "What do you want on the pizza?"

"Everything." I say, then ask, "Do you mind if I use the restroom?"

"You don't need to ask. You know where it is."

With a nod, I head into his bedroom as I hear him call in the order for our pizza, and by the time I come back out, he's off the phone and has a beer in his hand and pink-looking wine in a glass on the counter waiting for me.

"Thank you." I pick up the glass and take a sip.

"I know you filled in Miles and Tucker about what went down there for tonight, and I got your story from them, but I'd like to hear it from you."

I place my glass on the counter, then tell him about Carly saying that she was going out of town after her father's death, her message to me, calling her and texting her over and over, then finding out this evening that she had resigned from her position at the bank. As I talk, he listens with his face blank, but I can tell that he's taking every single word in and mentally taking notes.

"So that's why I went to her house this evening. Things just haven't been adding up and I was worried about her." I pick up my glass.

"Do you know anyone that she was close to besides you?"

"I know she mentioned making friends at the gym she started going to and you know about the guy she was seeing."

"Was she still seeing him?"

"As far as I know." I lift one shoulder. "At work we don't have a lot of time to sit around and talk, but the last time we really spoke, she told me they were going out after spending the weekend together."

"Do you remember his name?"

"Matthew, but I don't know his last name."

"How did they meet?"

I wonder if I should have told Tucker and Miles about him, then remember that I have to talk to them tomorrow and can tell them then.

"On an app, the same place everyone meets nowadays."

"Everyone except me and you," he says softly.

"I don't think many people meet outside of liquor stores and have their first kiss before they even know each other's names."

"I didn't need to know your name to know I wanted to kiss you." He smiles, picking up his beer to take a swig.

112

Laughing, I shake my head and take another sip of my wine. "The night that I went out with her was their first date—or kind of date anyway, because he had friends with him, but so did she."

"What was your impression of him?"

"He was nice enough. He was a little much for my taste, but Carly didn't seem to mind."

"What do you mean?"

"I don't know, he just seemed very familiar with her, even though they'd just —like placing her basically on his lap at the bar and calling her *his* when his friends showed up and he introduced us."

"You didn't like that?"

I know that question has nothing to do with Carly and Matthew. "It seemed strange with him. He just met her a few minutes before, and had only known her online earlier, so the claim seemed out of place." I shrug. "But, again, Carly loved it, so I don't know."

"Did she have any other friends?"

"She mentioned her best friend from back home but no one else that I can think of."

"What about her family?"

"Are you taking notes for you brothers?"

He steps into my space. "Tomorrow." His voice is softer than it was, almost soothing. "When you go to the station to give your official report, you might not feel as comfortable or as relaxed as you do right now. Talking about things with me will help you prepare for what you'll be asked."

"Do your brothers and you talk about the cases they work often?" I ask because I know my dad never spoke or speaks about his work, at least not with my sisters or me, and I don't believe he talks to my mom about them either.

"Can you handle a little honesty?"

When I nod, he places his beer on the counter then his hands wrap around my waist, and he lifts me off my feet. As soon as my ass hits the top of the island, he uses his hips to spread my legs apart.

When he's got me completely caged in with his hands on my thighs his eyes lock on mine. "I told you that Miles, Tucker, and Dayton are my foster brothers."

I nod.

"We also had a sister growing up. We were all close, then one day we found out that she was being adopted. When she left to live with her new family, she stayed in touch and would send us letters constantly, telling us about her new life." His jaw clenches. "Then those letters dried up and we lost contact with her, and no matter how often, or who we asked, we couldn't find out if she was okay."

"Clay," I whisper, reaching up to touch his jaw and he captures my hand then touches his lips to it before placing it on my thigh and covering my hand with his.

"When we all eventually aged out of the system, we went searching for her. That's when we found out that, when she was fifteen, she started talking to someone online, and over the course of a few months, they convinced her to meet up. That was the last time she was seen until she was picked up by the police almost two years later alive but not well, she was hooked on drugs and being pimped by some low life drug dealer after being trafficked out of state by the person she'd been talking to online."

My stomach churns and I fist my hands and dig my nails into my palms.

"By the time she was identified after being picked up by the cops for prostitution, her adoptive family wanted nothing to do with her, so she went back into the system, got lost, then fell back into the only life where she really felt she was wanted."

"Where is she now?" I ask scared to know but sure that was not the end of her story.

"She passed away from a drug overdose in Vegas while partying with a group of men who flew her in and paid to spend the weekend with her."

"No." My throat gets tight.

"She didn't know that we had been looking for her." His jaw clenches.

My heart breaks for him, for all of them.

"I'm so sorry." I know the words are meaningless. I can't imagine finding out that someone I loved was no longer alive and because of such horrific circumstances. And with his brothers and him all growing up in foster care, I imagine that would make them value the bond they share even more, so it had to be devastating for them to find out someone they considered family had passed away. And knowing what I do of him, I can't help but think that he would believe he failed her in some way— they all probably think that.

"The system failed her, then we failed her."

"You guys were just kids," I remind him gently, even though I'm sure he felt far beyond his age even when he was just a kid himself. "And now your brothers are working cases where women are being targeted, and you're somehow involved with helping them?"

He lifts his chin. "We—" He cuts himself off when his cell phone rings, and he reaches over to grab it off the counter. He puts it to his ear, then tells whoever is calling that he will meet them downstairs before he hangs up. "Pizza's here. I'll be right back." He steps back, then in a blink, he's out the door.

I sit there on the island and stare at where he disappeared for a long time, trying to wrap my head around what he just told me and what that says about him.

Clay Raven is beyond complicated, and something tells me I'm just now scratching the surface of who he really is. Logically, I know I should walk away and cut my losses before I'm in too deep, but he's already got his claws in me, and I doubt I *could* walk away, even if I wanted to. He's a good man—the kind of man who would do whatever is necessary to protect the people he cares about. Another thing I know is he's got his own walls, even if they are not as obvious as mine. His are made out of things like live-wires and hidden booby-traps that could possibly explode before you even realize they are there and that makes him dangerous for a multitude of reasons.

*W*AKING WHEN I register light behind my closed lids, I blink my eyes open and stare at the expanse of Clay's bare, tattooed chest that, at some point in the night, I must have decided to use as a pillow.

Last evening after he came back upstairs with dinner, we ate sitting in his kitchen, and there was no more heavy talk about his sister or Carly. Instead, we spoke about his trip to Colorado, where he went to check on a building he has that is being remodeled like the one here. We also spoke a little about my family, and his brothers.

By eight, even as early as it was, I couldn't stop yawning. Between the wine, a full belly, and an adrenalin crash, I was done and ready to crawl into bed and sleep for a week. And seeing this, Clay ushered me into his room, gave me the toothbrush I used last time I was here – a toothbrush he saved like he knew I was going to be back – and a t-shirt to wear to bed. Then, with a kiss to my forehead, he told me to shower and go to bed—that he had some phone calls to make. And not feeling even a little awkward or anxious, which goes to show just how exhausted I was, I did just that. Then, with my hair still damp, I got into his bed. I sent a text to my parents checking in, then a separate one to my dad filling him in on what happened, because I know that, even if he doesn't get it until they reach whatever port they land in next, that's better than not saying anything at all, especially when he could find out the news from someone else. And after that, I laid down and apparently passed out before Clay even came back into his room.

Careful not to wake the man that I'm basically sleeping on top of, I slide my thigh off his, then move my hand from off his waist, and roll to my side so that I can check the time. As I grab my cell phone, Clay rolls into me, wrapping his hand around my waist, and curving his body around mine.

"What time is it?" he asks his voice rough with sleep.

His warm breath brushes against my shoulder causing goose bumps to crawl across my skin.

"Six thirty." I set my phone down, then roll to my back. "I have to leave soon so I have time to make it home and get ready for work."

He gets up on his elbow, looming over me, then slides his fingers across my forehead. "I should have taken you home last night to pack a bag." His gaze locks on mine and his lip hitches up ever so slightly. "But I didn't want to risk you changing your mind about coming home with me."

"I wouldn't have changed my mind," I whisper, and he lowers his face toward mine and the first brush of his lips causes the muscles in my lower belly to clench and my eyes to slide closed. I grab onto him, not sure that I won't float away when he deepens the kiss, and I whimper when his hand moves to my stomach just under my breast. I arch my back, silently begging him to slide his hand under my shirt to touch me, but he doesn't. Instead he groans and drags his mouth from mine, leaving me with one final soft kiss.

"Let's get you up."

He rolls to his back then right out of bed, leaving me laying there looking at the ceiling, wondering if I did something wrong. Or I think I did something wrong until I glance over at him and find him looking at me with a dark look in his eyes as he adjusts the very obvious bulge in his boxers.

Rubbing my lips together I sit up, then laugh when Skye pops up on the side of the bed and places her face on mine. "Good morning to you, too." I rub her head and behind her ears as she places her front paws on my lap.

"Do you want some coffee or breakfast?"

Looking over at him, I find him still shirtless, but putting on a pair of grey sweats. I seriously wonder how many hearts he's broken. Probably a million.

"I wish, but don't have time." I get up off the bed and go to my clothes I folded up last night and set on the top of his dresser. Grabbing my pants, I shimmy into my tapered leg slacks, but leave his shirt on as I put on my bra. When I'm done, I turn around finding him staring, and heat curls in my belly while my pulse quickens. "Umm." I clear my throat as my cheeks warm. "Are you still taking me this evening to talk to your brothers?"

"Yeah." His chest expands as he scrubs his fingers through his hair, then he meets my gaze. "I'll call Miles and figure out what time they want you there."

"Thanks." I shift on my feet as energy pulses through the air between us then motion to the bathroom. "I'm going to just—" My words taper off and he jerks up his chin. I duck my head and walk across the room, then shut the door behind me and quickly brush my teeth and use the restroom.

When I step back out a few minutes later, he's no longer in the bedroom, but in the kitchen giving Skye her breakfast. As soon as he sees me, he motions me forward with a flick of his fingers and I walk to where he is. I don't know what I expect, but it's not for him to wrap his hand around the back of my neck to drag me forward and cover my mouth with his. The kiss puts the one in his bed to shame. My toes curl and my nails dig into his biceps, as his mouth possesses mine. When his hand grips my ass, I feel the length of him against my belly and moan while he growls down my throat. Lifting up on my tiptoes to get closer. He hefts me up with a quick jerk and I circle him with my legs.

"Clay," I pant, as his mouth leaves mine to trail down my neck, and my fingers slide into his hair while my head falls back on my shoulders. When he pulls back, I'm panting for breath and my heart is beating hard. My eyes flutter open, and I tip my head down to meet his gaze knowing what I'm feeling is being mirrored right back at me.

"Fuck!" he groans, dropping his forehead to my chest. "I thought it would be safer to kiss you out here, rather than in my bed where I'd want to take advantage." He lets me fall slowly to my feet but keeps hold of me, which is good since I'm pretty sure my legs wouldn't be able to hold me up right now. "I was wrong."

"I should get home and get ready for work." I say after my breathing and my heartbeat has slowed to something close to normal.

"Yeah."

He leans in to touch his lips to my forehead and my eyes slide closed. Kissing him might make me light up but the forehead kisses are going to be my undoing.

"Come on, we'll walk you down to your car." He takes my hand and walks me to the door, then calls for Skye to follow, and grabs the hardhat I wore upstairs last night. When we get into the elevator, Skye starts to prance in excitement, then the bell chimes and the doors open on the first floor and she takes off, disappearing out of sight before Clay even has a chance to place the hat on my head. While we walk through the building, I notice people starting to filter in to start work, and Skye stops to greet each of them on her way back to us, all of them acting like it's a regular occurrence to have her around.

"You need to get her a yard to run in." I tell Clay when we get outside, and she starts to roll around in a small patch of grass next to his jeep.

"She has access to the back of the building where we laid down grass, she just thinks we're going for a ride and is showing off."

"Now you need to take her on a ride, otherwise she'll be disappointed."

"She'll ride with me later today when I run a few errands."

He stops at the door to my car and opens it up, but before I can place my ass in my seat, he presses me up against the side of my car and cups my face in his large palms.

"I want you to stay the night tonight, are you good with that?"

"Yes." I answer without even having to think about it.

His face gentles. "That was easier than I thought it would be." He dips down brushing his lips across mine, then steps back enough for me to get in my car, and once I'm in my seat, he bends down to give me one more kiss, only leaning back enough to look me in the eye. "I'll see you when you get off work."

"Okay," I say, and he shuts my door. Then I hear him call Skye and as I pull away from the curb, I watch the two of them in my rearview mirror as they both watch me drive off.

WITH MY FEET hurting from being in heels all day I get off the elevator and head down the hall to my apartment, flipping through the mail I picked up from the box on my way into the building. Like always it's mostly junk and a few clothing catalogs that I plan on looking at later, then will likely toss in the trash because I won't actually order anything from any of them.

As I get closer to my door, I lift my head and stop when I see Tucker leaning against the wall with his arms crossed over his chest and his eyes on me. Dread instantly fills my stomach, causing the soup I had this afternoon for lunch to crawl up my throat.

"What happened?" I barely whisper.

"Shit." His eyes scan my face, and he shakes his head holding up his hands. "Nothing happened, I just need to talk to you."

"Okay." I take my bag off my shoulder and get out my keys as I walk to my door. "Clay should be here soon."

"He's actually what I want to talk to you about."

I pause with my key in hand and look up at him. "You want to talk to me about Clay?"

"You need to cut him off," he says quietly, tucking his hands into the front pockets of the vest he's wearing. "I know you've been spending time with him but he's not the kind of man you should get attached to."

"And why is that?" I ask, feeling a little annoyed and whole lot anxious about where this conversation is going.

"Because he doesn't care about anyone but himself, and as soon as he's done with you, you'll be left picking up the pieces. I know your dad, he's a good guy and I feel it's my obligation to look out for you."

"Where is this coming from?"

"There have been a hundred women just like you in and then right back out of Clay's life. You're not special, Willow." His expression fills with sympathy. "But I can tell you're a good person and you deserve better."

His words cause a knot to form in my stomach and my hands to ball into fists. Everything he's saying just reminds me that I still don't know what exactly it is that Clay wants from me, I really know very little about him.

"I gotta go, but just think about what I said."

I turn to watch him walk away, then let myself into my apartment and shut and lock the door behind me.

Going right to my bedroom I change out of my work clothes, and put on a pair of jeans, a sweater, then slip on a pair of flats. Clay told me that he would be here by six at the latest, which doesn't give me very long to come to terms with what Tucker said or how I should feel about it.

One thing I know is I'm annoyed—annoyed that he would show up at my door to basically talk shit about his brother. Even if he thinks he's doing the noble thing of looking out for me, it's still messed up. I would never—not ever go to someone one of my siblings was seeing and tell them that they should back off. First, because I don't know how they feel about that person, and for all I know that person could actually be their person and I could mess that up. Second, if I ever did that to one of my sisters or brothers, they would lose their flipping minds. Third, it's just dickish. Okay, so maybe I do know how I feel about it, and it's not good.

I already knew that I needed to be cautious when dealing with Clay and it's honestly not surprising that he's dated hundreds of women. Plus, who am I to judge when I've dated more than my fair share of guys. For me, Clay is different than any of the guys I've spent time with and maybe he feels that way about me. Only time will tell.

Coming out of my thoughts when there is a knock on the door, I go to it and check the peephole, finding Clay standing on the other side.

"Hey," I greet, swinging the door in.

His eyes do a scan of my face before he leans down touching his mouth to mine. "How was work?"

"Busy." I stand back to let him in. "How was your day?"

"All right." He looks around then asks. "I thought I saw Tucker leaving the parking lot when I was pulling in. Did he stop by?"

"He did." I walk to the kitchen and open the fridge, grabbing a bottle of water.

"You're supposed to show at the station at seven for your statement."

"He wasn't here to take my statement." I put the bottle of water to my lips and tip it back, hating that Tucker placed me in such an awkward position. One where if I lie it could blow up in my face and if I don't, I could hurt their relationship.

"Then why was he here, Mouse?"

I let out a breath and meet his gaze and decided that honesty is the best course of action in this situation. "He came to talk to me about you."

"About me?" He walks around into the kitchen then stands a few feet from me, planting his feet wide apart and crossing his arms over his chest. "And what exactly did he want to tell you about me?"

"I feel like you should ask him."

"I'm asking you."

"All right." I shake my head. "He told me I need to be careful when it comes to you."

"Careful?"

That one word sounds like a question, and I shrug. "Yes, careful."

"All right what else did he say?"

"Nothing." I take another drink of water.

"So, he took the time out of his day to come knocking on your door, just to tell you that you need to be careful when it comes to me."

"He was actually waiting for me when I got home." I say, then instantly regret opening my mouth, because his expression that had been blank gets hard.

"He was waiting for you?"

"Don't we need to go?" I ask, hoping to get out of this.

"What the fuck else did he say, Willow?"

"Don't fucking curse at me, Clay." I snap then add. "And what does it matter? You're obviously inside my apartment, so I'm not taking his suggestion to heart."

"It matters, now what else did he say? Was it about me and Naomi?"

"What?" I shake my head, wondering what he's talking about."

"His wife—did he tell you about me and his wife?"

"You were with his wife?" I breathe.

"Fuck no, I went on a couple of dates with her before she even met him, then one day he tells us that he's dating someone and it's getting serious, and it was her."

"Oh." Relief swamps my system. "Why would you think he would have told me about her?"

"Because a while back she showed up at my house and she tried to shove her tongue down my throat."

"She what?" I gasp totally horrified.

"It doesn't fucking matter, now what else did he say?"

"I think it does matter because who the heck does something like that firstly when they're married and secondly when it's their husband's brother. That is just—" My nose scrunches, "so messed up, not to mention gross."

"Don't be cute right now, Willow, not when I'm so fucking pissed that I'm seeing red. Tell me what he said to you."

"Seriously." I toss my hands in the air. "He didn't say anything. Just that I need to be careful when it comes to you and not get attached because you date a lot and none of your relationships last long. But who the heck cares about that." I roll my eyes. "I mean you've seen firsthand that I've not been sitting at home, knitting, waiting for the right suitor to knock on my door and ask for my hand in marria—" The word marriage tapers off when he takes two steps across the kitchen to where I'm standing and curls one hand around my waist and the other around the back of my neck so he can drag me into him. When his mouth lands on mine, I gasp and then moan and latch onto him. Okay, so the forehead kisses are nice, but lord, the man can kiss. When he pulls his mouth from mine, I blink my eyes open and find him staring down at me.

"I don't need to hear about all the men you've dated, I'm sure I'll meet them all eventually." He grins.

The tension I didn't even know was in my muscles loosens. "Whatever! Now, are you ready to go? I want to know if Miles has found anything out about Carly, then I need to eat because all I had today was soup, so I'm starving."

"We can go." He stands me up then reminds me. "Make sure you pack a bag for tonight."

"I will." I lift up on my tiptoes to kiss the underside of his jaw, then I head to my room to pack an overnight bag, because even if it might be reckless to trust Clay, I'm going to do just that.

Less than forty-five minutes later I sit with Clay in a dimly lit conference room at the police station with his hand wrapped around mine. Since we were ushered in here to wait, my leg has not stopped bouncing. I count the minutes as they tick by on the clock each one seeming to take longer than normal. How criminals are able to sit in these rooms for hours while being interrogated is something I can't fathom doing. We've only been in here for a few minutes and I already feel like the walls are closing in on me.

"Hey."

Clay startles me, making me jump and I look over at him.

"Relax. Remember, you already know what they are going to ask you."

"I know." I sit up when the door opens, and watch Miles walk into the room with a notepad in hand and a gentle smile on his handsome face.

"Hey, Willow."

"Hey, Miles." I smile or try to, as he starts to take a seat across from me.

"Where's Tucker?" Clay asks.

Miles focuses on him as he sits. "He's sitting this one out."

"I bet he is," Clay mutters.

I squeeze his hand.

"Did something happen?" Miles asks, looking between the two of us.

"He and I just need to have a conversation," Clay mutters.

"Sounds cryptic," Miles says, looking at me and raising a dark brow.

I press my lips together to keep from laughing because that would be inappropriate, especially right now.

"All right, well, let's get this over with." He leans back in his chair, then begins asking me questions about Carly.

I respond to each one the best I can, but there are some that I just don't have an answer to, and those questions make me feel like the worst kind of friend. I wish I had taken time to find out more about her family and why she wanted to move to Tennessee to begin with, when she didn't know anyone here. But I didn't and now I don't know if me not having that information will hurt the chances of her being found.

"That's it." He taps his pen against the notepad where he jotted down the information I gave him. "But if you think of anything else, just call."

"Sure. Have you guys found anything out since last night?"

"Not yet."

I nod, I should have known that, I mean it's only been a few hours since anyone even knew she might be missing, so it's not like they could have closed the case or even got a timeline for when she disappeared.

"As soon as we know anything, I'll let you know."

"Thanks. And thank you for bringing my car back to Clay's last night."

"Not a problem."

"If you're done, I'm gonna take her to get something to eat." Clay stands and Miles follows suit.

"Yeah, we'll talk later," he says.

Clay lifts his chin, placing his hand against my lower back as Miles opens the door.

As soon as we step over the threshold into the hall, I feel a change in energy in the air around me and that's when I spot Tucker at the entrance to the station, talking to a female officer who is in uniform.

"Please don't say anything to him, I'm hungry and these are all his friends. I'd rather not spend the next few hours trying to bail you out of jail for beating up your brother in the middle of a police station," I mutter under my breath, as we walk toward the two of them.

Tucker takes his attention off the woman he's with and looks between Clay and me with a blank expression.

"What did I tell you about being cute when I'm pissed?" Clay asks, grabbing my hand.

I glance up at him. "I'm not trying to be cute."

"I know," he grumbles, then he lifts his head as we pass Tucker.

I hold my breath, not sure what is about to happen.

When we pass him without a word said between the two of them, I sigh in relief. My brothers use to fight all the time growing up and it's something they never really grew out of. They still argue and get pissed at each other to this day and there are times that we wonder if it won't come to blows. Thankfully it's been years since that's happened, but it still could, and you never know what might set them off.

Men are so weird.

"Do you think that Miles will be able to do anything with the information I gave him?" I ask when we get outside to Clay's jeep.

He opens my door for me. "He'll do his best." He stands in the open door as I climb inside and start to put on my seatbelt. "Now that they've got a case opened, they'll be able to dig into Carly's past along with her phone records and see if they can find out who she's been talking to and hopefully spending time with. There is always someone who knows something—they just need to figure out who that person is."

"I just hope they can find Matthew. Maybe she is with him. Maybe this is all some big misunderstanding."

"Maybe."

I bite my bottom lip because the feeling I've had in my chest for days hasn't gone away and I know that there is something wrong even if I don't want to admit it to myself.

Clay

Twelve

WITH WILLOW SITTING across from me, I watch her as she talks on the phone to her roommate, and listen as she fills her in on what happened with Carly. From what I've gathered listening to her side of the conversation, her roommate is out of town and, up until a few minutes ago, she had no idea that anything was even going on with Carly. And now Willow's filling her in which doesn't seem to be going over well.

"Sorry," she mouths to me.

I lift my chin then watch her rub her forehead as she continues talking.

"You're right, I should have told you, but I didn't want you worried. I know you're already stressed, dealing with your parents." Willow meets my gaze and then closes her eyes. "You're right, sorry." She rubs her lips together then drops her eyes to the table. "I promise I'll keep you filled in on what's going on. Right now they don't know much. Okay." She lets out a long breath. "Okay, and let me know if you need me to come rescue you and I'll be on the next flight." Her gaze meets mine once more and she bites her bottom lip before whispering. "I'll let him know—Love you, too. Bye." She hangs up and places her cell phone on the table next to her drink.

"What are you supposed to let me know?" I ask.

The worried look on her face slides away. "That Leah will hurt you if something happens to me."

"Should I be scared?"

"She's a doctor with access to lots of drugs, so probably." She shrugs.

I smile. "You hadn't told her about Carly?"

"No." She picks up the diet coke she ordered when we sat down and takes a sip. "She is in Florida with her mom and dad who just moved there. Her mom is a lot on a good day, and I didn't really want to worry her with this when I wasn't sure my imagination wasn't being overactive. I was going to call and tell her about things this afternoon when I had lunch, but I only had a couple minutes between clients so there wasn't really time to explain things properly. This is the first time I really had to talk to her."

"Have you told your dad?" I ask only because it's obvious this is something he would want to know.

"My parents and siblings are on an Alaskan cruise right now. I sent him a text but I'm not sure when he'll get it because service on the boat is non-existent."

"You didn't want to go with them?"

"I wasn't invited." She laughs. "I should have clarified that it's a cruise with my parents and my married siblings and their kids. I haven't joined that cool club yet."

"Do you want to?" I pick up my drink.

"What? Get married and have kids?" She fiddles with her straw.

"Yeah."

"Eventually." She looks across the restaurant then she quickly looks down and mumbles something under her breath before grabbing her bag from the seat next to her and starts digging in it. Looking to where she had been, I notice a guy sitting at a table with a woman, and chuckle.

"Another boyfriend?"

"What?" She keeps her head down as she pretends to look in her purse.

"How long did you date him for?"

"A while." She groans glancing up at me. "You know until you started coming around, I never ran into any of my ex-boyfriends as often as I do now. I swear you must be putting some kind of signal in the sky showing them my location."

"He's here with someone and not even paying attention to you." I say then look up when a shadow falls over the table and barely keep from laughing because it's the guy who had been sitting across the room most likely on a date.

"I thought it was you," he says to Willow in greeting.

She kicks me under the table when I chuckle.

"Hey Abe, how have you been?"

"Good, I've been meaning to call you and check in, but life's been busy." He glances at me.

"Sorry, I'm Abe, Willow and I are old friends."

"She has a lot of those." I grunt when she kicks me again harder this time.

"Abe this is my—"

"Boyfriend." I cut her off and hold out my hand, the claim startling her but feeling right when it rolls out of my mouth.

"Cool," he says, then looks over his shoulder when his name is called, and I glance over finding the woman he was sitting with motioning that their food arrived. "I gotta go." He focuses back on Willow. "Call me and we'll catch up."

"Sounds good." She smiles then avoids looking at me when he's walked away.

"Did you befriend every guy you've dated or just most of them?"

"They're nice guys," she huffs, placing her bag back on the chair next to her.

"They all seem great." I agree and she glares at me. "That said, you're not calling him."

"Only because I wasn't going to anyway." She rolls her eyes and I get up from my chair and walk around the table to where she is, and her eyes widen as I bend down and get in her space.

"For however long this lasts, you're mine." I slide my fingers into the hair at the back of her scalp, grip and tip her head back. "And I'm not sharing you with anyone." I kiss her and she doesn't hesitate to open up for me.

Fuck, I've never been big on kissing, never done it just because I wanted to, it was always a means to an end, but I could take her mouth over and over and never get tired of it. When I pull back, her lashes flutter open and I rub my thumb across her bottom lip.

"Umm, I'll be back," I hear behind me, and I stand and turn to find our waitress holding a tray of food backing away from our table.

"We're ready." I take my seat and she awkwardly hands me my plate while she blushes then gives Willow hers.

"Thank you." Willow tells her taking her napkin and placing it on her lap, then her eyes meet mine when my phone begins to ring. Taking it out of my pocket I check to see who it is then place it face down on the table next to my plate. "You're not going to answer it?"

"It's business, I'm out with you." I watch her face go soft in a way that makes her impossibly more beautiful, then she nods and digs into her meal.

By the time we've both finished eating it's after eight, and I can tell that like last night, the day has taken a toll on her. "Tired?" I ask when she leans into me as we walk to my jeep.

"A little." She glances up at me. "Last night I slept better than I have in a while, but I still feel like I could sleep for a week straight."

"You've had a lot going on so that's understandable." I open the passenger door for her and she climbs in.

Slamming her door I head around the back, pulling out my cell when it beeps. When I see it's a message from Miles, I open it up and scan the text. After reading it I draw in a tight breath and message him back before I swing open my door.

"I think I might need to unbutton my jeans." She laughs as I get in behind the steering wheel. "I really should not have ordered that dessert, but I'm such a sucker for carrot cake and that one was delicious."

"It was good," I mutter, pulling out of our parking spot.

"Is everything okay?"

Glancing over at her I wish I could tell her "yes" but it's not—not by a long shot.

"Miles and Tucker want to speak to us back at my place."

"Did they find something out about Carly?" She pales.

I reach over for her hand and place it on my lap. "We'll talk when we get somewhere that I can hold you."

Her fingers dig into my thigh where I've got her hand trapped. "Clay?"

"Five minutes, baby." I drive to my place wondering what the fuck it is she's done to me in such a short time. My insides are raw just thinking about how much pain I'm about to cause her, and I wish I could keep driving to avoid the conversation we are about to have.

Miles said he and Tucker would share the news that Carly's body was found, but I don't trust them, not with this and not with her. Miles might not go in with the intention of being harsh, but Tucker would rip that shit off like a Band-Aid, not caring about the kind of damage he'd leave behind. And as things stand right now between Tucker and me, I'm not sure I wouldn't end up putting my fist in his face if he caused her more pain than she's already going to be feeling.

When we arrive at my building, I park behind Tucker's SUV, then put the engine in park and unhook her belt. "Come here." I urge her over the middle console and once she's settled on my lap, I wrap my hand around her lower jaw and wait for her to meet my gaze. "I don't know all the details, we'll have to wait to get those from Miles and Tucker, but Carly's body was found."

"No!" she gasps. She closes her eyes, dropping her forehead to my shoulder. "Are they sure?"

"I'm sorry, Mouse." I slide my hand into her hair and hold her as she silently cries. Feeling her pain soak through my shirt is enough to make my gut twist. I hate that I'm so fucking helpless to do anything for her right now but hold her.

I don't know how long we sit like that, in the darkness of the interior of my jeep, but eventually she lifts her head from where she had burrowed it into the crook of my neck and looks at me. "Sorry for crying all over you."

"You don't have to apologize for that." I wrap my hand around the side of her neck as she drags in a breath.

"I hate this."

"I know, Mouse." I scan my eyes over her face while I wipe the wet from her eyes and cheeks.

"I'm ready to go talk to them if you are?"

"Are you sure?"

"Yes, I want to find out what they know."

"All right." I open the door and help her out, then take her hand in mine and lead her into the building and through it. When we get to my door, I open it and let her in, then send a text to Miles to let him know that we are home. "They should be here in a few minutes, do you want a glass of wine?"

"Yeah." She wanders to the couch after kicking off her shoes.

I pour her a glass of the rosé she had last night and grab a beer from the fridge. I take both to the living room, handing her the glass, then grab the remote for the fireplace to turn it on.

As a glow fills the room, I take a seat next to her and she slouches into me, lifting her legs and pressing her knees into my thigh. I wrap my arm around her shoulders and lean back on the couch, watching the flames dance in the fireplace. I look over the back of the couch when the door opens behind us and watch both Miles and Tucker step inside. I'm not surprised when Tucker avoids my gaze. Him speaking to Willow behind my back was a violation and he knows it. He thinks that this thing between her and me is just temporary, but it's not, or it won't be if I get my way. But what he did today could have caused her to run once again, and if that had happened, I'm not sure I'd be able to forgive him.

"Willow," Miles greets, taking a seat on the couch across from us while Tucker stands with his arms crossed over his chest. "I'm guessing that Clay explained why we're here."

"He did." She leans into me.

I smooth my hand up her arm while he nods and leans forward resting his elbows on his knees.

"Now I—" He stops himself and looks up at Tucker. "We can't go into a lot of detail about the case since this is an open investigation, but I can tell you that her body was found in Percy Priest Lake this morning by a fisherman. And as we speak, the coroner is performing an autopsy to see when exactly she died and what the exact manner of death was."

"Was she—"

"I don't want to tell you 'yes' before that information has been confirmed." He cuts her off.

We both know she's asking if her friend was murdered. And since his message to me told me how she was found, it's easy to assume that she was murdered. Not many people go diving into that lake fully clothed in the midst of fall with cinderblocks tied around themselves. "We would like to ask you a little more about the man she was seeing, and if you could talk to a sketch artist and give him a description."

"I can, yes, but his photo was on the dating app I told you guys about."

"We've not been able to find him on there." Tucker chimes in then adds. "And it might take a little while to get a warrant for the app company, and until then they won't hand us over any of Carly's profile information."

"What about his job? He said he dealt in shipping expensive things around the world, that doesn't sound like a normal job, could you find him with that?"

"We're looking into that." Miles assures.

"Is there a reason why you're trying to avoid sitting down with a sketch artist?" Tucker asks.

Willow stiffens, while I come out of my relaxed position.

"I'm just asking." Tucker holds up both his hands. "If you're unsure or nervous."

"I'm not, I just don't know how good of a job I'll do." She rubs her forehead. "I remember him, but I also don't, that night is blurry and so is he."

"You mentioned that your roommate had been with you the night you met him," Miles says.

She sits forward, placing her glass on the table. "Leah, yeah, she was, but she's out of town right now. She'll be back in a few days. She might do a better job than me."

"When she gets back, we'll want to speak to her, but in the meantime don't talk about this guy with her. I'd like the two of you to each go into your meeting with the sketch artist with your memory of what he looked like if that makes sense."

"Okay." She agrees then asks softly, "Should I find out who Carly used as an emergency contact at work and try to get in touch with them?"

"We'll take care of that," Tucker tells her.

She nods.

Tucker's gaze moves to Miles. "Can you think of anything else right now?"

"No." Miles pushes up to stand. "We'll get out of your hair and let you get some rest."

"Thank you both." Willow stands, wrapping her arms around her middle. "For believing me."

"We just wish we could have had a different outcome," Miles tells her gently.

"Me too." She lets out a breath.

She leans into me, and I wrap my arm around her waist as they both tell her goodbye.

As they start toward the door, I squeeze her hip and she tips her head back to meet my gaze. "I'm going to step out with them for a couple minutes, you gonna be okay?"

"Yeah, I think I'm just going to get into the shower."

"All right." I bend and brush my lips over hers. "Be right back." I follow my brothers out the door and as soon as I close it behind me, I prowl toward Tucker, and he starts to back up.

"Clay." Miles steps between us and I shake my head keeping my eyes locked on Tucker's.

"Did he tell you he went to Willow?" I ask Miles without looking at him.

"What the fuck, Tuck?" he asks, looking over his shoulder.

"She seems like a nice girl, you don't—"

"And fuck if I deserve her, right?" I cut him off as I push my chest against Miles, while he tries to hold me back. "Someone good, something good."

"You don't care about her." He shakes his head. "You don't give a fuck about anyone but yourself."

In a flash before I even know what I'm doing, the space between us is closed, I have my hand wrapped around his neck and am shoving him against the wall. "You don't know shit."

"Clay." Miles grasps my wrist.

"Stay the fuck away from her." I let him go and step back.

"Like you stayed away from Naomi?" he asks when I turn my back on him and start to walk back down the hall.

I don't even bother turning around to respond. It's obvious he's set on blaming me for his failing marriage and there isn't shit I can do about that.

"You know that's fucked up," I hear Miles tell him.

My eyes land on Willow standing in my doorway looking concerned. When her face softens as our eyes lock, I know Tucker's right, I don't deserve her, not even a little but I'm still not fucking letting her go.

Willow

Thirteen

*W*ITH SKYE'S LONG body resting on the bed in front of me I run my fingers through her soft fur and stare out the window, watching the rain fall in thick sheets while lightning flashes sporadically through the grey cloud-covered, early morning sky.

I've tried to convince myself numerous times to get out of bed since the storm woke me, but I don't mentally feel ready to face the day. And with Clay still asleep behind me with his big warm body curled around mine I have even less motivation to move.

When I was little, I would crawl into bed between my parents and cuddle up between the two of them, and sleep my best sleep because I was warm and safe. And over the years when I've had relationships with men where I'd sleep over at their house or where they've slept at mine, I've hoped I'd feel that same sense of security and warmth, but I never have, not until Clay.

"How long have you been awake?" Clay's deep sleepy voice asks in my ear and my eyes slide closed.

"A while." I say then feel the bed move and his lips brush the shell of my ear.

"You should have woken me up."

"Why? So, we can both stare out the window?"

"Yes." His hand moves to my jaw, and he puts pressure there until

I look at him. "I don't want you keeping shit bottled up if you need to talk."

"I'm okay."

"You're not, but I'll make sure you are," he says quietly.

His words make my chest feel heavy because I know that he will. There is something about him that makes everything okay which is terrifying.

"What time can you call into work and let them know you won't be in?"

"I'm not calling in." I shake my head.

"You're not going to work today," he denies in a tone that states he's the boss and I shouldn't argue.

"I am. I need to be there."

"Mouse."

"No," I cut him off and turn toward him, resting my hands on his bare tattoo-covered chest. "I don't want to tell Katy what happened to Carly over the phone, and I don't want Miles or Tucker telling her either. I need to do that."

"Fuck." His jaw shifts and his eyes scan over my face. "Fine," he gives in, "but I'm dropping you off then picking you up."

"Okay."

"And you'll cut out early if being there is too much."

"I can do that." I agree softly but he doesn't look any happier, even getting his way.

"And Skye isn't allowed on the bed."

"She was just keeping me company, it won't happen again." I move my hands up his chest to his shoulders.

"Right," he grunts, and I barely keep from smiling.

"Are you always this grumpy when you wake up in the morning?"

"I've have you in my bed more than once, Mouse." His hand smooth's up my stomach to just under my breast causing my breath to catch. "And I still haven't been inside you, so until that happens, you're gonna have to deal."

"Oh." My heart does a summersault inside my chest and the muscles in my core clench tight.

"Yeah," he mutters.

I start to lift my head wanting more than my next breath to kiss him, and to have him kiss me back, but just when his lips touch mine Skye stands and bounds over to us as she starts to bark.

Then in a blink Clay is up off the bed growling, "Stay here."

As he prowls through the bedroom door with Skye and shuts it behind himself, I toss the blanket back and roll out of bed. I don't even bother looking for pants to put on, his t-shirt that I wore last night is longer than some of the nightgowns I normally wear. When I reach the door, I swing it open and instantly relax when I spot his brother Dayton who was here the first morning I woke up in Clay's bed.

"I see you don't listen," Clay says, and I turn my head his way.

"I'm not good at following orders." I shrug one shoulder then watch his lips press into a thin line.

"You remember my brother Dayton."

"I do," I look over at Dayton then lift my hand. "Hey."

"Hey." His eyes scan over hair and face then down my torso and my bare legs as he grins, then he moves his gaze to Clay. "She's back."

"She is and I'd appreciate you not checking her out again."

"Just taking it all in." He lifts a hand out toward his brother.

"Well don't," Clay grumbles then he looks at me. "You want coffee, baby?"

"Yeah." I shift on my feet then motion with my thumb over my shoulder. "I'm going to go get dressed."

"You want me to bring you a cup in there or you wanna wait until you're done?"

"I'll wait," I tell him, then look at Dayton. "I'll be back."

"All right, sweetheart." He smiles and I spin on my heel and head back into the room hearing him say, "If I knew she was staying here I would have crashed with Miles."

Closing the door, I cut off whatever Clay's reply is, then grab my overnight bag and take it with me into the bathroom.

It takes me about forty minutes to get through my full morning routine and after I'm dressed, I slip on my heels and open the bedroom door. When I step out of the room, I find not only Dayton sitting at the island in the kitchen, but Miles and Winter are as well, along with a woman with long dark hair.

As soon as Winter spots me she jumps down off her stool and runs across the room shouting "Willow."

"Hey, sweet girl." I smile and cup the back of her head as she wraps her arms around my waist.

"My mom is here." She jerks her head back to grin up at me.

"Oh yeah?" I lift my head and look at the woman who had her back to me earlier and I'm stunned by how beautiful she is.

"Nice to meet you, Willow." She slides off her stool with ease and smiles as she walks toward us. "I've heard nothing but good things about you from Winter."

"Your girl is the sweetest."

"She is." She smiles down at Winter then holds her hand out toward me. "I'm Hazel."

"But everyone calls her El," Winter tells me.

"They do." Hazel laughs. "I was getting to that."

"Nice to meet you." I laugh as Miles calls Winter over to finish her breakfast.

"You, too." She focuses back on me when Winter is up on her stool. "And I'm sorry about your friend. Miles told me when he got home last night."

"Thanks," I say quietly, and she nods.

"Baby, come eat some breakfast." Clay calls out and I look in his direction.

"So, you locked down the un-keepable Clay, huh?" she asks under her breath.

"Umm," I mumble, not sure how to respond. I want to think that I've got my claws in him as deep as his are in me, but I honestly don't know if they are.

"Never mind, I don't think you keep a man like him, I think you just accept that you're his after he's claimed you." She winks at me then walks away.

With a breath, I head into the kitchen and as soon as I'm within touching distance, Clay reaches for my hand, grasps it, then pulls me close enough to touch his mouth to mine. "Love the shoes," he whispers, before he leans back.

I swallow from the look in his eyes.

"Willow," Miles calls and I look his way. "I told Clay, but I have a sketch artist meeting you at the station this evening."

"Oh, okay sure." I accept a cup of coffee from Clay, then feel his hand against my lower back, his touch putting me at ease.

"It shouldn't take long."

"Okay."

He looks down at Winter and I notice then that she has a pair of headphones on her head and is watching an iPad that is set up in front of her.

"I also want to fill you in on the news we got back from the coroner last night," he says gently.

My muscles bunch.

"Miles," Clay growls.

"Would you rather her find out at work when people start talking?"

"No, but I'd also appreciate you letting me fill her in when she's not in the kitchen, surrounded by people and able to let go if she needs to."

"Just tell me," I say quietly, cutting into what I can see becoming an argument between the two of them.

"Mouse." Clay slides his hand across my back and squeezes my hip.

"It's okay." I tip my head back to look up at him. "I just want to know." I focus back on Miles. "Tell me."

"She was murdered, beaten pretty badly then strangled."

Closing my eyes, I let that information sink in and try to understand why or how someone would do that to her. It doesn't make any sense.

"Baby." Clay turns me to face him and takes the cup from my hands before hugging me.

"She never hurt anyone, I just don't get it." My throat starts to ache like I'm going to cry.

"You never will, Mouse." He presses his lips to my temple and holds them there.

I fight back tears, refusing to give into them. It would be easy to call into work, then spend the day crying, but that's not going to help get answers or justice for Carly. Someone has to know something, and even if Miles and Tucker can't get Carly's account information for the dating site without a warrant, that doesn't mean I can't see if I can.

"I'm okay." I tell him after a few minutes, and he leans back enough to look me in the eye.

"Are you sure?"

"Yeah." I drag in a deep breath through my nose. "I just want to know who did that to her."

"We're going to do everything we can to find out," Miles says.

I look over at him and nod.

"I want you to eat something," Clay tells me.

I shake my head as I pick up my coffee. "I'm not hungry."

"I'm sure you're not but you need to eat."

"I will at lunch."

"You need to eat now," he argues.

"Is this weird for anyone else?" Dayton asks.

Miles chuckles while Hazel laughs.

"Just asking." He mutters and I imagine that if I looked up at Clay, I'd see him glaring at Dayton.

"I think it's sweet." Hazel shrugs.

Miles looks over at her. "You think it's sweet?"

"Yes."

"If I ever told you that you need to eat, you'd lose your shit."

"Probably, but I still think it's sweet that Clay is trying to take care of his girl."

"Whatever," Miles mutters.

I look between the two of them. Honestly, they look like they would be perfect together, like they would just make sense, which makes me curious about why they are no longer together.

"Here." Clay holds out a piece of toast to me. "Don't argue just eat it while I go get dressed." He drops a kiss to my mouth then takes off.

I watch him walk to the bedroom, then with a sigh, I take a bite of the toast in my hand because he's probably right. I should eat something even if I don't really want to.

"So El, how long are you in town for?" Dayton asks.

"I head back to Colorado tomorrow," she says, resting her hand on the back of Winter's head and that's when I catch the glitter of a diamond on her ring finger.

"Darn I was hoping I'd have a drinking partner this weekend."

"Sorry, I wish I could stay, but I have an open case on my desk that's sucking up all my time."

"Where do you work?" I ask her and she looks at me then over at Miles, which is a strange thing to do for such a simple question.

"She works for the FBI," Miles says.

I blink. "Really?" I look at her. I don't know why that news shocks me, but it does. Maybe because in my head FBI agents are bald guys in dark suits like I see around the president.

"I do." She smiles.

"Wow, that's awesome."

"I think so too," she agrees.

Miles grunts.

"Ready?" Clay asks, coming out of the room dressed in a pair of jeans and a hooded sweatshirt with a baseball cap on his head. After seeing him dressed to ride his motorcycle, shirtless in just sweats, in a suit at my bank and now this, I don't know my favorite look on him. Who am I kidding, the guy could wear a paper sack and I'd think he was attractive, but him shirtless and sleepy is by far my favorite.

"Babe," he mutters.

I snap out of my thoughts and chug the rest of my coffee as everyone laughs.

"Sorry." I grab my purse from where it's resting on the counter before I look at Hazel. "It was nice meeting you."

"You, too, and I'm sure I'll see you around."

"Yeah." I smile then look at Miles. "I'll see you this evening."

"You will."

"Bye, sweetheart," Dayton says.

I give him a wave then get Winter's attention. "I'll see you later."

"Can we have our ice cream party tonight?" She holds her hands up and looks between Clay and me.

"Not tonight kid, but tomorrow I'll pick you up from school and we'll go to the store and pick everything up," Clay tells her.

"Aww please?" she begs.

"You and I have a date this evening," Hazel tells her, kissing the top of her head. "We're getting our nails done."

"Can I choose any color I want?"

"Yes," her mom says.

Winter narrows her eyes. "Even black?"

"Why do you need black nails?" Miles asks her.

"Because it's going to be Halloween, and black is my favorite color."

"Technically, black isn't a color," Dayton says.

Winter rolls her eyes at him.

"You can get whatever you want," Hazel tells her as I walk toward the door where Clay is waiting for me then listen to him say goodbye before he takes my hand and leads me to the elevator.

When we get outside a few minutes later he opens the door of his Jeep for me and I climb in, then watch him walk around the hood and get in behind the wheel.

"So, what is the story with Miles and Hazel?" I ask as soon as he starts the engine, and he glances over at me.

"It didn't take you long to ask."

"I'm curious, it seems like they get along and they obviously have a great co-parent relationship."

"They used to work together and were friends." He starts the engine then pulls out onto the road. "And since they got along so well, they figured they'd be good in a relationship."

"But they weren't?"

"No." He reaches over for my hand. "Miles is as laid back as they come but he also likes control, and Hazel wasn't down with giving him that."

"How old was Winter when they broke up?"

"She wasn't born." He squeezes my fingers. "They've gotten back together a few times over the years, but it's never lasted long."

"I saw a ring on her finger."

"She's engaged to a lawyer back in Colorado. He's a good guy, he comes out to visit when he can but not as often as Hazel does. I'm sure you'll meet him eventually."

"So why doesn't Winter live with her mom?" I shake my head. "Not to be sexist, I'm just use to the mom having custody of the kids when the parents have split up."

"We're all here," he says easily and something about that makes my chest warm and it also makes me like Hazel even more because she's giving her daughter that without a fight. "Things might change when Winter gets a little older but right now she likes living with her dad and having her uncles close. Plus, she's in a great school here."

"She's a lucky girl to have so many people who love her."

"She saved us."

"What do you mean?"

"Her coming into this world gave all of us something outside of work and Arya to focus on."

He looks over at me as he comes to a stop at a red light, and there is something there that I have never seen before, and I wish I could read his mind to know exactly what it is that he's thinking because I'm honestly too afraid to ask.

"Hazel works for the FBI and you said Miles and her worked together…" I let my sentence trail and he squeezes my fingers.

"You're smart, Mouse, anyone ever told you that?"

"I just listen."

"Both Miles and Tucker work for the FBI," he says and my stomach drops. "I won't go into why they're here, but no one can know who they really work for."

"I won't tell anyone."

"I know you won't," he says softly.

My throat itches because him trusting me with that information is huge.

"You should probably send your dad another message, and let him know what's going on."

"I will, and I'll call my brother and fill him in just in case he somehow gets a hold of Dad before I do."

"Your brother?"

"I have three, only one of them isn't on the trip with our parents."

"Sisters?"

"Two of those, one of them is my twin, and the one not on the trip with our parents is also in Colorado."

"Jesus, we need to talk more," he mumbles.

I laugh. "We talk all the time, there's just been a lot of stuff going on."

"Tonight, you'll tell me everything."

"Only if you do the same."

"You've met my family baby."

"Yeah, but I don't know what you actually do for a job or who all those people are in the frames in your living room."

"What people?" he asks as he pulls into the parking lot for the bank.

"The frames in your living room, I haven't met any of those people," I say, and he tosses his head back and laughs.

"The decorator who styled my place put those there, I don't have a fucking clue who those people are."

"Oh." I bite my bottom lip and he reaches over grasping me behind the neck then pulls me over until we are face to face.

"I'll tell you about my job tonight. It's not exciting," he says but something tells me he's lying.

"Okay." I agree then he leans in to kiss me and I kiss him back. When he lets me go, I grab my purse and start to reach for the door handle, but stop and look at him when he grabs my wrist.

"Call me if you need to leave early and I'll be here as soon as I can to pick you up."

"I'll call." I promise before I open the car door and hop out. When I reach the door to the bank, I glance back over my shoulder where he's still parked watching me and lift my hand. It would be easy to go and get back in his jeep, but I know if I do that, I won't have a chance to dig into Carly's information and try to find out what happened to her myself.

WITH MY FOOT tapping nervously on the floor under my desk I look through the glass that surrounds my office and gives me a full view of the lobby then back at my computer.

This morning when I arrived, I found Katy in her office and told her what I could about Carly, but left out the information Miles gave me, not wanting to jeopardize the case in any way. As I knew she would be, she was visibly shaken and stunned and so was everyone else when we sat the entire bank staff down at our morning meeting and told them the news.

I had known that Carly made some friends working here but I had no idea how close she had gotten to her co-workers, and it was hard seeing the same pain I've been feeling reflected back at me. No one could understand how someone could do that to her or why, and I wished more than anything I could reassure them somehow that the person responsible would be caught.

Biting my lip, I log into my management account and run a search for Carly's file, praying that it hasn't already been removed from the company's database. Once I find it, I open it up then glance at the lobby to make sure no one is coming my way. When I see that the coast is clear I quickly hit print and the printer on my desk shoots out her resume, along with her application. Snatching it out of the plastic tray, I fold it in half then tuck it away in my bag before I start to shut down my computer. My hope is that I can somehow use the information Carly had to break into her e-mail account and gain access to her dating profile then share Matthew's information with Miles and Tucker.

After the screen of my desktop goes black, I pick up my bag and head to the door, shutting off the light before I leave my office. Seeing everyone waiting in the sitting area for me to let them out, my stomach clenches. Today was a long, difficult day for everyone and I'm sure even the customers could feel the weight of the black cloud hanging over all of us.

"Everyone ready?" I ask, taking out my key from my pocket as I walk to the door to let everyone out.

"We've been ready," Troy gripes as he gets up from his seat.

"Don't be a dick, Troy," Indigo hisses at him as she gets up, tossing her long braids over her shoulder.

"Don't call me a dick."

"Don't act like one," Becca rolls her eyes at him.

I see a few heads nod in agreement.

"Troy." I step between him and Becca when it looks like he's going to say something more. "It's been a long day. Let's all just go home and relax."

"Whatever, just open the door." He glares at me, and I let out a long breath and remind myself that emotions are running high and that everyone deals with difficult situations differently. Who am I kidding? Troy is always a jerk.

Turning, I open the door and feel a sense of ease when I see Clay standing next to his jeep with his hip leaning against his door and his arms crossed over his chest.

"Who's is that?" Indigo whispers as she walks out through the door, I'm now holding open.

"He's mine," I tell her, and she smirks at me.

"You go, girl."

"Thanks." I laugh then say goodbye to everyone else as they file out. Once the bank is clear I step back inside, set the alarm system then walk back out as it begins to beep. When I turn from locking the door, Clay is standing on the sidewalk between me and his jeep and my feet take me to him before I even know what I'm doing. As his arms wrap around me, my muscles relax, and I swear my soul sighs in happiness.

"You okay?" he asks as his lips touch the top of my head.

"Better now." I tip my head back and look into his eyes.

"Long day?"

"Very." I nod and he bends down brushing his lips across mine.

"Sorry, baby." He takes my hand and leads me to the passenger door. "After you meet with the sketch artist you can relax for the rest of the night."

"I hope so." I climb into my seat, and he reaches across me and pulls out a familiar white cup and hands it to me. "What's this?"

"Hot cocoa."

He steps back slamming the door while my heart trips all over itself inside my chest.

Willow ⸺ Clay

Willow

Fourteen

"ALL RIGHT, HERE'S what we've got." Johnny, the sketch artist I've been working with for the last two hours says while turning the paper note pad in his hands around to face me. I stare at the image of a man who looks familiar but also not, and twist my hands in my lap. He looks like he could be anyone, or no one. "Do you see anything else you want to add or anything you think I should change?"

"I don't know." I close my eyes and drop my face into my hands as I try to remember Matthew's face. I wish that night wasn't so blurry, that everything didn't seem to be shrouded in a thick layer of smoke, but that's what it's like every time I try to recall anything from my time with Carly at that bar.

Hearing a knock, I lift my head, then a second later the door is opened behind me, and I turn around.

"Dad," I gasp, jumping to my feet before I rush across the short distance between us. "What are you doing here?"

"I got your text when we hit Juneau and I caught the first flight I could back here." He wraps his arms around me, and tears start to fill my eyes.

"You didn't have to do that."

"Miles and Tucker filled me in on what went down. How are you holding up?" he asks, ignoring my comment as he palms the back of my head.

"I'm okay, just wish this wasn't happening," I tell him softly, then tip my head back. "Where's mom and everyone else?"

"Finishing the cruise. They wanted to come but I told them to stay," he says, and I nod then look to my side when a shadow fills the doorway.

Seeing Clay standing there, my stomach flutters then sinks. My dad has never liked any man I've dated or spent time with. He's always found them lacking and usually he was right in his assessment, but I need to believe that Clay is different; I want him to think that Clay *is* different. But I know my dad, and asking him to give Clay a chance would be like asking the moon not to pull the tide to shore.

"Hey," I whisper, letting my dad go then hesitate for just a second before I walk to Clay and take his hand.

"Were you done?" he asks gently, reaching up with his free hand to touch my cheek with the tips of his fingers.

"I can't remember him," I say quietly, and his face softens.

"It's okay." He squeezes my hand.

"My dad is here."

"I see that." He smiles softly.

I nod, then rub my lips together before I turn to face my father who I can feel watching us. "Dad, you remember Clay, right?"

"I do." His jaw clenches as he looks between the two of us and that sinking feeling in my stomach suddenly feels like a lead weight.

"He's been taking care of me through all this," I try, hoping that will soften him up. "I—"

"If you're done here, I'll get you home," Dad cuts me off.

My chest gets tight. "I'm staying with Clay," I tell him quietly and I feel Clay's hand around mine jerk.

"Kid, do you think that I'm going to let you go home with this man after I just flew across the country to make sure you're okay?"

"Saturday, I can come over for breakfast and we can talk," I say softly, and he crosses his arms over his chest.

"Willow."

Oh lord I know that tone; I remember it from when I was a teenager. It's the tone he would use right before he got pissed.

"Dad, I appreciate you showing up, but between Miles and Tucker working to figure out what happened to Carly, and Clay making sure I'm okay, I'm good. If you had called, I would have told you that."

"Mouse," Clay says, grabbing my attention.

I glance back at him. I don't even know when I stepped in the space between him and my dad.

"How about you go take your dad out to dinner, then come to me after you two have had a chance to catch up."

"I—"

"That's a great fucking idea," Dad agrees, cutting me off again.

I drag in a deep breath hoping for a little patience.

"I love you, Dad, but I don't want to go to dinner." I look between both men. "I want to have a glass of wine, take a shower, and crawl into bed." I turn my attention to Johnny who's been sitting quietly watching this train wreck. "I really appreciate you taking the time to sit with me, and I wish I had more to offer but I really think that your depiction is exactly what I can remember right now."

"You sure, darlin'?" he asks.

I look down at his sketch knowing it's useless. "Yes."

"All right, you can call Miles or Tucker if you recall anything else and I'll come meet with you again."

"Thank you." I grab my bag off the floor next to the chair I was sitting in, then turn around and start toward the door, daring either of the men standing almost in front of it to try to stop me. After I bypass the two of them, I step out into the hall and stop where Miles is waiting.

"You all right?" Miles asks looking over the top of my head.

I can only shrug. The truth is I'm not. I'm tired, and stressed, and everything in between. And more so now than I even was before.

"I gave Johnny what I could, which wasn't much. I'm sorry."

"Any little bit helps." He reaches out, rubbing my arm.

"Did you get a hold of Carly's emergency contact or anyone in her family?"

"I'm waiting for a call back; I left a message."

"Will you pass along my number? I mean I know it's probably against some rule, but I'd like to talk to them and share how sorry I am for their loss."

"I can do that." He agrees quietly and I nod, then look behind me. My dad doesn't look any happier than he did just a minute ago. Actually, he looks like he wants to pick me up and toss me over his shoulder, while Clay looks like he's worried, only I'm sure that he's only worried about me. Not surprisingly, he doesn't seem to care at all that my dad is here.

"Wish me luck," I tell Miles.

He grins. "Something tells me that you'll be just fine."

"Hummm." I start walking through the station toward the front entrance with both men following close behind me. As soon as we all get outside, I stop on the sidewalk and focus on my dad when he calls my name.

"You and I need to have a talk," Dad says.

I feel Clay get close, so close that his arm brushes against mine.

"I know and we will, just not tonight, please." I really don't want to be interrogated by him—not after today—and I know that's what any conversation with him would consist of: a million and one questions that I might or might not be able to answer and some that I probably just won't want to.

"All right," he agrees after a long moment and my muscles relax.

"Thanks, Dad." I walk toward him, and he opens up his arms. As soon as I'm in his embrace he wraps me in a tight hug.

"You've always had to be so fucking stubborn, just like your mom."

"I know." I don't even deny it because ever since I was little, I've pushed back and driven him crazy by not doing exactly what he wanted. I love my dad, I love the way he loves our family, and I appreciate that he's always made keeping us safe a priority, but there have been times where his protectiveness has been suffocating. Especially when it comes to my sisters and me. My brothers always had a chance to grow and stretch their wings, and we did too, but within limits. And that's probably why I've tended to rebel when I've felt too stifled.

"I love you, kid."

"I love you, too, and I'll call you tomorrow." I promise and his chest expands before he lets me go.

"You hurt her or if harm comes to her while she's with you, you won't be able to run far enough to get away from me," Dad says to Clay as I walk to where he's standing on the sidewalk

Besides the jerk of his chin in my dad's direction, he doesn't respond to him. "Ready?" he asks once I'm within reach.

"Yes." I take his hand then head down the sidewalk with him, but glance over my shoulder to see my dad heading back into the police station. "So that was fun, huh?"

"Your dad is protective, I'd be worried if he wasn't." He opens the door for me to get into his jeep and as soon as my ass is in my seat, I lean my head back against the headrest and close my eyes. "When we get home, I'll order dinner and we can eat in bed."

"You can just drop me at my place." I open my eyes to meet his gaze as he pulls my seatbelt around me. "I know you didn't plan on me staying with you again, I just didn't want to be interrogated by my dad all night."

"It's cute you think I'd give you a choice, Mouse." He brushes his mouth against mine, then steps back and slams the door before I can respond to his highhanded statement.

"Whatever, his bed is more comfortable anyways," I mutter to myself as he walks around the hood.

"What do you want to eat for dinner?" he asks as soon as he opens his door.

"I have food at my place that's going to go bad if I don't cook it and I need to get clothes anyway, if I'm staying with you, so if you're good with it, I can make us dinner there."

"Are you sure you're up to that tonight?"

"I like cooking, so I don't mind," I say as he reaches over for my hand then brings it to his thigh.

"All right." He puts the engine in drive then fifteen minutes later we arrive at my building.

As soon as we get upstairs and into my apartment, I flip on the lights then kick off my heels by the door and walk to the kitchen to set my bag on the counter. "I'm going to go change real quick."

"I'll be here." He takes a seat on one of the barstools and I go to my bedroom then change into a pair of sweats and a tank top with a long sweater and slip on my slippers.

When I walk back out, he's on the phone, so I go to the fridge and start pulling out the stuff I picked up a couple of days ago to make chicken and mushroom risotto. I place all the ingredients on the counter, half listening to him talk quietly about some building supplies that need to be approved and a trip that needs to be planned. As I start to chop things, adding them to the pan I already have heating on the stove, he comes into the kitchen to join me with the phone still to his ear and steps up behind me caging me in.

"Do you want wine?" he whispers against my ear and my thighs clench together.

"Y—yes please," I stutter out. "There's a bottle of white in the pantry. I'll also need some for this." I say then feel his lips trail down the side of my neck to my shoulder where my sweater has slid off before his warmth leaves my back.

A few minutes later he places a glass of wine next to me along with the bottle. I add what I need to the cooking risotto, then stir as I sip from my glass while he leans against the counter next to me. Just listening to him talk on the phone, the wine in my stomach and the repetitive stirring of the rice after I've added the chicken stock is just what I need to relax, and clear my head.

"How long until it's done?" he asks, stepping behind me and looking over my shoulder when he hangs up his call.

"A while, it's a process." I glance over at him as he slides his hand around my waist leaving it to rest on my stomach.

"It smells good."

"It's one of my favorite comfort foods," I tell him, focusing back on my task. "You mentioned on your call that you have to go on a trip?"

"I need to fly down to Florida for a couple of days to close on a building I just purchased there."

"Oh," I say quietly, feeling more disappointed than I should that he's going to be going out of town. "Do you travel a lot for work?"

"A couple times a month, depending on what's going on."

"So that's what you do, purchase buildings around the US?"

"It's a little more complicated than that, but essentially, yes." His fingers slip under the bottom of my tank top causing the muscles in my lower belly to twist and dance while he keeps hold of my hip with his other hand.

"H-how d—did you get into that?" I get out on a strangled breath.

"Albert." His lips trail up my neck while his large palm moves up my stomach, coming to rest just under my breast.

"Clay," I breathe as his teeth nip my ear.

"Keep focused baby, you don't want to fuck up dinner." He cups my breast while his other hand slides forward then down under the band of my sweats. How he expects me to keep focused on anything but the way his hands feel on me, I do not get. Not when his fingers slip under the edge of the lace panties I'm wearing and smooth over my pubic bone, and his hand cupping my breast tightens. "You're so soft." His warm breath brushes against my ear making my toes curl. "Let's see if you're wet." His fingers dip lower and brush across my clit causing me to gasp. "Do you know how many times I've wanted to do this, wanted you at my mercy?"

"Ohh—" I lift up on my tiptoes when he suddenly fills me with two thick fingers.

"Jesus, you're tight, and so goddam wet."

"Oh my god." My head falls back to his shoulder, and I bite my lip hard as he fingers me slowly, so slowly.

"Sleeping next to you, waking up with you, having you in my space and in my life but not fucking having you has been torture." He nips my neck. "Did you enjoy torturing me, Mouse?"

"No," I deny, and he pinches my nipple making me whimper

"I think you did." He slides his fingers in then back out slowly, lightly skimming his thumb over my clit with each thrust. "Drop the spoon and turn off the stove." He orders roughly squeezing my breast.

It takes a second to get the stove off but as soon as I do, he spins me around and lifts me up off the ground. My legs go around his waist and his hands go to my ass while I dip my chin to look him in the eye. The dark look in his gaze makes my pulse thunder and my core clench. Lifting my hands, I spear my fingers though his thick hair and drop my mouth down to his, as he carries me through the kitchen, and the living room into my bedroom.

When my back hits the bed I expect him to follow me down but instead he stands back and rips my legs from around his waist, then takes off my slippers, tossing them to the floor. He curls his fingers in the band of my sweats. I lift my hips on instinct and then cry out when he shoves my legs apart and his mouth is suddenly on me. He doesn't go gentle; he works me with his tongue, his teeth, and his fingers like he can't get enough, like he's trying to consume all of me. My back arches off the bed, my fingers tangle in his hair and the skin on my thighs starts to tingle as he pushes me over the edge before I even have time to prepare for it.

As I come down from the high of my orgasm, I feel him kiss my clit and I open my eyes. "Clothes off, Mouse," he orders, standing up and ripping the hoodie he's wearing over his head leaving him in nothing but his jeans.

Sitting up I take off my tank top, then start to unclasp my bra while I watch him kick off his jeans leaving him in a pair of black boxers that mold to his thick erection, and sit just below the defined V of his hips. As my eyes move up his abs and over his tattooed chest, my breath catches when our gaze locks. From one look I can see that he's on edge and although that should scare me, it doesn't. If anything, it turns me on even more than I already am.

Slipping my bra off my shoulders, I let it fall to my lap exposing all of me to him for the first time. He doesn't move or even seem to take a breath as he devours every inch of me that is now bared to him. When he finally reaches for the waistband of his boxers and begins to take them off, my insides clench. I might have wanted him to be perfect in every way, but didn't think that would be possible because no man ever is. Of course, he would be the one to prove me wrong with his perfect cock.

"You keep looking at my dick like that, Mouse, I'm gonna fucking lose it before I even get inside you," he groans, stepping toward the bed wrapping his fist around himself.

I hold my breath, the anticipation of him touching me again almost too much to even think about. When he grabs my ankle and tugs, I fall to my back with a gasp then a mewl slides up my throat as he captures my breast in his mouth and cups the other one.

Wrapping my legs around his thighs, I move my hands up his sides that are hard yet smooth under my palms. When his mouth travels to my other breast my hips raise off the bed. "Clay."

"I'm right here." He lets my breast go with a pop, then his lips trail up over my collarbone, along my neck. Then, his mouth is on mine. I open for him, his tongue sliding between my lips as his hips press forward. I feel the tip of his cock against my clit before he pulls back, then in one brutally beautiful thrust he fills me completely.

When he stills deep inside me and pulls his mouth from mine, my lashes flutter open. Staring into his gorgeous eyes as his search mine, I know I'm stuck, that I'm wrapped up so tight in his web I will never get free. This man who I've tried to avoid has consumed me completely and I don't stand a chance when it comes to him. Lifting my head to break our connection, to stop feeling so much, I kiss him and move my hands from his sides to his shoulders.

"Fuck me." I breathe against his mouth

"No." He captures my wrists in his hands and pulls them up over my head pressing his body down the length of mine leaving no space between us.

"Clay," I cry as he slowly thrusts inside me, keeping his eyes locked on mine. My nails dig into his hands that are holding me hostage and my heels move to the back of his thighs. My eyes slide closed, knowing it's all too much but his teeth nip my chin causing my eyes to fly open.

"Eyes on me when I'm inside of you."

"It's too much," I whimper, feeling vulnerable and completely overwhelmed.

"Never." He pulls back and thrusts forward harder than before.

I gasp. "Clay."

"Who do you belong to, Willow?"

I attempt to lift my hips off the bed, to try and gain even a little bit of control back.

"Say it."

"You say it," I bite back

He grins at me. "I'm not the one who needs to be reminded." He pulls out so slowly that I feel every single inch of him drag along my inner walls that cling to him. "Feels like your pussy knows it's mine already, Mouse." His lips brush across mine then they move to my ear. "You belong to me."

"For how long?" I ask without thinking and instantly wish I could take that question back, but it's too late. The question that I've been asking myself since the moment we met is now floating in the air between us and his muscles tightening lets me know he heard me.

"Until you realize that you're too good for me," he says quietly after a long moment.

My throat instantly gets tight. "Please, let me go," I whisper, and he hesitates a second, but soon he lets my wrist go. Once I'm free, I curl my hands around the back of his neck and pull his mouth down to mine and lift my head up off the bed. I kiss him hoping that he can feel what he's come to mean to me in such a short time, hoping that he knows that he's got just as much of me as I do of him. Because even if I'm still terrified of losing myself in him, I'm more afraid of losing him, of losing this.

As we kiss, he slides in and out of me his pace never faltering, each thrust sending me closer to the edge of euphoria. As my skin starts to tingle like lightning is dancing across it, and my core pulses around his length, I listen to the sound of his breathing pick up as his heart beats just as hard as mine against my chest. Clinging to him with every part of me, I fall over the edge, while the walls of my sex pulse around his length.

I hear him groan as he drops his forehead to mine then he thrusts deep one last time, stilling there as he comes inside me.

I don't know how long we stay like that but when he rolls, taking me with him, I know I'm already half asleep. "You gonna pass out on me, Mouse?"

"Yes." I don't even attempt to lie.

He laughs, the sound vibrating against my ear making me smile.

"As much as I'd normally be down with that, you need to eat and we need to get home; Skye is going to be upset if we don't show up," he says, placing his fingers under my chin and tipping my head back until we are eye-to-eye, then his gaze searches mine for a long moment. He doesn't say anything but that doesn't mean I don't feel the look he gives me all the way down to my toes before his mouth touches mine.

I PARK MY car outside of the restaurant where I'm meeting my dad for brunch then grab my bag off the passenger seat and pull out the papers I printed off a couple of days ago and haven't had a chance to look at until now.

As I start to look over her information, my cell ringing makes me jump and I quickly answer the call with a press of a button on my steering wheel. The sound of a baby crying, and a child yelling fills the interior of my car in an instant, and I turn down the speakers as I say. "Hello."

"Hi umm is this Willow?" a woman asks.

I glance down at the monitor in the middle of the car seeing a Florida number I don't recognize there.

"It is."

"This is Annie." She clears her throat. "Carly's best friend."

My eyes slide closed. I saw Miles just last night after he came to pick up Winter from our ice cream party and he didn't mention getting in touch with anyone, so he must have talked to her this morning, which means she just found out about her friend.

"I'm so sorry for your loss," I say quietly, knowing that is the worst thing to say. But what else is there?

"Me too." She sniffles. "I just spoke to her, she said she was going to come visit me and the boys for Christmas. Now I don't even know what to do."

"Did she have any family there?" I ask quietly.

"No, none that she talked to anyways."

I listen to her drag in a shaky breath.

"I—" She starts to sob, and I drop my forehead to the steering wheel as my heart breaks for her. "Th—The detective gave me the number to have her body rel—released. I—I don't have any money, I just—I can't afford to have her buried," she cries, and I shut my eyes.

"Don't worry about that, I'll take care of her," I promise softly.

"She di—She didn't want to be buried, she told me that once."

"I'll make sure she's cremated."

"I hate this, I hate that I can't come there and see her—that I can't help," she says as a tiny voice in the background asks why she's crying, and she tells him that her heart is hurt. Then the baby who had stopped crying starts again. "I have to go."

"Okay, sure," I whisper.

"Will you—Will you see if you can get me her chest? I—I know it's weird, but she had kept all of our concert tickets and stuff from when we were in school in there and I'd like to have all of it."

"I'll see what I can do, and Annie?"

"Yeah?"

"Call me anytime."

"Okay, bye." She hangs up and I lift my head from where it's still resting against the steering wheel then check the time. My dad should be here in about ten minutes but knowing him he'll be early because he always is. Lifting the papers off my lap I find Carly's personal e-mail along with some pieces of information that might be helpful to get into her accounts and type it all into the notes app on my phone. As I'm tucking the papers away, I hear the rumble of an engine and look out the driver's side window.

"Great." I mutter under my breath as my brother Bax parks his sixty-four mustang in the spot next to my car. When he looks my way, I lift my hand and wave and he jerks up his chin. It figures that my dad would call in reinforcements. Even though my brothers are all younger than me and Harmony they have always acted like Nalia, Harmony and I are their little sisters and that we need constant protection from the outside world. Opening the door, I get out and walk to where Bax is standing on the sidewalk in front of the restaurant.

"You didn't call me," he greets, giving me a quick hug.

I hold back the urge to roll my eyes.

"You're working, and there is nothing you can do."

"I might be working but you know you can always call," he says as I lift my purse higher on my shoulder. "Dad's flipping the fuck out."

"Should we go in and put our names down for a table?" I ignore his comment and start toward the door to the restaurant. "It's probably packed."

"He mentioned a guy you're seeing."

"And?"

"He doesn't like him."

"What guy have I dated does Dad like?" I step inside and like I assumed it would be, there is already a line from the podium to the door of people waiting to be seated.

"True," he mutters.

"It must be nice having a penis and having every single choice you make just accepted without even so much as the raise of a brow."

"You think Dad doesn't give me shit for the things I do?"

"When has Dad ever given a crap about who you date?"

"Never."

"Exactly. The power of the penis is a magical thing." I step up to the podium when it's our turn and then give the girl there our name, then walk back to stand next to the door to wait.

"Who is this guy? I mean Dad was worried about your friend, but he wouldn't stop talking about the guy you went home with."

"His name is Clay," I sigh, looking up at my little brother who is not so little anymore. "He's a good guy and if Dad gave him a chance, he'd probably like him."

"You've said that about every man you've gone out with."

"Yeah, because I have great taste."

"Obviously not, since none of them have stuck."

"Really? And how many of your female friends have had what it takes to stick around?" I raise a brow and dare him to lie. I know he's broken more hearts than he probably even knows. Heck, even when I was in school the girls in my class would talk about how cute he was. And now his cuteness has turned into heartbreaking handsomeness.

"Whatever," he grumbles.

I bite back a smile.

"Did you put in for a table?" At that question coming from behind me I turn and find my dad in all his badass glory.

"We did." I say as I step forward and give him a hug, then I watch as he and my brother share a chin lift. *Men.* "Is Mom and everyone on their way back?"

"They get in tonight late," he says, looking me over. "You okay?"

"I'm good." I let out a breath. "But I might need some help though," I say, and both my dad and brother instantly go on alert. "It's not for me, I talked to Carly's best friend from Florida, she's Carly's only contact, and she can't afford to have her cremated. I need to figure out how to go about getting that done."

"I'm sure I can make a few calls," Dad says softly and as I lean into him, he wraps his arm around my shoulders.

"Has Miles or Tucker told you anything?" I look up at him and he shakes his head in the negative but I don't honestly know that he'd tell me if they did.

"Mayson." The girl at the podium calls and I walk with my dad and brother to her, then we all follow her through the maze of tables in the center of the room to one that is clean near the window. After we're seated with me next to Bax and our dad across from us, I pick up the menu she left us with and begin to look it over.

"Now, let's talk about Clay," Dad says.

I slowly draw in a deep breath, I knew this was coming. I knew that he would want to talk about Clay, but I don't want to have this conversation. I have no desire to try and convince my father that he should give Clay a chance. Even if I told him how good Clay is to me, how he makes me feel important, validated, and safe, my dad would brush that all off as infatuation. He would point out all the times I've given those same qualities to other men I've been with in the past. The thing is none of those guys had all of the qualities I was looking for in a partner. They were all lacking in one way or another.

"No." I shake my head. "I don't want to talk about him."

"Willow."

"He means something to me." I shake my head again. "Actually, he means a lot to me and right now what he and I are or what we might be is just for us."

"I don't like him," he rumbles, and I feel my face soften.

"You don't know him."

"I know guys like him."

"Mom told me that falling in love with you was the scariest thing she ever did in her life." I lower my voice. "But she never regretted taking a chance on you."

"You're falling in love with him?" he asks.

I want to lie to him. I want to lie to myself, but the truth is I know that I'm quickly falling over the edge with Clay, and I don't think there is anything I can do to stop it from happening.

"Yes," I whisper and his jaw clenches. "I don't know how he feels about me, I don't know if he feels like I do, I don't know what will happen a week or a year from now, but I do know that in this moment I'm trusting him to catch me if I fall."

"Shit." Bax mumbles from my side.

But I don't take my eyes off our dad's.

"All right, kid," he says softly.

My throat gets tight. I might not have his approval, but I do have his acceptance and that is more than I expected to have from him.

"Thank you," I say softly, and he reaches across the table with his tattoo-covered hand, and I take it like I have since I was little and likely will until the day I have to say goodbye to him.

"Now, tell me what you know about your friend." He gives my fingers a squeeze and I let his hand go and sit back against the booth behind me.

Then for the next hour and a half, while we eat, I fill him and my brother in about Carly, Matthew and what has happened over the last week. And when I leave the restaurant and get back in my car, I feel more at ease then I have in days because like always, I know my father and my family will be in my corner no matter what happens.

SITTING ON THE couch in my living room with my computer on my lap, and my cell phone in my hand, I bite my bottom lip as I stare at the password box on Carly's email. Since I got home an hour ago, I've accumulated a dozen potential passwords for her account from the information on her resume and what I knew of her. But I have yet to try any of them. Like all websites now days, I know I only have a limited number of tries before I'm locked out for good, and I do not want to risk that happening.

Checking the time on the clock I see that I have about two hours before I need to leave to head to Clay's place. After telling him that I spoke with Annie, he wanted me to come right to him after brunch, but I told him when I was leaving the restaurant that I had stuff to do around my place, which wasn't a total lie. Besides trying to break into Carly's account, I need to catch up on laundry, run down to the mailboxes to see if there is anything there, then clean up since Leah will be home in a few days.

Holding my breath, I type in my first password option then click enter and almost instantly it kicks me back to the sign in page to try again. After the fourth try with no success I close my eyes. The chance of this working is almost impossible, and although I knew that it's even more apparent now. Looking at the screen, I pull up the dating app and my eyes land on the sign up now link. I haven't used this dating app, but I'm familiar with others just like it. Rubbing my lips together, I hit the sign-up button and start to fill in the information required. It doesn't take long at all for my account to be approved and once I'm on their site, I search for Carly's profile. Once I find it, I start to look through her photos and my throat gets tight when I come across one of her with two little boys and a woman who I bet is Annie. When I slide to the next picture, I smile at the photo she and I had taken at dinner one evening a couple months ago. Then I laugh when I slide to the next picture, I forgot that she, Becca, and Indigo had dressed up like bunnies one day for work before Easter.

After saving the pictures to my computer I try to see if there is a way to find out who she had been matched with but there isn't.

Exiting out of her profile I begin searching for Matthew, but not knowing his last name, it's going to take me a while to get through all the men with the same name. Not to mention he could go by a different name, so I might as well be searching for the lost ark. After thirty minutes with no luck, I hear the buzzer for the dryer go off. I set my stuff aside and head for the laundry room. As I'm folding up the last of my stuff from the dryer there is a knock on the door, so I leave everything as is and head across the apartment. I don't know who I expect to see when I look through the peephole but it's Clay.

"Hey," I swing the door in. "I thought that I was meeting you at your place."

"I decided to come to you instead." He wraps his hand around my hip and dips his head so that he can kiss me.

When he drags his mouth from mine a minute or seconds later my lashes flutter open and I meet his gaze. Yep, I'm totally falling in love and if he isn't too, this is going to be a disaster. "Um—" I clear my throat. "Why the change of plans?"

"I wanted to see you." He walks me backwards with his hands still around my waist then kicks the door shut. "I needed to see for myself that you were really okay after meeting with your dad and talking to Carly's friend."

"I'm all right." I melt against him smoothing my hands up his chest to his shoulders.

"You keep saying you're all right, Mouse, but you're dealing with a lot."

"It sucked hearing how upset Annie was, but I'm glad I got to talk to her." I drag in a breath. "I asked my dad to help me figure out how to get Carly cremated and Annie wanted a box from Carly's place, so I want to get that for her."

"I'm sure Miles can make that happen," he says softly.

I nod, knowing he's probably right.

"I just want whoever did this to her caught so that everyone can have some closure."

"I get that," he says as his phone starts to ring.

"You get *that.* I need to finish folding my clothes before they wrinkle." I lean up to kiss his jaw then step out of his grasps and head for the laundry room.

"It was Dayton," he says stopping in the doorway as I'm pulling out a shirt from the dryer.

"Dayton? Is everything okay?"

"He wants to go out tonight but doesn't want to do that solo."

"He's still here?" I ask because I haven't seen him since the other morning.

"He's been crashing at Miles's place."

"Well, I'm totally okay hanging at home tonight, so don't worry about me if you want to go out."

"He wants all of us to go out."

"All of us?" I look at him from where I'm bent over in front of the dryer.

"Me, you, Miles, and whoever Miles is currently dating."

"Miles is dating someone?"

"Miles is always dating someone."

"Hum," I murmur, and he grins.

"Are you up for going out?"

"Sure, where does he want to go?"

"The Rooftop, have you been there?"

"No, I've never even heard of it."

"It's more lounge than bar. We can go for a couple hours then sneak out after everyone has had a couple of drinks and forgotten about us," he says.

I laugh. "That works."

"Are you still catching up on stuff here?"

"Yeah, I need to put stuff in the dryer then I need to run down to check the mail and clean up a little. I should be another hour or so. When I'm done, I'll just pack my stuff and ride with you to your place, if that works."

"It would, but you should bring your car. Tomorrow morning I need to fly to Florida early."

"I thought you were leaving Monday," I whisper, feeling all sorts of disappointed.

His face goes soft. "Sorry, baby, I gotta meet with some people tomorrow afternoon, then I close on the building first thing Monday."

"Okay." What choice do I have?

"Do you want to go with me?"

"To Florida?"

"That's where I'm going."

I wish I could, but I know I can't, not with everything going on and everything I need to do. "I have to work. And I want to plan a small service for Carly to give her a proper goodbye. My mom is coming home tonight, so I'm hoping I can get her and my family to help me do that."

"I guess I'll have to try and survive without you for forty-eight hours then."

"You did it for years," I remind him, and he shakes his head as he steps up to me and wraps his hand around my hip.

"I didn't have you before, now I do." His lips touch my forehead causing my lashes to fall closed. "Finish up, baby, so we can get home."

"Okay." I watch him walk out of the laundry room knowing I'm not just tangled in his web, he's trapped me there, and I have no shot at getting free.

And really, I don't want to.

Willow ❦ Clay

Clay

Sixteen

$\mathscr{A}$FTER SLIPPING MY belt through the loops on my slacks I tuck in my shirt, finish doing the buckle, then grab my suit jacket off the end of the bed. I walk to the bathroom door and knock as I push it in.

"Mouse!" I shout over a song she has playing through her phone speaker, then curse my fucking brother for wanting us to go out tonight when I find Willow half bent over the counter wearing one of my t-shirts.

"Yeah?"

I pull my eyes off her ass and meet her gaze. Fuck, she's beautiful.

"Clay."

"I'm gonna be waiting in the kitchen," I tell her after a second.

She smiles. "Okay, I shouldn't be much longer, I just need to finish my makeup and get dressed."

"Don't rush." I step back and shut the door, knowing if I don't put some space between us, there is no way we're going anywhere but back to my bed. Because now that I've had her, I can't get enough. I'm addicted, not just to her pussy, but to everything that makes her who she is.

When I get to the kitchen, I grab my cell and look over the information Tammy sent me for my flight tomorrow morning. After I send her a message back letting her know I got it, I open an email from Tucker that contains the names of a few men and women along with some of their personal information.

"Ready," Willow calls.

I lift my eyes from my cell and my gut clenches as she walks into the kitchen holding a small, shiny bag in her hand.

Her hair is down in a mass of messy waves, the top of her dress loose on top and falling off one shoulder before skimming her waist and thighs tightly then ending mid calf, with a pair of high as fuck heels on her feet. The outfit is different than the one she was wearing the first time I met her, but that same feeling of want that I had then washes through me, only now it's tinged with possessiveness.

My jaw clenches and I toss my phone to the island, Tucker's email forgotten.

"Come here," I order when she starts putting stuff from her purse in a smaller bag.

"Just a second," she mutters absently, focused on what she's doing.

"Come here, Willow."

Her eyes come to me and as soon as she meets my gaze, she licks her lips, stops what she's doing and slowly walks toward me.

"Okay, I'm here," she says quietly when we're toe-to-toe.

I wrap my hand around the back of her neck then slide it up into her hair, tightening my grip. When she gasps, I cover her mouth and thrust my tongue between her lips, tasting her while my free hand smooth's over her ass then down the back of her thigh.

Gripping the material of her dress in my fist, I drag it up until it's around her waist. "Up," I growl, helping her off her feet. Once her ass is on the island, I unbuckle my belt and free my cock then slide my hand between her legs and run my fingers along the front of her panties over the lips of her sex. Her hips lift on the counter, chasing my touch, making my cock throb. Fitting myself between her legs I slide the lace covering her to the side, finding her glistening and line myself up. I had her this morning, then again before we left her place, and I know I'll have her again later tonight. Like I said I'm fucking addicted.

"Clay," she whimpers.

I slide the tip of my cock up and then down her sex.

Lifting my eyes to hers, seeing them dark with desire and need, I rumble, "Hold on to the counter, Mouse."

Her fingers wrap around the edge of the marble she's sitting on, and I slide into her with one harsh thrust. I don't go gentle. I fuck her hard and she takes every inch of me with her head thrown back and her eyes closed. When I start to circle her clit with my thumb, the walls of her pussy begin to pulse around my cock making me see stars. "Jesus, this pussy is going to kill me." I grab her ass with my free hand and drag her until her ass is hanging half off the counter and my cock is the only thing really keeping her up. Almost instantly she starts to come on my dick, the tight wet heat of her making my balls draw tight. After two more thrusts, I wrap my hands around her throat, tip her head back and kiss her as I come hard— so hard my knees get weak, and my vision turns black. As I come back to myself, I drag my mouth from hers and look into her pretty eyes.

For years, I did nothing but live and breathe the idea of taking down those who lead Arya to killing herself with drugs and alcohol, whether it was by putting them behind bars for the shit they had done to others or by taking away everything that they owned and loved. I thought of nothing but the satisfaction I'd feel when every last person who played a part in her demise was destroyed the same way they helped destroy her. Then this woman came along and became my new obsession. She has no idea the lengths I'll go through to keep her. And I know that when she finds out about the kind of man I am and the things I've done, I'll have to do more then pretend I'm walking away from her in order to make sure that she's mine for good.

"Are you okay?" she asks, sounding breathless.

I touch my lips to her forehead to break our connection. "Yeah, baby." I slowly slide out of her. "Are you?"

"Besides not being sure that I'll be able to walk, I'm okay." She laughs and I smile at her then grab some paper towels and clean myself up before I do the same to her. Once she's good, I lift her off the counter then help her adjust the skirt of her dress. "I'm just going to go check my makeup." She looks up at me, blushing and I touch her pink cheek with the tips of my fingers.

"All right." I bend down brushing my mouth across hers, then watch her take off toward the bedroom as I tuck my shirt back in. When she comes back out a few minutes later she still looks well-fucked, but her hair is back in place and now a dark stain that looks the color of red wine is covering her swollen mouth.

"Now I'm ready," she tells me, grabbing the gold bag she carried out earlier.

"You look gorgeous, baby."

"I kinda got that's what you thought when you put me on the counter." She smiles.

I chuckle as I follow behind her to the door.

When we get downstairs to my jeep, I hold the door open for her, then wait until she is buckled in before I walk around the back and get in behind the steering wheel. "Anytime you're ready to take off tonight, let me know and we'll leave."

"How about you let me know since it's obvious you don't want to go." She places her hand on my lap before I can reach for her like I normally do, because I like having her connected to me even when we're sitting right next to each other.

"I never said I didn't want to go."

"You didn't have to say it." I can almost hear her rolling her eyes. "You've asked me a dozen times today if I'm sure I'm up to going out."

"I know that you wanted to rest this weekend?" I squeeze her hand and before she can reply her phone starts to ring and she takes it out of her bag.

"It's my sister." She puts her cell to her ear. "Hello." A second later she starts to laugh. "You know how Dad is."

I can feel her looking at me, and I glance her way, finding her eyes soft as her gaze dances over my skin.

"I'll ask him, maybe we can all have dinner next weekend." A pause. "Nothing like any of them."

This makes me curious about what her sister is asking.

"I know… Um we're going to the Rooftop, it's a lounge close to downtown… Really? Okay hold on a second." She squeezes my thigh. "Harmony wants to know if she and her husband can come tonight."

"Sure."

She relays that to her sister, then a second later she says goodbye and hangs up.

"She's going to talk to Harlen and send me a text if they're coming." She pulls down her visor and looks in the mirror as she nervously rambles. "I promise my sister is much more chill than my dad and her husband is awesome. You'll like him. Miles actually reminds me a little of him."

"Relax, babe, it will be all good."

"I know, I just want you to know they're cool." She sighs, leaning back in her seat and flipping the mirror back into place.

"Have they ever met any of the guys you've dated?"

"My whole family met Brodie. My dad hated him, but everyone else loved him."

Fuck, if my hands don't get tighter on the steering wheel hearing his name. "What happened between you two?"

"His job." She gets quiet a second then adds. "I don't know if you recognized him, but he plays hockey in Nashville." I listen to her drag in a breath. "He traveled all the time, which was understandable, but I hated that even when he was home, he was out with his teammates more than he was with me. Then there were the women."

"Women?"

"Yeah, there were constantly women throwing themselves at him and again I understood that would be one of the things I'd have to deal with when we got together. I mean, I'm not stupid—he's a good-looking guy with money who's famous, so that was inevitable. What I didn't appreciate was how he played into their attention by flirting back or feeding into it. And when I told him how I felt, he ignored my feelings, and made it seem like I was just acting like a jealous girlfriend. And yeah, I was jealous, but it was more than that. I never felt secure with him, and I didn't feel like a priority, so without those two things, I knew that I couldn't be with him." She let out a breath. "So that's why things between us ended."

"A lot of women would have put up with that bullshit, baby, and just pretended everything was okay. Says a lot that you chose your own happiness."

"No, a lot of women will put up with stuff like that for a time but eventually it will eat away at them. And then they'll either get out, or become so resentful that the man can't deal, so he cuts ties."

"You're right about that, Mouse." I pull into a parking garage close to the lounge.

After I find a spot to park, I get out and then help her into the coat she brought with her before taking her hand. When we make it across the street I lead her inside, then scan the open, dimly lit room. The space is filled with small tables, couches, and chairs that are all set up in a way that each is an intimate place to gather with friends or a date.

"There's Dayton." Willow points, tugging on my hand and I find him sitting with a cute brunette that I don't recognize. "Come on." She starts to walk in their direction, dragging me with her.

I watch my brother stand and smile, as we get closer.

"I wasn't sure you two were coming." Dayton greets Willow by kissing her on the cheek, before reaching out to touch his fist to mine.

"Where's Miles?" I ask, while Willow takes off her coat, laying it over the back of the couch.

"Said he was picking up his date." He motions to the woman now standing awkwardly at his side. "This is a friend of mine, Grace." His hand flicks out to me, then Willow. "My brother Clay and his girlfriend Willow."

"Nice to meet you." Grace smiles pushing her black framed glasses up the bridge of her nose.

"I love your dress," Willow tells her, and pink spreads up her cheeks.

"Thanks, I love yours, too." She nervously smooths her hands down her sides, then looks up at Dayton. "I'm going to get a drink. Do you want anything?"

"I'm good, babe," he mutters, lifting the beer in his hand and she nods then looks at Willow and me. "Do either of you want something?"

"I'll come with you," Willow tells her, and then she tilts her head back to meet my gaze. "What are you drinking?"

"Brandy on the rocks." I take out my wallet but before I can pull out some cash, she's taking Grace's arm and the two of them are walking away.

"So, she's a friend?" I raise a brow at my brother once both women are out of earshot, and he shrugs.

"Yep, she used to work as an assistant to the DA in Denver but recently moved out here." He looks toward the bar. "I tried for years to get in there but she's so fucking shy that it's almost painful." He shakes his head then looks past me and I turn to see Miles and Ivy walking our way. I told Willow that Miles is always dating someone, but Ivy has been a pretty steady fixture for the last few months. She just hasn't passed whatever test Miles has mentally set up in order for her to meet Winter. Then again, more than once I've caught glimpses of her true personality and if I haven't missed it, I doubt Miles hasn't either.

"What's up?" Miles grins, giving me a one-armed hug while Dayton greets Ivy. "Where's Willow?"

"At the bar."

"You let her out of your sight?" He raises a brow.

"She's where I can see her."

He laughs as he touches his fist to Dayton's.

"Do you want a drink, babe?" he asks Ivy.

She scrunches her nose. "Yes, but just a Vodka and soda, I promised myself that I wouldn't go overboard with calories this weekend."

"Right." He shakes his head. "Be right back."

As Ivy takes a seat on the couch and pulls out her phone, I look to the bar and watch Miles walk up to Willow and touch his hand to her back. When she spins to face him, a smile curves her full lips and she gives him a hug, then motions to Grace, who looks about ready to pass out when he turns his attention to her.

"Tucker's here."

At that statement from Dayton, I feel my jaw get tight. "You didn't tell me he was coming."

"He's our brother," he says under his breath, right before he grins and says loudly, "Look who made it."

As he greets Tucker with a fist bump, and Naomie with a wave, I glance back toward the bar and see Willow, Grace, and Miles coming our way. As soon as Willow sees Tucker, her eyes fly to mine, and they do a scan of my face.

Jesus, I'm done for.

"We good?" Tucker asks, stepping up to my side and I pull my attention off of Willow to focus on him.

"You tell me."

"I overstepped."

"You did," I agree, and he lifts his chin.

"Are you not even going to say hi to me?" Naomie asks, fitting herself under Tucker's arm and he stiffens at the contact.

"Naomie," I rumble.

She smiles then looks up at Tucker. "I need a drink."

"You know where the bar is." He steps away from her, and her expression gets tight.

If I didn't know the kind of woman she is I'd feel bad for her, but I do know and I wish my brother would see that he'll never find happiness as long as her nails are clawing away at him.

"Brandy for you." Willow glides up to me placing the short glass filled with dark liquid in my hand before fitting herself to my side and turning toward Naomie holding out her hand. "Sorry to intrude. I'm Willow."

"I've heard about you," Naomie says, taking her hand. "I'm Tucker's wife Naomie."

"Clay's mentioned you."

"Has he." Naomie's eyes glitter and she looks up at me.

"He told me that you two had gone on a couple of dates. It must have been super awkward when you realized that you were dating his brother." She laughs.

I press my lips together to keep from smiling. Leave it to her to get the bullshit out in the open before Naomie can even think about sideswiping her with it.

"Very." Naomie smiles tightly, then looks around. "I'm going to go get a drink."

"The blueberry martini is amazing." Willow calls to her back as she starts toward the bar.

Naomie lifts her hand without so much as a backwards glance.

"You're evil." I turn Willow toward me, capturing her waist in one hand.

"Why would you say something like that?" she gasps as she places her palm against her chest.

"You know why." I dip my head and brush my mouth across her smiling lips.

When I pull back her smile slides away and her gaze searches mine. "Are you okay?"

"Don't worry about me."

"Why, because you're a big badass who can take care of himself?"

"Yes."

"Whatever." She rolls her eyes.

"Is your sister and her husband coming tonight?"

"She hasn't messaged, so probably not. She and Harlen might not have been able to get a babysitter for Ava on such short notice." She takes a sip of her drink then looks toward the couch and whispers. "Grace seems really sweet. Are she and Dayton dating?"

"Just friends." She nods, not seeming at all surprised by that news.

"I'm going to keep her company for a bit if you're good being here alone in your badassness."

"I'm good." I tap her bottom and she steps out of my hold. As she takes a seat on the couch between Grace and Ivy, Tucker comes to stand next to me.

"You really care about her."

"I do." I don't even bother looking at him as I watch her say something that makes Grace toss her head back and laugh, the sound grabbing both Miles and Dayton's attention.

"Naomie wasn't supposed to come tonight." At that I turn my head to look at my brother and find his eyes across the room with his jaw hard, and when I glance to where he's staring. I see Naomie leaning over the bar with her ass in the air as she talks to the bartender. "She's having an affair. She thinks I don't know about it, but I do."

"Jesus, Tuck."

"I'm meeting with a lawyer Monday." His eyes meet mine. "She quit her job when she found out she was pregnant, and I've been supporting her since then. I need to make sure that I'm not going to have to pay her alimony."

"You told him?" Miles asks, joining us and Tucker jerks up his chin.

"Do you have proof she's cheating?" I ask.

"Guy's a cop at the station. She met him at a dinner we went to a while back. His wife called to let me know that her husband was sleeping with my wife."

"Does the husband know that you know about the affair?"

"No, his wife hasn't confronted him yet. She's trying to get a job and to tuck away some cash before she contacts a divorce lawyer." His hands ball into fists. "They have a son who's just three, so she's been a stay-at-home mom for the last few years."

"Dick," Miles mutters.

"Yeah." Tucker takes a swig from his beer. "I can barely stomach to be around her, I don't even want to think about what it would be like if we had a kid."

"You'd figure it out." I tell him.

He clenches his jaw. "I should have fucking listened to you," He scrubs his fingers through his hair. "I should have—"

"Don't think about that, right now you need to sort this shit out and deal with whatever comes."

"I'm gonna need a place to stay after I do hand her over the divorce papers."

"I always have a spare room." Miles puts in then adds. "And Dayton's place is almost done, I'm sure you could crash there for a while until you figure out what you want to do."

"Are you staying in Tennessee?" I ask because he never wanted to move here but with the case he's working he didn't have a choice.

"For now." He mutters.

"She's on her way back," Miles says

I lift my chin then watch her come up to Tucker and wrap her arm around his waist.

"It took forever to get my drink," she says, then asks while looking at the couch. "Who's the chubby girl?"

"Don't start your shit, Naomie," Miles bites out.

She holds up her hand. "It's just a question. I've never seen her before," she says softly like she actually feels bad, but I know that's a fucking lie.

"Oh my god, you came!" Willow shouts and when I twist around, I find her running across the room toward a woman who looks similar to her but not exactly identical.

"Who's that?" Dayton asks, watching the two of them embrace while a man stands back shaking his head at the two women.

"Willow's sister Harmony and her husband," I tell them as she gives Harlen a hug before letting him go, then hooking her arm through her sister's who she drags our way.

"My sister came." She beams at me looking so fucking beautiful in her happiness.

"I see that, Mouse," I tell her, holding out my hand.

"Clay."

"Mouse?" Harmony raises a brow at her sister as she takes my hand.

"Long story," Willow mumbles.

"I can't wait to hear about that." Harmony looks at me and motions with her thumb to the guy next to her. "This is my husband, Harlen."

"What up, man?" I reach to shake his hand then introduce him to my brothers as Willow takes her sister to the couch to introduce her to Grace and Ivy who hasn't moved from her spot.

"Do you wanna drink?" I ask Harlen.

He glances at his wife then lets out a breath. "I got a feeling I'm gonna need one."

"That bad?" I raise a brow.

"When any of the Mayson girls get together you never know what's gonna go down." He looks back at his wife who is now sipping from Willow's drink. "The only reprieve I had is when Harmony was pregnant with Ava." He focuses back on me.

"Advice?" I lift my chin.

"You get in that deep my man, knock her up then keep doing it."

My stomach muscles clench as an image of Willow pregnant with my baby flashes through my mind. A serious relationship isn't something I ever considered before her, and idea of a family of my own was never even on my radar. In such a short fucking time, everything I thought would bring me solace has changed. And now one tiny woman has complete control over my future and my sanity.

Jesus, I knew I was fucked but that's now more apparent then ever. Because I want that with her, all of it, and I know until I have it, I won't be completely satisfied.

*W*ITH BOXES OF half-eaten Chinese food containers on the counter I sit on a stool at the bar in my kitchen with Leah on the one next to mine, and Skye lying on the floor at our feet. For the last four or more hours we've been scrolling through the dating app website hoping that we'll eventually come across Matthew.

Unlike me, Leah clearly remembers what he looked like and this afternoon as soon as she got off the plane from Florida, I took her to the police station where she was able to give Johnny a full description of him. And when Johnny finished talking with Leah and showed me the sketch, I knew it was Matthew. Where my memory of him had been blurry and unfocused, Leah's brought him to life. And seeing him again made me even more determined to find the guy who had been dating Carly and who has not made another appearance since her disappearance.

"What time is Clay getting in?" Leah asks.

I drag my eyes off my computer and look at the clock on the microwave seeing it's a little after seven. "Eight. He said he'd call when his plane landed." I raise my arms up over my head as I yawn.

Even with yesterday and today off, I'm exhausted. Sunday after Clay woke me up to kiss me goodbye and do other things to make sure I wouldn't soon forget about him—*not that I could if I tried*—I couldn't go back to sleep. So instead of lying in bed, tossing and turning, I got up and showered, then packed Skye in my car and went to my parent's house. We spent the day with my mom and dad coming up with a plan for the week ahead, which I more than appreciated. Then today I called out of work and spent the morning on the phone getting Carly's body released and set for cremation and things in place so that Saturday we can have a simple memorial for her. And by the time I was done with all the items on my to do list, it was time to pick up Leah, then she and I spent the afternoon at the police station.

"Are you sleeping over at his place?"

"Are you okay with that?" I ask instead of answering her question.

She rolls her eyes as she slides off her stool. "Of course. Plus, I have to be up early to get to the hospital."

"Could you take an extra day off?"

"No, two weeks is even more than the hospital wanted to give me." She goes to the fridge and pulls out a jug of water, then grabs a glass from the cupboard. Seeing the exhaustion in her features I shut my computer.

"You should go to bed." I slide off my stool and Skye, who's been stuck to my side like glue since Clay left, gets up and does a doggy stretch.

"I will. I'm gonna shower, then watch some TV until I pass out."

"What's your schedule this week?"

"Hectic." She sighs. "Dr. Nice Bottom is taking a few days off to go golfing, so I'll be covering his workload."

I smile, Dr. Nice Bottom's name is not actually that but when Leah first started working at the hospital, he came in every day wearing bicycle shorts and so that's the nickname he was gifted.

"When is your next day off?"

"Next Monday."

"Ewww." My nose scrunches.

"I couldn't agree more." She starts to help me as I close up the containers from our dinner. "Will you be home at all this week, or have you traded me in for unlimited orgasms?"

"I love you, but orgasms are pretty amazing."

"I bet they are." She laughs.

"Honestly, I'm not sure what this week will look like, but I'll definitely see you at the memorial Saturday."

"Yes, you will." She tips her head to the side and asks, "Is Annie coming for that?"

"No, but she's going to do something similar with her sons and her husband." I say quietly and she nods. "Hopefully with your sketch, Tucker and Miles will be able to find Matthew and get some answers."

"I hope so." She walks to where I am and wraps her arms around me. "I love you."

"Where is this coming from?" I hug her back.

"I just want you to know, you're a great friend—the best kind of friend."

My throat gets tight, and I squeeze my eyes closed to keep from crying. The truth is I wish I had been a better friend to Carly, that I had spent more time with her that I had gotten to know her better. But I can't change that now. "You're going to make me cry."

"No crying." She leans back to meet my eyes. "I just hope you know that you're amazing."

"Thanks," I whisper, letting her go so that I can press the sleeves of my shirt into my eyes and cut off the tears.

"Now, I need to shower, and you need to go get an orgasm, and while you're at it get one for me too."

"I don't think that's how it works." I give her a watery smile.

"Sucks that it doesn't." She steps out of the kitchen and stops to bend over and give Skye a rub down before looking at me. "While I'm in bed I'll keep scrolling the site, eventually we'll come across him."

"I hope so," I say, and she rubs her lips together before standing to her full height.

"I'll see you Saturday, but if you need me, call."

"I will. Love you."

"Love you, too," she calls over her shoulder, then a second later I hear her door close.

Going to my room I pack a bag with my shower stuff, something to sleep in and clothes for work tomorrow, then head out of my bedroom and grab Sky's leash off the door handle. Once I have her hooked up, I make sure that everything is shut down, and since I can hear the shower on in Leah's bathroom, I lock up and head out with my bag over my shoulder. When I get downstairs to the lobby, I push the door open and lead Skye over to the small grassy area that's designated for dogs.

As I watch her sniff around, my cell starts to ring, causing a flutter to fill the pit of my stomach when I take it out of my pocket and see Clay's name on the screen. He's called me a lot over the last few days, way more than I expected him to, and I appreciated him putting in the effort to keep in touch. Even if we were only to talk for a couple of minutes, those couple of minutes reassured me that he was missing me as much as I was missing him.

"Hey," I answer and can hear a shuffling sound in the background.

"Hey baby, getting off the plane now. Are you at home?"

"Not yet, I'm waiting for Skye to potty then we will be on our way."

"All right. I need to pick up my car from valet, so you'll probably still beat me. Did you eat?"

"Did you?"

"I had dinner at the airport, but I want to make sure you ate something."

"I ate." I bite back a smile then scream when Skye barks and I'm practically knocked over as a weight crashes into me from behind, knocking my phone out of my hand and almost sending me to my knees.

"Fuck, Jeb no, down." I hear Brodie command but that does nothing to stop Jeb from jumping up to greet me as I hear Clay roaring from my phone that is now on the grass.

"Calm, buddy," I tell Jeb, grabbing his collar to try to control him as I pick up my phone. Once I have it in hand, I quickly put it to my ear. "I'm okay," I tell Clay. I swear I hear him running. "It's just Jeb and Brodie."

"Fuck!" he shouts. "Do not fucking ever scare me like that again."

"I didn't do it on purpose," I remind him softly.

"I don't give a fuck," he growls, causing my temper to flare.

"Don't fucking curse at me," I hiss. "I'll see you at home." I hang up, cutting off whatever he's about to say.

My phone starts to ring again so I put it on silent.

With a deep breath that does nothing to ease my annoyance, I tuck my phone away in my pocket, then lean down to give Jeb, who I've still got a hold of, a hug. "You scared me." I grab his face and he barks, which makes Skye get up and come over to join us. After giving each of them some attention, I look over at Brodie.

"Hey."

His eyes wander over me. "Haven't seen you around much."

"I've been busy." I tuck my hands into my pockets. "How have you been?"

"Good, busy. I'm transferring teams in a couple months so that's taking up a lot of time."

"You are?"

"Yeah, I got an offer to play for Florida."

"Really?" I can't help but to smile at the news because he told me more than once that that was his dream team. "I'm happy for you."

"Thanks." He shifts on his feet, and then looks around. "I know our last conversation didn't go well."

"That's a little bit of an understatement."

He smiles. "I'm sorry about that. I shouldn't have laid all that on you, and you were right, trying to make you jealous to get you back was a really, really stupid idea."

"You know better for next time." I shrug.

He lets out a breath as his eyes lock on mine.

"Can we go back to being friends?"

"No." I blurt then cringe. "Sorry, it's just, I've made a promise to myself that I'll no longer be friends with my exes."

"You do have a lot of those." He smirks.

"You're not one to talk." I laugh.

"True." He tucks his hands into the front pocket of his hoodie. "Are we at least cool?"

"Yeah, we're cool," I say softly, and he nods then looks at Jeb and gently tugs on his leash.

"Come on dude, let's get inside," he orders.

Jeb hesitates to leave where he's sitting next to me for a second, before he gets up and follows his dad.

I watch the two of them until they are out of sight then look down at Skye.

"Well, are you ready to get home?" I ask her and she lets out a huff.

"Let's go see your dad," I say, hoping that Clay has had a chance to calm down by the time we get to him.

After I toss my bag in the trunk, I get Skye into the front passenger seat since I learned Sunday that she is not a fan of riding in the back if the front seat is empty. Once I get situated behind the wheel I head for Clay's building, and as I pull onto his street I search for his jeep, but its nowhere in sight. I do see Tucker's SUV so he must be here visiting Miles.

Deciding to just wait for Clay in my car, I turn off the engine and grab my phone. Ignoring the slew of missed calls on the screen, I pull the dating app up, figuring I can use the time to look little more. As I'm sitting in the dark with my phone in hand, I see the reflection of headlights coming up behind me in my side mirror and with how low they are to the ground I can tell it's not Clay's Jeep. Before long the car pulls in behind me and parks and that's when I see that the driver is Naomie.

Being around her Saturday confirmed what I already knew, which is that I don't like her, not even a little.

I know you shouldn't judge people by their past actions, but within a few minutes of being in the same room with her, and witnessing the way she flirted with every man she came in contact with, I could see exactly the kind of woman she is. That is the kind of woman who uses her beauty to get attention from men, no matter who those men are or whom they might belong too. In her head, I'm sure that if a guy is willing to break whatever vow or code he has with his wife, brother, or friend, who is she to stop them from flirting or doing more?

My lip curls even thinking about that.

How she's married to Tucker is not something that I get, not with how much of a rule follower he seems to be. I imagine him with someone more like Grace, who is not only pretty but is also sweet and shy in that cute way that makes her more endearing.

Coming out of my thoughts when a door slams, I look in the rearview mirror and watch Naomie adjust the dress she is wearing before she heads into the building. When she's inside I go back to my app and less than a minute later I see the reflection of another set of lights and know in an instant that they belong to Clay's Jeep. When he parks behind Naomie's car I tuck my phone away in my purse then grab Skye's leash and push open my door.

"You hung up on me then ignored my calls," he says in the way of a greeting, as he slams his door closed.

I cross my arms over my chest and fight to keep myself where I am. Letting Skye go so that she can run to him the way I want to, I watch him bend to pet her while his eyes stay locked on mine. I've missed him, everything about him, even though he's only been gone a couple of days.

"You were mad at me for something I had no control over, and you cursed at me."

"You scared me," he bites out then growls. "Why the fuck are you standing all the way over there."

"Because I'm annoyed with you for being a jerk." I toss my arms in the air.

"I don't give a fuck if you're annoyed with me, come here."

"No, and stop cursing at me."

"Mouse."

"Clay." I watch his jaw clench, then he starts walking my way. As he gets closer, I brace while Skye starts to dance between the two of us.

"You're lucky I missed you so fucking much." He wraps one hand around my hip, then uses the other to grab me behind the neck so he can haul me against him. As I soak in his scent and warmth my entire being sighs in happiness.

"I missed you too, you big jerk." I curl my arms around his waist and press my ear to his chest over his heart.

"You scared me, Mouse. I can't stand the idea of something happening to you."

"I know, but nothing is going to happen to me." I listen to him take a deep breath before he places his fingers under my chin and uses them to tip my head back.

"What did Brodie say?"

"He's being transferred to Florida in a couple of months," I say, leaving out the rest because I never told him about what happened between Brodie and me the last time I saw him. And really none of what went down between us matters now.

"That's it?"

"Yeah." I shrug and his eyes search mine for a moment before he touches his lips to my forehead then my mouth.

"Let's get inside." He looks at me then my car. "Do you have a bag?"

"It's in the trunk." I use my key to pop it open then watch him grab my duffle before he takes my hand and leads me to the back of his jeep to get his suitcase.

When we get inside a couple minutes later, I use the keycard he gave me to let us onto the elevator, and as soon as the doors open, I'm assaulted by the overwhelming scent of perfume.

"Naomie's here," he grumbles, while the expression on his face says clearly that he smells something unpleasant.

"She showed up a few minutes before you did."

"What did she want?"

"I didn't talk to her, but Tucker's SUV is here so she's probably with him." I lean into his side as the doors shut and his arm wraps around me.

"I need to change the code for the elevator."

"Why?" I tip my head back to meet his gaze.

"I'll explain later." He bends to kiss me, then lets me go to grab the bags when the doors open. As soon as we step off the elevator, Skye begins to bark, and I see why a second later when I spot the door to Clay's place open an inch with low light coming from inside.

"Stay here," he orders, and I roll my eyes at his back as I follow him and Skye through the door.

"What the fuck are you doing here and how did you get in?" Clay barks and I peek around him to see Naomie parched on a stool in the kitchen holding a glass of wine with the bottle in front of her and a short glass filled with dark liquid on the counter.

"I came to talk to you about Willow," she says.

My spine stiffens. "You came to talk to him about me?" I step around Clay and her eyes widen ever so slightly because she obviously had no idea I was here.

"Yes." She looks apologetically at Clay then lowers her lashes. "I didn't want to be the one to tell you this, but I overheard Tucker and Miles talking about how she's on a dating app, but they didn't want to tell you."

I snort, I can't help it, the sound just slips out, but Clay obviously doesn't think this is as hilarious as I do, and I know that when the air in the room seems to thicken and he slowly turns his head my direction.

"What are you doing on a dating site, Mouse?"

"Obviously she's looking for men," Naomie ever so helpfully chimes in from where she's still sitting.

"I'm not looking for men." I roll my eyes. "I'm looking for Matthew."

"Have you lost your fucking mind?" he shouts.

My hands ball into fists. "No, but maybe you have," I shout back, going from annoyed to pissed in just seconds.

"What are you going to do if you find him? Are you going to ask him to meet you for coffee and have a chat about the weather?"

"Don't be a dick, or absurd. Obviously, I'm going to give his information over to Miles and Tucker. I'm not an idiot."

"Are you sure about that?" he asks.

I take a step back from him. "You know what, screw you." Since I still have my purse on my shoulder and my car keys are in it, I spin around and start to stomp toward the door.

"Where the fuck do you think you're going?"

"Home. You've obviously lost your mind and I have zero desire to help you sort yourself out."

"You're not leaving, Willow."

"Try to stop m—" I gasp when arms wrap around my waist, and I'm lifted off my feet. "Put me down."

"Oh my." I hear Naomie whisper as Clay carries me across the living room and I kick my feet.

"Naomie, get the fuck out of my house," Clay orders, as he takes my purse and tosses it toward the couch.

"No, stay," I cry, trying to break the hold he has on me but it's no use he's to flipping strong.

"Leave now," he growls.

"Put me—" I start to yell for him to put me down again but instead I yelp when I'm tossed unceremoniously into the air and land on the bed with a bounce. Scrambling to my knees, I push my hair out of my face, then watch in confusion as he storms back toward the door. Breathing heavy with my heart going a million miles a minute I scurry to my feet and start to rush after him but before I even make it halfway across the concrete floors, he slams the door.

"I'll be back," he growls from the other side of the door just as I reach it and I grab the handle, finding resistance when I attempt to turn it.

"No way." I tug the knob and smack my fists against the wood. "Let me out of here right now, Clay."

"Do not fucking hurt yourself by pounding on the door," he barks, and I glare at the door and pound harder than I was. When my palms start to sting, I stop and spin around. Chest heaving, I go to the windows and look out, from this far up I'd hurt myself if I tried to jump, not to mention there is no way to even open the windows, so I'd have to break one of them to get out.

So angry that I swear I can feel my blood boiling through my veins, I toss my head back and scream as loud as I can, then fall to my bottom and start to cry. The tears are absolutely stupid, and I hate that being angry makes me sob like a baby, but with no other way to release my emotions, here we are.

I don't know how long I sit on the cold ground for but eventually my tears dry up and a headache kicks in. Going to the door I try it again, but it's still locked. Giving up on getting free, I go to the bathroom and find some Tylenol in the cupboard, taking two out then I capture some water in the palm of my hand and wash them down while looking in the mirror.

I look like crap. My eyes are bloodshot, my face is so red that I look almost sunburnt and even my hair is in disarray. After splashing some cool water on my face, I go to the bed and lay down. I don't plan on sleeping because as soon as Clay gets back, I'm going to kick him in the nuts and leave whether he likes it or not. Or at least that's my plan but before long my eyes get to heavy to keep open.

Clay

Eighteen

$\mathscr{S}$TANDING ON ONE side of the island in Mile's apartment, I look between my brothers then scrub my hands down my face. When I got down here forty-five minutes ago, I was ready to kill both of them. Brothers or not there is no way they should have sat back, knowing Willow was on the same dating app Carly was using before her death.

Then they filled me in on what's been going down since I left town. With help from a source within the FBI they were able to push through a warrant for the dating app this afternoon. A warrant which gave them access to retrieve the information about who Carly was talking to and allowed them to monitor everyone who might have visited her profile while she was using the app and those who have clicked on it since her body was found.

After receiving the warrant, their first order of business was to find Matthew, which they did within just a couple hours. And what they found is that he had not been active on the site since Carly's disappearance. And after some digging, they got in contact with his job and a family member who both brought up the fact that he has been missing since around the time Carly quit her job, and that a missing person's report was filed. Only since he actually lived and worked in Kentucky, not in Nashville, no one even had him on their radar here in the city.

So, with two missing people, Tucker started digging deeper into

Carly's account this evening hoping to find some kind of lead. That's when he noticed a ping on her profile from someone who recently signed up for the app. And when he dug into who it was, he found that the new person was Willow, and of course the woman used her real name along with her photo, so they were easily able to verify it was her. And since he was at home with Naomie when he called to inform Miles of the situation she overheard and was all too happy to share that news with me this evening.

"Like I said earlier, unlike what my wife said," Tucker spits out the word wife like it taste bad, "we never said we weren't going to tell you about her being on the app. We were waiting to do it face-to-face so we could reassure you that you have nothing to worry about."

"What she's doing is harmless," Miles adds, then lifts his hands in front of him when my eyes narrow. "I get why you're pissed, but she's only been looking through the photos of men named Matthew on the site. She hasn't made contact with any of them." His tone softens. "She wanted to help, and if by chance she had come across Matthew's photo twenty-four hours ago she would have been."

In my gut, I know he's right, just like I know Willow was telling the truth, that if she did come across Matthew, she would have given that information over to Tucker and Miles and probably her dad. Still, the idea of her being in danger of any kind is something I can't even stomach. Tonight, when we were on the phone and she screamed, I thought my world was coming to an end. I swear I actually saw the life I could have had slip right through my fingers.

"Just talk to her," Tucker says.

My jaw clenches.

"She'll understand why you were pissed," Miles assures.

I almost laugh. Before I locked her in my room, she might have been willing to hear me out. Now I'll be lucky if she hasn't created some kind of weapon to kill me with as soon as I open the door.

"Do you want us to come with you? We can explain what we know about Matthew and assure her that we are looking for him.

"No, stay here. I'd rather not spend the rest of the night in jail."

"Why would you be going to jail?" Tucker asks, going on alert.

"She tried to leave me."

"And?" Miles asks, staring me down.

"I locked her in my room."

"Jesus, Clay," Tucker bites out.

I shrug. "It seemed like the best place to keep her safe while I dealt with the two of you."

"You've lost your mind." Miles shakes his head, then his expression becomes serious. "She's changed you."

"She has." I don't bother trying to deny it.

"Are you done helping us?" Tucker asks.

I drag in a breath, and I look between my brothers before I answer honestly.

"I don't know that I'll ever stop searching for the person who led Arya down the path she took, but the desire to hold others just like them accountable no longer consumes me."

"Good." Miles says and my head jerks back. "I'm happy for you, happy that you found something more important to focus on."

I look at Tucker.

"I'd never ask you to put your past in front of your future."

"Shit Dayton would be so fucking proud of us right now." Miles mutters and I bite back a smile while Tucker chuckles.

"I better get back upstairs."

"Maybe we should go up with you to make sure Willow doesn't kill you." Tucker says and I shake my head.

"I should be okay."

"You better hope she doesn't tell Nico about this," Miles sighs.

"You two can handle him for me." I call over my shoulder as head for the door.

When I arrive upstairs a few minutes later, silence greets me as soon as I get inside. Going to the kitchen I toss the glasses Naomie had out into the dishwasher then dump out what is left from the wine bottle. After shutting off all the lights, I go to the bedroom door and listen for a minute before I unlock and slowly open it. The overhead light is on so I can clearly see Willow laying on the side of the bed that she's claimed as hers and know in an instant that she is asleep. I can also see that she had been crying, which makes my insides twist painfully.

Shutting off the light, I walk to the bed and strip out of my clothes before I lay down and toss the blanket over the two of us. With my temper settled but my mind still reeling from what I learned this evening and what I know I'm going to face the second Willow wakes up, I put my hands behind my head and focus on the sound of her steady breathing. The reminder that she's okay, that she's here with me.

What I don't do is sleep.

I'm not sure what time it is when I know she's woken up, but the second she moves to get out of bed, I grab her by the wrist.

"Let me go!" she screams, trying to tug free.

"Calm down. We need to talk."

"Screw you." She kicks and tries to pull away. Not wanting her to hurt herself, I quickly roll onto her, placing my weight against her body and lifting her arms above her head.

"Listen to me, Mouse."

"Never!" she hisses, writhing under me, trying to get free.

"I fucked up."

"Yeah, I know!" she yells in my face before she tries to headbutt me.

"Jesus, Willow, calm the fuck down."

"No, let me go," she pants, and I do the only thing I can think of. I kiss her and in an instant her body under mine stills and she kisses me back. Then in the next second she stiffens and bites my lip so hard I taste blood.

"Fuck."

"Get. Off. Me."

"Not until you listen to me."

"Fine," she whimpers, as tears fill her eyes. "What? What do you want to tell me, since I don't have a choice but to listen to you?"

"Please, don't cry."

"Do you think I want to cry?" Her chin wobbles. "I don't. I hate that I'm so weak that I can't get away from you even when I want to."

Closing my eyes, I drop my forehead to hers. "Okay," I whisper. "I'll let you go, but you have to promise to hear me out before you leave me."

"Fine," she whispers back, and after a second of hesitation, I release my hold on her wrist then sit up on my knees.

As she scrambles away from me and off the bed, I watch with my muscles on fire ready to chase her down if need be.

"Talk!"

My heart starts to pound as I look into her eyes, because I know after I admit my truths, I might not ever see her again.

"My parents were both druggies, the two of them were in and out of jail so often, I don't have many memories with them before I went into the system at nine. After I was taken from their custody, I bounced around from house to house, because no one wanted an older kid and especially not one with issues." She holds my gaze. "I moved in with the Patrick's when I was twelve. They were good people, but they had a family of their own and we all knew that we were not apart of their family." My jaw twitches. "When I was thirteen the Patrick's got me a job at a steak house, washing dishes because they thought that a little responsibility would be good for me.

"Is there a point to this?" She bites out and I can't even fault her for being so angry.

"When I started working there, I met Albert, the owner, and after a few months he took a special interest in me. He had multiple businesses all over Denver, and before long I was going everywhere with him. And as a kid who never had an adult looking out for him before, I soaked up every word he said and thought that he cared about me." I watch her swallow. "I had no idea how wrong I was about him until it was too late." My hands ball into fist. "By that point in my life I was so used to being mistreated and used by the people in my life that were supposed to look out for me, that I didn't fucking say a word. Or maybe I thought no one would believe me even if I did."

"Clay, stop."

"It didn't last long, I grew up fast," I tell her but remind myself because the memory is almost enough to bring me to my knees.

"Please, no more." She presses her fist to her mouth as tears fill her eyes.

"I hated him, everything about him but I was so fucked up that I stuck around and stayed in his life for years, wanting to prevent what happened to me from happening to someone else." I swallow down the bile crawling up the back of my throat. "He died when I was nineteen. A week after his funeral I was called by a fancy ass lawyer and asked to come in for a meeting. He left me everything he owned, and every penny he had, like it was some kind of fucked up apology for what he did to me."

My jaw clenches.

"Millions of dollars along with properties all over the US I didn't want. But I knew that I could use that money to right some wrongs, to make men and women just like him pay for every fucked-up thing they've done. And that's all I've thought about for the last fourteen years of my life. Until you." I shake my head when she starts to take a step toward me. "You're the first good, clean thing to touch my life and being in love with you is my only weakness."

"Clay."

"Let me finish," I cut her off, watching tears race down her cheeks. "I'm fucked up, Mouse. I can't handle the thought of something happening to you and I know that if something ever hurt you, it would send me into a darkness that I doubt I'd be able to escape from. So, if I need to lock you away to keep you—to keep you safe, I will."

"Nothing is going to happen to me."

"You might be right, but you can't guarantee that."

"You're right, I can't." She shakes her head as she takes a tentative step around the bed toward me. "But you also can't lock me in a box and think I'll ever be okay with that." She takes another step. "I love you."

Her chin wobbles as her hands land on my chest over my heart that is now pounding from hearing those words from her, words that from anyone else would just be that, words with no feeling or emotion behind them.

"But if this is going to work, you are going to have to trust me to never knowingly put myself in danger."

Shaking my head, I cup her face in my palms and she lifts her finger to my lips "And you'll give me that because you love me and you trust me."

"Willow."

"I hate what happened to you." Her eyes search mine as a fresh wave of tears falls from between her lashes. "And if Albert wasn't already dead, I would kill him myself. No one deserves what you went through. You did not deserve to be mistreated by someone you trusted when you were a kid." She reaches around me with her arms and rests the side of her head against my chest. "I'm sorry. I know those words are not enough, but they are all I have."

Resting my chin on the crown of her head I stand there with her in my arms and close my eyes.

"I'm so fucking scared of loosing you, of you realizing that you deserve better than me."

She tips her head back and I open my eyes to meet her gaze.

"I will never find another man who makes me feel as safe or as complete as you do." Her fingers trail down my jaw. "I deserve that, the kind of love you give me, the way you make me feel."

"Mouse."

"I love you, and I choose you, don't ever forget that." She leans up, pressing her lips to mine, whispering there, "But if you ever lock me in a room again, I'll kill you."

"Noted." I whisper against her mouth as I walk her backwards to the bed. When she falls backward onto the mattress, I go down with her and take her mouth in a deep kiss.

And as I lose myself inside her I know I'm home, that she's my home and no matter what happens in life as long as I have her, I will always belong.

Clay

Nineteen

STANDING IN MY kitchen I look around at the people who have come today to celebrate Carly, and I let out a breath. For the last three hours I've watched Willow put on a positive face as she's talked and laughed with the people she invited, but I can tell this whole thing is taking a toll on her. I glance at my watch and wish that I could just kick everyone out, but I know if I did that Willow wouldn't be very understanding even if I was doing it for her. If we had been at the park where today was supposed to take place, I'd be able to use the weather as an excuse to usher her away, but when she saw that rain was on the forecast she asked if she could have everyone come here. And since I want her to get used to the idea of this place being her home, I agreed.

"We need to talk," Nico says, stepping up to my side

I raise a brow. Since he arrived with Sophie, Willow's mom, early this morning to help set up, he's kept his distance even at the frustration of his daughter and his wife.

"Outside," he mutters.

I lift my chin then start to follow him through the room.

"Is everything okay?" Willow grabs my hand, stopping me, and I bend to brush my mouth over hers.

"All good, baby. Be right back,"

She looks to where her dad is standing, then back at me. "Okay. Love you."

Fuck, I don't think I'll ever get used to hearing those words from her. Every fucking night I go to sleep wondering if I'll wake up in the morning, the happiness and contentment I've been feeling just a dream I made up. But somehow, I've started each day with her in my arms and that connection to her just a little stronger than it was the day before.

"Love you, Mouse." I squeeze her fingers then let her go.

When we reach the front door, Nico opens it, then waits for me to step outside before he shuts it behind himself.

"They got Matthew."

My shoulders jerk back in surprise at this news coming from him and not Miles or Tucker. "A hunter came across his body this morning and the coroner just confirmed it was him."

"He's dead?"

"His body was found near Percy Priest Lake. He suffered a single gunshot wound to the side of his head, and after going over the scene, they believe the wound was self-inflicted."

"So, they think it was a murder-suicide?" I surmise.

He nods.

Looking at the door, I don't even want to think about what Willow will think or feel when she finds out this news. "I'm not sharing this with her now, not with all these people around."

His jaw clenches.

"What?"

"I looked into you. I know some of your story. Know who Dayton, Miles, and Tucker are to you and about your sister. What I need is for you to tell me that what you've been through, and the shit you're doing now, isn't going to blow back on you and, in turn, my girl."

"I love your daughter and I'd never let anything touch her."

"You can't always prevent shit like that from spreading through your life and contaminating everything."

"I can. And my family knows where I am with Willow and that my priorities have shifted."

His eyes stay locked on mine. "I don't want to like you."

"You don't need to," I tell him as the door starts to open.

"You haven't been around long enough to know that's not true," he says, focusing on Sophie when she pokes her head outside.

"Is everything okay out here?" She scans me then Nico before locking her eyes on his.

"All good, baby, just filling Clay in on some news I got," he tells her, ushering her back into the house and following her inside.

With a deep breath, I step back in behind them, not sure what the fuck to think about whatever the fuck that was.

"You're not bleeding so I guess whatever Dad wanted to talk to you about wasn't bad," Willow says as soon as she sees me.

I take her into my arms.

"Is everything okay?"

"Yeah, I'll explain when we're alone," I tell her softly and her eyes search mine.

"Is it about Carly?"

I nod and she drags in a breath then takes my hand and just keeps hold of it like a lifeline until people start to leave.

With Leah and Sophie helping to clean up the plates and cups that were left around by guests, the place is straightened fast. I turn when the front door is opened and watch Miles step inside carrying a small wooden chest.

"Where's Willow?" he asks me.

I motion across the room where she's sitting with her dad.

"What's that?"

"The chest Carly's friend asked us to get for her."

"Right," I mutter, then call out, "Mouse."

"Yeah?" She turns to look at me, then sees Miles and gets up. "You got it." She gives a relieved smile, and her eyes start to water.

"I did. I figured you could mail it to Annie."

"Of course." She takes it from him and places it on the counter, but doesn't open it. Instead, she smooth's her fingers over the warn wood before giving him a hug. "Thank you."

"Anytime." He hugs her back, then looks around the room when she lets him go.

"How did today go?"

"It was nice having everyone together to share stories about Carly."

"Good," he mutters, looking across the room at Nico before he meets my gaze. "I gotta get to the station."

"We'll talk later." I touch my fist to his then watch him walk out.

"I'm going to leave too," Leah says, wiping her hands on the dishcloth next to the sink. "Unfortunately, I have to work tonight."

"Okay." Willow hugs her then I hear her whisper. "Thank you for helping today."

"You know I always got your back." Leah looks at me and hesitates before giving me a hug.

"I think we're taking off as well," Sophie says, going to pick up her coat. "I'd rather not drive in the rain if we can avoid it."

"Except you're not driving," Nico tells her, and she rolls her eyes before looking between Willow and me. "I expect to see the two of you at dinner sometime soon."

"I'll make sure that happens," I assure her, then watch as she hugs her daughter.

"I love you, sweet girl."

"Love you, too, Mom," Willow whispers, then she goes to her dad and falls into his arms. "Love you, Dad. Thank you for coming and helping with everything."

"Anytime, kid." Nico kisses the top of her head then meets my gaze. "Take care of my girl."

"Always." I tuck Willow into my side then open the door for her mom, dad, and Leah, then wait until they are out and have said goodbye one last time before I close the door behind them.

"Okay, tell me." Willow twists around to face me.

I run my fingers through my hair. "How about we get a drink."

"No, I want to know. Just tell me."

"All right." I lead her to the couch then pull her down onto my lap. "They found Matthew's body." She gasps as her eyes widen. "He shot himself in the head and they believe he did that after killing Carly."

"Oh my god."

"I'm sure Miles and Tucker will have more information, but that's what your dad took me outside to tell me." I wrap my hand around the side of her neck and run my thumb up and down her pulse.

"I can't believe this. Why would he do that?"

"I don't know, Mouse." I lower my voice. "Maybe something happened between them, and he killed her on accident then couldn't handle what he did."

"Maybe." She closes her eyes. "I know I should feel better, but I don't."

"Finding out what happened was never going to cure your hurt, baby; that's going to take time."

"You're right." She tucks her head under my chin.

I wish I didn't have to keep giving her news that reopened that wound for her.

"Hopefully this news will give everyone a little closure."

"Hopefully, baby." I know that's what she needs to hear, even if I know that it's the furthest thing from the truth, because now everyone is just going to be left with a million unanswered questions.

"ALL RIGHT, BABY, my plane is boarding. I'll see you in a few hours," Clay says through my car speaker system, and I smile at the reminder that he's on his way home.

It's been five days since Carly's memorial and two days since he left to fly to New York for work. I hated that he had to leave, but when he told me that it would be the last trip for at least a couple months, I felt a little better about him going away. Plus, this trip had nothing to do with his past or what happened to Arya, or at least not completely anyway. He and a few donors will be opening a house in Manhattan that will work to help get women off the streets, by getting them into jobs and then eventually their own apartments. And even if I'm sure he's right about doing some fucked up things, the world could use more people just like him—people that will do whatever is necessary to help others and make sure that harm doesn't come to those who can't protect themselves.

"You there, Mouse?" His question drags me out of my thoughts, and I blink at the road and notice that I've already reached the bank.

"Yeah, sorry," I say as I pull into the bank parking lot that is completely empty. Normally, Katy opens and I close, but today she has a dentist appointment so we traded schedules, which worked out perfect, since Clay will be home by the time I get off work. "Love you, I'll see you at home."

"Love you, too, Mouse," he says quietly before he hangs up.

After parking, I get out of my car, taking my purse with me, then go to the trunk to take out the chest that Miles brought to the house a few days ago. Since I haven't been able to pack it up, I figured that I could do that this morning with stuff from our recycle room then drop it off this afternoon at the mailing center down the street.

Using one hand to hold the trunk, I open the door, then quickly scoot inside so that I can shut off the alarm before it times out. After punching in the code, I go back to lock the front door, since Troy, who should be here to help open, has a key that Katy gave him yesterday.

As I'm turning from locking the door my bag gets caught on the handle, tugging me back a step which knocks me off balance and sends the chest in my hands tumbling to the ground before I have a chance to catch it.

As soon as it crashes against the tile floor in the entryway the lid flies off and skids across the floor while the contents explode out scattering across the glass-enclosed space.

"No, no, no, no, no." I drop my purse and grab the lid before I fall to my knees and frantically flip the box over to assess the damage. When I see that the worn brass hinge that attached the lid to the box has snapped in two, I want to cry. There is no way I will be able to put the chest back together without somehow replacing the hinge and I have no clue how to do that.

With a breath I start cleaning up all the ticket stubs, photos, and tiny trinkets from the floor then I notice more than one piece of paper, each about the size of the Post-it notes we use here at the bank. When I pick up the first one, I frown at the messy writing and the single line question.

You think you can block me?

I pick up another and find the same messy writing.

I told you I loved you.

I grab another, then another, each one from someone who was obviously harassing Carly and angry that she didn't return their feelings. As I look at the stack of them in my hands, a sinking feeling fills the pit of my stomach. It was assumed that Matthew committed suicide after he killed Carly, but what if he didn't kill her? What if he was murdered, too, and Carly's killer is still out there.

When a loud bang hits the glass, I scream, and my eyes fly up. Seeing Troy standing on the other side of the door shoving his key in the lock a wave of fear spreads down my spine and the hair on my arms stands on end.

As quickly as I can I shove the pieces of paper in my hands into the box then start picking up the rest of the stuff off the ground.

"What happened?" he asks opening the door.

I shake my head. "Just being klutzy." I get to my feet as he bends over. When his eyes drop to the paper he picks up off the ground, I freeze. Slowly his head turns my way and my heart that is already beating hard, begins to thunder away behind my ribcage. "I dropped Carly's box that I have to mail to her best friend."

"What else is in there?" he asks quietly as he watches me with a look in his eyes that makes my skin crawl.

"I didn't go through it, I was just putting everything that spilled out back in when you knocked on the door," I say, and am proud of the evenness of my tone when I'm so scared, I'm sure I might pass out.

"Let me see."

"Why?" I back up a step and his eyes narrow before he lunges for me. Throwing the box at him as hard as I can, I hear it make contact, but don't stick around to see where it got him. I spin and run into the bank then slam my palm against the security panel by the front door. No alarm sounds so I don't know if it did any good.

"You bitch!"

He plows into me from behind when I'm almost to my office and I stumble in my heels. My knees hit the floor then my chin makes contact next and pain explodes across my lower jaw. When he grabs a handful of my hair and rips my head back, I scream and roll from my belly to my back catching him off guard and sending him tumbling to his side. I don't have long before he's back up and when he tries to climb on top of me, I fight him with every ounce of strength I have. I kick, scratch, punch, and bite and just when I think there is hope, he grabs my face, lifts my head off the ground, and pounds my head into the floor causing everything to go black.

Clay

WITH MY COMPUTER in front of me on the tray table I look over the spreadsheet my accountant sent over and double-check that things are as they should be. As I click to the next page a message pops up at the bottom of the screen from Miles and the moment I read his text my heart stops.

The alarm at the bank was activated twenty minutes ago
I was just informed from the officers who arrived on
scene first that there was a woman being held hostage
and I just confirmed it's Willow. I know you're in the air.
Tucker and I are on our way to get your girl.

I look around the packed plane and squeeze my eyes closed. I could have hired a plane to take me to New York and back, I didn't. I never want to get too comfortable with having the kind of money I have access to. I should have fucking got a plane. I open my eyes and flip over my wrist, we still have forty minutes before we're scheduled to land, anything could happen in that time. My entire life could change by then.

Tell her I'm on my way

I write Miles back, then reaching above me, I press the button to get the stewardess attention then wait until she makes her way over to me.

"Is there any chance we'll be landing sooner than planned?"

"I…" she starts and just then a ding sounds from the speaker above me.

"Hey ya folks, it looks like we'll be landing about ten minutes ahead of schedule in Nashville." The pilot says and the stewardess smiles as he starts to talk about the weather.

"Looks like the answer is yes." She touches my shoulder before she walks off.

It seems to take forever for the plane to touch down and I feel like a caged animal as I listen to the sound of belt buckles being undone and people talking on the phone as we taxi across the tarmac.

As soon as I have a signal I press send on Willow's number and listen to it ring. When her voicemail clicks on, I close my eyes then look down at my phone and dial Tucker.

"We're outside the bank," he answers. "A negotiator is on the phone with the guy holding her."

"What the fuck happened?"

"The guy inside is an employee, we're trying to figure out what set him off."

"I'm going to kill him."

"Good thing you're forty thousand feet in the air."

"We're on the ground, just waiting to get off the plane."

"Then let's hope we can get this guy out before you get here," he says and my jaw clenches.

"If he hurts her."

"I know," he says quietly.

"She has to be okay." My throat gets tight with a feeling I haven't felt in years.

"She will be. Nico just showed. I'm going to go fill him in," he says before hanging up.

Tucking my phone into my back pocket I make my way to the front of the plane and the moment the doors open I push out.

Following the signs, I jog toward the exit then down to the carport with my bag in hand. When I make it to my Jeep, I swing open the door, toss my bag onto the seat next to mine and shove the key in the ignition.

It takes me thirty minutes to make it out of the airport and across town to the bank, each minute feeling like an hour. As I pull into the lot, I see dozens of police cars, a couple of news trucks and an ambulance parked out front. I park where there is an open spot then shove my door open. Before my boots even hit the ground Miles and Tucker join me at the side of my Jeep.

"What's going on?"

"He's been stalling," Miles says. "Guy's name is Troy. He works here. We asked to speak with Willow, but he's refused to put her on the phone."

"Does he have a weapon?"

"No, not one we've been able to see."

"Then what the fuck is everyone doing out here?" I bark.

Miles presses closer. "We need to make sure that it's safe to go in, and we don't want to risk him getting scared and hurting Willow."

My chest heaves while my hands ball into fists.

"I know you want to rush in there to her, but you need to keep your shit tight right now. There are too many people with eyes on this situation, you can't go off half cocked."

I jerk up my chin and he steps back then turns and watches a uniformed officer approaches.

"SWAT is on the way."

"How far out?" Tucker asks.

"Twenty, maybe thirty minutes," he says, before walking off.

"Hopefully this will be over soon," Miles says.

My jaw shifts.

As they walk away to go talk to a group of officers, I stare at the bank and catch the shadow of the man inside moving past the door and a couple seconds later he passes by again. The man inside is obviously agitated and that emotion is only going to get stronger when he sees the SWAT team pull up. And not knowing what condition Willow is in, only that she has not been allowed to speak to anyone to confirm she is okay is sitting wrong in my gut.

Glancing around I check to see if anyone has eyes on me. No one does. Everyone is preoccupied. Walking around to the opposite side of my Jeep I open the back door then press a button that releases the bottom of the seat and shove it up. Taking my key out of my pocket I unlock the black box that runs the length of the seat and then look inside. It takes me just a second to decide on my M9, and to tuck it into the back of my jeans. Pulling my shirt over it, I grab my key set and slam the door. I do a scan of the parking lot then dart across the pavement to the bank and jog down the side of the building. If there is a front door, there is a back one and if his attention is on the parking lot where all the action is happening, he won't be expecting me.

I stop at the next corner and look around the side of the building, then jog to where the door is. Taking my key kit out, I pull out the pieces I'll need and squat down so I'm eye to eye with the handle.

Hearing footsteps, my head shoots up and I see Nico come around the corner with his gun in hand.

"You got a gun?" he asks low, once he's close.

I stand. "What do you think?" The lock clicks open, and I meet his gaze. After a single look, he takes the handle, turns it, then peeks inside. When he jerks his head to the side, I move to the opposite side of the door, then slip inside and he follows. There are no lights on back here, so the two of us move slowly through the dark toward a strip of light coming from under a door. Listening close, I try to hear something, but I can't make out a single sound. When Nico taps my shoulder, I step to the side, and he slowly turns the handle then pulls the door in toward us.

"It's clear." He meets my gaze. "I'm going out first, and stopping at the first door on the left, follow me after ten."

I lift my chin then watch him open the door and disappear out it. At the count of ten, I leave my position and swing into the kitchen opposite of where he is now squatting. Then, the two of us work our way up the hall. When the lobby comes into view, Nico places his back to the wall, and I clear the doorway and duck into an open office. Just as I'm about to move again I notice a stocking covered foot peeking out from the edge of the desk in the middle of the room. I get down and with my heart pounding I move around the back of the desk swallowing bile when I find Willow covered in blood. My hands shake and my throat gets tight as I reach out my hand and search for her pulse. Feeling the steady beat of her heart under my fingers, relief swamps me. Then she gasps and her eyes fly open. Covering her mouth with my hand when she starts to scream, I press my mouth to her ear.

"It's just me, baby. We're going to get you out of here," I whisper, pulling her behind the desk when footsteps start heading our way, then I force her under it. "Stay," I order quietly. Her fear-filled eyes meet mine as she nods. After pushing the rolling chair in front of her, I move to the door and I steal a glance around the corner, finding Nico with his gun raised and pointed at Troy who is standing with his hands above his head.

"Look. I didn't do anything, this was all a mistake," Troy says.

If I knew I wouldn't be arrested and have to spend time away from Willow, I'd put a bullet between his eyes. Stepping out into the hall with my gun out in front of me I point it at the guy.

"How is she?" Nico asks as he quickly glances my way.

"Alive." I tell him and he nods then orders Troy to his knees.

"Please," Troy begs, looking between Nico and me. "Let me explain things."

"You can explain to the judge." Nico tosses me a pair of cuffs and I catch them midair.

Going to Troy, I shove him between the shoulders forcing him to fall face first into the tile floor, then I put a knee in his back and slip the cuffs on him.

"I think he killed Carly." I hear Willow whisper and my head jerks back. Seeing her up gives me relief, but I'm still terrified by the amount of blood on her face, in her hair and down the front of the dress she has on.

"I—" She wraps her arms around her middle and shakes her head. "I found some notes that someone left Carly, that she had put in her chest." Her eyes go to him, and she shivers. "I think he killed her."

"She doesn't know shit," Troy yells.

Willow flinches.

I push his face into the cold ground.

"We'll get that sorted out, Mouse. Please just go wait for me to come to you." I whisper, my throat tight. I can't stand having her this close to him after he put his hands on her.

"You take her out," Nico says, and I look at him. "Get her to the ambulance, I'll deal with him."

With a jerk of my chin, I push away from Troy, then hand Nico my gun, watching him place it in the back of his jeans before I prowl toward Willow and scoop her up into my arms. I hold her against my chest and walk with her to the door, then use my shoulder to push it open. As I step out into the cold air, chaos erupts. Then Miles and Tucker jog toward me yelling orders for everyone to stand down.

"You couldn't fucking help yourself," Miles growls, touching his hand to Willow's face, turning it first one way then the other.

"Nico's inside, he has Troy detained," I tell them, and Tucker curses before turning around and heading back toward the building.

When two EMTs approach us with a stretcher it takes everything in me to release my hold on her ass they place her in the back. I stand outside and watch them check her over and ask her questions and she starts to talk about what happened to cause her injuries. Listening to the details, I fight the urge to go back into the bank to deal with Troy myself. It doesn't take long at all for them to assess that she needs to go to the hospital to get stitches under her chin and checked for a concussion, so I toss my Jeep keys to Miles then get into the back of the ambulance with her and one of the EMTs.

"Call Miles, tell him what I said," she says, grabbing my attention when the doors close and I focus on her beautiful face. "As soon as he saw one of the notes from inside the chest, he changed, I—" She closes her eyes. "It was like something took over him in an instant and—" She whispers. "I knew he did it and he knew I'd figured it out."

"I'll tell him, but right now I want to get you taken care of." I lean down and press my lips to her forehead, and she lifts her hand to my jaw.

"I tried to get away, I tried to fight him."

"You did good, Mouse, so fucking good."

"I was weak." The tears in her voice cause pain to slash through my chest. I know she hated that—despised that she couldn't stop him from over-powering her.

"You're not weak." I clench my jaw tight to fight back the emotion I feel burning the back of my throat. "You're strong, so fucking strong." I drop my head and hold her fingers wrapped around mine to my forehead and close my eyes.

When we arrive at the hospital, she's rolled into a room then everything happens in quick succession as she's cleaned up, has twelve stitches placed in her chin and is sent to have a CT scan done after doctors say they are concerned about the lump on the back of her head.

With no choice but to wait, I go to the waiting room and sit with my head in my hands hoping it doesn't take long for the doctor to come out and say she's fine and we can go home.

"Any news?" Hearing that question, I lift my head from my hands and watch Sophie walk across the waiting room toward me with Harlen and Harmony following her, along with others I recognize from photos

Willow's shown me.

"Not yet." I get up to give Sophie a hug.

"She'll be okay."

"She has to be," I tell her, and her face softens.

After greeting Harmony and Harlen, Sophie introduces me to Willow's siblings; Talon and his wife Mia, Sage and his wife Kim, and her brother Bax. Then she tells me that Willow's sister Nalia is flying in. When Nico shows up about fifteen minutes later his eyes lock with mine as he enters the room, and he jerks up his chin.

"I see it took you less time to win him over then it did me," Harlen mutters, and his wife elbows him, making him grunt.

"Willow Mayson." A woman calls as she steps into the room and each one of us stand up which makes her eyes widen. "Well okay." She looks at all of us. "The doctor will be releasing her to go home in about thirty minutes. Two of you can go back to wait with her until then."

My hands ball into fists. I don't want to have to fight with Willow's family, not when I know they are worried, but I'm not sure I have it in me to stay away from her much longer.

"Baby, you go in with Clay," Nico says.

Sophie nods before leaning up to give him a kiss, then she turns to me and smiles reassuringly.

The two of us follow the nurse down the hall, and when we enter the room Willow is in, her eyes open and she smiles a tired smile at us. I stand back and watch the two of them embrace and talk quietly for a few seconds before Willow looks at me holds out her hand.

I walk to the bed, and I wrap my fingers around hers, smoothing my thumb over her ring finger, trying not to dwell on everything I could have missed out on if things had gone differently today.

"I love you," she says quietly.

I look into her eyes, reminding myself that I didn't lose her. She's still here with me and if I have my way, we'll have a lifetime together and one day when she leaves this earth, I'll follow her into the next lifetime and do this all over again.

Willow

Twenty-One

*A*FTER BRUSHING MY teeth, I dry my face then head into the closet to put away a little more of my stuff. Listening to the soothing sound of his deep voice I put stuff on hangers and place my things inside the drawers he cleaned out for me.

I figured at some point that Clay and I would move in together since I have been staying here with him every night since we officially became a thing. I just didn't think it would happen so soon. But a few days after I got out of the hospital, while the two of us were lying in bed, he asked me to move in and I knew that there was no point in saying no. With him, I feel my safest, and after what happened, I didn't want to put off being truly happy for any reason, so I said "Yes". Thankfully Leah understood, so over the last few weeks I slowly packed up my stuff at her place to bring it all here.

Picking up a pair of pants from the floor, I realize they are the ones Clay had on earlier today, so I fold them in half and reach for a hanger. As I'm hanging them up, I hear a thud land against the carpeted floor and look down at my feet. When I see a small red box with gold etching around the edges my brows draw together and I pick it up, flipping open the lid without thinking.

"Oh my god!" I breathe, staring at the single princess cut diamond ring glittering back at me.

"I was going to ask you this weekend after I had a chance to talk to your dad." Clay says from behind me, and I spin around to face him with my heart now beating a million miles an hour. "I even had a photographer scheduled to show up and capture the moment." He steps toward me and takes the box from my now shaking hands.

"Clay," I whisper, watching him pull the ring from the black velvet cushion protecting it.

"I love you."

He captures my hand as my world starts to spin.

"I don't even know the moment that happened, but I know you own all of me." He lifts his head and his eyes lock with mine. "I promise if you agree to marry me that no one will ever love you more completely than I do, that you will always be safe with me, and that not a single day will go by where you do not feel just how vital you are to my survival." He drops his gaze from mine to the hand he's holding. "But there is no going back from this, Mouse. If I put this ring on your finger, it's staying there forever, we fight, we fuck, and we work it out."

"I wouldn't want it any other way." I capture his jaw with my free hand, and he lifts his eyes to mine. "I don't even want to think about what I would be missing out on if you hadn't been so—"

"Obsessed?" he cuts me off.

"Yes." I laugh as I lean into him. "So, the answer to your question is 'yes' and it will always be 'yes'." The word yes ends on a gasp of breath when he presses into me and covers my mouth with his.

As he thrust his tongue between my lips, his hand slides up my sides taking the tank top I'm wearing with it, and I run my hands down his bare chest and under the edge of his sweats grasping his cock in my hand and squeeze.

"Fuck," he groans, and I smile against his lips, then whimper when he lifts me off my feet and his cock bumps against my sex through the simple cotton covering me.

"Oh god," I breathe, my head falling back to my shoulders as he carries me out of the closet and toward the bed, while his mouth works across the tops of my breast. When he lowers me to my back on the bed, my lashes flutter open.

"Clothes off," he orders, standing back.

I watch him kick off his sweats.

Swallowing, I slip my panties down my thighs then sit up and take off my tank top. Once I'm naked, he climbs onto the bed with me using his knees to push my thighs apart and when his weight settles over me, I wrap my legs around him and lift my hips. "I need you."

"You have me."

"Then I want you inside of me."

"Patience." He sits back and then wiggles the ring I totally forgot about until right now off his pinky. "Now let me see your hand so that I can get down to properly fucking my fiancée."

Laughing, I give him my hand, then with my breath stuck in the back of my throat, I watch him slide the ring down my finger. Once it's in place he lifts my hand to his lips, kissing it before locking his eyes on mine.

I expect him to be sweet, but maybe I shouldn't. His hands go behind my knees and he jerks my hips up onto his lap, slides his hands up my thighs, then his fingers slip through my wet sex and his eyes darken.

"Always so ready for me," he grunts sliding the head of his cock over my clit then thrusting in so deep I whimper.

Wrapping my legs around the back of his thighs I dig my nails into his chest relishing in the pressure I can feel building in my lower belly. "Clay."

"Who do you belong to baby?" He comes down on top of me, grasping my hands linking our fingers together then bringing them up over my head.

"You, always you."

"That's right." He pulls his hips back then slides back in slower. His mouth takes mine in a slow sensual kiss while he keeps the slow, brutal pace of sliding in and out of me. Then his mouth leaves mine and he leans back to look at me and tears fill my eyes. The amount of love I see in his gaze is almost overwhelming and I know he's right, I will never find another man who loves me as completely as he does.

"I love you." I whisper and his face gentles before he leans down, pressing his forehead to mine, circling his hips. A knot forms in my lower belly and tingles spread across my skin from my scalp to my toes as my hold on him tightens in every way.

When he rolls his thumb over my clit, I don't know how long I will be able to hold on. "Come for me, Mouse." He rolls my clit faster and faster, and my legs start to shake as his thrust speeds up. Not being able to hold off any longer, my breath gets stuck in the back of my throat, and I listen to him groan as his hips jerk. When his weight crushes me into the mattress, I tuck my face into the crook of his neck and the aftermath of my orgasm and the feel of his steady breath dancing across my skin almost lulls me to sleep.

"I need to clean us up," he mutters, kissing the side of my neck as he rolls us so that I'm sprawled out across his chest.

"Not yet." I yawn, cuddling closer to him and he lifts up ever so slightly so he can grab the blanket from the bottom of the bed and drag it over us.

"I'm not ready for you to go back to work tomorrow." His words pull me from the sweet bubble we've built around ourselves and I'm instantly wide-awake.

I let out a breath, then pull my head back so that I can look down at him. As hard as this whole thing has been on me, I know it's affected him just as much maybe even more. Not only did he sit down with his brothers and tell them that he was done helping them, but he also told them he's no longer going to be actively looking for the person or people who lured Arya away from her adoptive family. I was not happy about this, I didn't want him to feel like he had to give up something that was so important but then he explained that his future is now more important than his past so how could I argue with that.

"I know, me either." We've been inseparable these last few weeks and I love having him around constantly, but I also know its time for us to get back a little normalcy. And now with there being no possibility of Troy being released from jail anytime soon, I don't have that hanging over me.

Miles, Tucker, and the entire police department have worked tirelessly to build a case against Troy for the murders of Carly and Matthew. Something they had zero evidence of because while I was passed out,

Troy had gotten rid of each and every note he wrote to Carly and that she had kept. What no one knew, including me, is that Carly and Troy had dated for two months when she first started working at the bank. And where he saw their relationship going somewhere serious, she did not, so she eventually ended it and began seeing other people.

This obviously did not sit well with him, and my guess is he started leaving her notes at work after she refused to respond to his texts or calls. Then she signed up with the dating app, started seeing Matthew, and that pushed him over the edge. At his home the police found proof that he had become obsessed with Carly, and on his computer, they uncovered the evidence they needed to charge him with not only Carly's murder but also Matthew's, something Miles and Tucker, both initially warned me would be more difficult to prove since Matthew was found with the gun used to kill him. Also, that gun had been registered under Matthew's name, and his prints were the only ones on the weapon. They kept digging though, until they found what they needed.

Now with the case they have built against Troy that is solid as a rock, he's set to go to trial next year. And I will be in the courthouse every single day staring him down because he did not kill me like he had planned. In fact, by hitting that alarm at the bank I prevented him from getting away with everything, since the police showed up almost right away.

When Troy goes to prison for life *hopefully,* I will finally be able to rest easy knowing that Carly and Matthew are able to do the same with their murderer behind bars. And Troy will rot away in prison never experiencing the joys of falling in love with someone who actually loves him back, start a family or have simple things like clean air or a warm home ever again.

"I'm not sure I'll be able to make it through the day."

Clay's statement drags me from my thoughts and the fear I hear in his voice hurts me. "You can come have lunch with me." I move and straddle his waist.

"That'll be good since my ass will probably be sitting in the parking lot all day anyway."

"It's going to be okay." I cup his jaw and it clenches. "I'm going to work and when you have your next trip, you'll go on it and we'll start planning our wedding, then at some point after we're married, we'll start talking about having babies." I lean down to kiss him. "We have a whole bunch of stuff to do and none of it will get done if we live our lives worried about something that might never happen."

"I love you."

"I love you, too," I whisper back, knowing that those three little words that used to feel so huge, don't even encompass the way I feel about him. He's everything I ever wanted and I'm so happy that fate shoved him in my path.

Clay

Epilogue

5 years later

*W*ITH THE THUNDER of voices filling the loft I stand at the edge of the island in the kitchen watching Willow, her sisters, and her mom fuss over the turkey I just pulled out of the oven for them. My wife looks stunning always, but these last few months have changed her in little ways that take my breath away. The bump and the extra curves she's carrying now make her look like a goddess come to life and in just a couple of days we should be welcoming our son into the world. And although I'm excited to meet our boy I know I'll miss her being pregnant.

"Oh no," she gasps, and my muscles bunch when I see pain slide across her features.

"Oh no what, Mouse?" I move to where she's standing now holding her belly.

"Nothing, it's just a contraction."

"What?" My muscles clench and my stomach drops.

"It's normal, they've been happening all day." She pats my chest.

"Are you fucking kidding me?"

"Honey, what do you mean they have been happening all day?" her mom asks, now looking concerned.

"I've been having them all day," she gasps and grabs her lower back.

"Now what?" I bark.

"It's just another one, I'm fine."

"It might have been a while since I had a baby but that's not normal, honey."

"What's not normal?" Nico asks, getting off the couch in the living room where he's been watching the football game with my brothers and his sons as the kids play in the back entertainment space.

"She's having contractions," I tell him.

"I'm fine." She waves her hand out. "My water hasn't broken, and I read online that it's normal to have some contractions as you get ready to give birth."

"So now we're using Google instead of a doctor?" I ask sarcastically and she glares at me. "Were going to the hospital, I'll grab that bag you've been packing and repacking for the last month."

"I'm not going to the hospital, it's Thanksgiving."

"I think you should go to the hospital," Harmony tells her.

"I'm not going to the hospital," she argues.

"You are, even if I have to carry your ass kicking and screaming out of the house, you're going to the hospital and staying there until a doctor tells me that you can leave."

"I'm not having our son on Thanksgiving." Her chin wobbles and fuck if that isn't a kick right to the gut.

"If he's coming you don't have a choice," Nico puts in, and she looks at her mom.

"Honey, you need to get checked out," Sophie tells her.

"Oh no, no, *no*." Willow pants as everyone who was hanging out in the living room comes to stand around the island.

"It's safe to say that your water broke," Harmony says, and I look down finding the floor wet.

"Shit." I carefully pick her up and start walking with her toward the door.

"I need to change." She says and when I drop my eyes to her and see the tears on her cheeks I give in and carry her to our room.

After I help her change into a pair of sweats, I grab the baby bag from the closet and then lead her into the living room where everyone is running around.

"I'll drive," Nico says, stepping in front of me, so I toss him my keys.

"We'll lead the way in Nico's truck," Tucker says as he and Miles head for the door.

"We'll be right behind you," Sophie says as Willow stops walking and whimpers.

Picking her up I kiss her forehead then head out the door with everyone.

I load her into the backseat then climb in with her as Nico gets in behind the wheel. When Miles and Tucker pull out ahead of us with the lights on, I breathe a little easier because I know we should be to the hospital soon.

"I feel like I need to push," she whispers, squeezing my hand and any ease I felt a second ago is swiped out from under me.

"Don't pus..."

"Push if you need to," Nico cuts me off.

My palms start to sweat. I mean I've read some baby books, but I do not know how to deliver a baby.

The moment we pull up to the emergency room I'm so relieved that I might pass out and as I help her out of the car, a nurse comes out with a wheelchair and places her in it. After explaining that her water broke, and her contractions are close and she's feeling the urge to push she's rushed right to a room while I fill out paperwork and Nico goes to park.

When I make it to her room a couple minutes later it's filled with people, and she's already changed into a hospital gown.

"Okay Dad, she's already at a ten so it shouldn't be much longer," a nurse tells me as I walk to the bed and take Willow's hand.

"I really did not want to have him on Thanksgiving."

"Baby." I laugh, leaning down to press my lips to her forehead. "He's ready to come—you can't stop that."

"I know."

She whimpers when another contraction hits and her hand squeezes mine so tight that I'm surprised she doesn't break bones.

"Okay, Willow, I'm going to have you start pushing on the next contraction," the doctor says from the end of the bed and Willow looks up at me.

"I'm so scared."

"I'm here," I whisper, and she draws in a breath, then over the next ten minutes I watch her work hard to bring our son into the world and then hear him cry for the first time before he's placed on his mom's chest.

"Did you guys have a name picked out?" the doctor asks, wiping him down a little more.

"Rowen," Willow tells her, kissing our son's head and I bend resting my hand on Rowen's bottom while kissing his mom.

"You did good, baby."

"We did good." Tears fill her eyes. "He's so small, and I'm already in love with him."

"Me too." I lean back, feeling humbled by what just happened and what I've been entrusted with.

Willow

LYING IN THE hospital bed with my mom lying next to me, Clay and my dad in the chairs next to my bed, and my siblings and Clay's around the room and Leah holding Rowen, tears fill my eyes.

I have always been grateful for my family and my friends but looking around I know exactly how lucky I truly am. Not many people have what I do, the love of a good man who would do anything necessary to protect me, unwavering love from family and friends that are there anytime I need them, and people who are supportive when things get difficult.

I probably would not be where I am today without the people in this room, each of them have given me the strength to fight through my fear and face each and every day head on, even when I haven't wanted to. Especially during Troy's trial years ago before he was convicted and sentenced to life in prison.

And seeing the way everyone I love, my dad included, has accepted Clay and his family has made my life that much more complete because not only does Clay have me, but now he has dozens of people who care about him and his family the way I do.

I've been blessed beyond measure, and I don't know what I did to deserve all the goodness I've received but I will never take any of it for granted.

Author Notes

I know this book touched on some difficult topics. More of them than I was even expecting. Getting to know Clay and his brothers was difficult but inspiring for me, given their past and the things they went through. The foster care system around the world is overwhelmed and far to often children are left feeling like they don't have a voice. Or that they don't want to rock the boat when they are in a bad situation because they know the outcome could mean they are left with no place to go. If you'd like to help a child without fostering, you can reach out to your local big brothers big sisters program and volunteer your time. Often kids just need someone to show up and show interest. If that's not an option you can assemble welcome boxes for kids going into foster care, or donate to a foster care organization close to you.

As the story about Arya unfolded it made me think a lot about social media and how it's so easy for kids now days to connect with complete strangers online through games or other social media platforms. As a parent we'd like to believe that the people are children are talking with are who they say they are but the hard truth is some are actually predators preying on young minds and taking advantage of the vulnerability that comes along with being a teen or preteen. If you're looking for ways to protect your kids while they explore the new norm of online you can get the bark app which allows you to block sites, monitor content, or limit time online. But honestly I believe that the biggest resource you have when it comes to protecting your babies is honesty, and open communication.

I really hope that you enjoyed this book, I can't remember a time I fell so deeply in love with my characters. And YES a new series with Tucker, Miles and Dayton is coming, I'll announce more information about that later in 2023.

If suspect sex trafficking you can reach out to the Department of Homeland Security at 1-866-347-2423 24 hours a day, 7 days a week.

If you suspect that a child is being abused you can contact your local police department to file a report with them.

Thank you

Thank you for reading, if this isn't your first Aurora Rose Reynolds book THANK YOU for being on this journey with me. And if this is your first thank you for taking a chance on me. I'm so grateful for every reader, blogger and word lover out there because I would not be living this dream without you.

Thank you to my amazing designer, editors, proofreaders, and formatter for putting so much care and love into this book. You are so appreciated.

And as always thank you to my little family, my son, and husband who put up with me disappearing for hours on end to spend time with the people who live in my head.

XX

Aurora

USA TODAY AND NYT BESTSELLER

AURORA ROSE REYNOLDS

Aurora Rose Reynolds is a *New York Times* and *USA Today* bestselling author whose wildly popular series include Until, Until Him, Until Her, and Underground Kings.

Her writing career started in an attempt to get the outrageously alpha men who resided in her head to leave her alone and has blossomed into an opportunity to share her stories with readers all over the world.

For more information on Reynolds's latest books or to connect with her, contact her at auroraroser@gmail.com

Printed in Great Britain
by Amazon

26098168R00146